INNER TURMOIL

INNER TURMOIL

PROVENANCE

DUSTIN HENSHAW

INNER TURMOIL
PROVENANCE

iUniverse books may be ordered through booksellers or by contacting:

iUniverse
1663 Liberty Drive
Bloomington, IN 47403
www.iuniverse.com
1-800-Authors (1-800-288-4677)

ISBN: 978-1-4917-5060-5 (sc)
ISBN: 978-1-4917-5061-2 (hc)
ISBN: 978-1-4917-5059-9 (e)

Library of Congress Control Number: 2014918559

Printed in the United States of America.

iUniverse rev. date: 12/03/2014

To my mother, Rose, for her love and support,
my father, Ab, for always believing in me,
and my wife, Jenn, for never letting me give up.
This dream came true because of you.

Prologue

"Can't stop ... have to keep moving ..." Demetri gritted his teeth, repeating those words over and over as he limped forward. One eye was partially shut from the swelling on his brow. Bruises and lacerations decorated his face with black hues and bloodstains. His left leg was limp from multiple stab wounds on the upper thigh, severing nerves but luckily not damaging any arteries. His wounds were intended to inflict the maximum amount of pain without causing a lethal strike. One arm was firmly pressed against the right side of his abdomen in an attempt to stop the bleeding from the puncture that grazed the side of his ribcage. This injury occurred from an enemy's knife when Demetri made his escape. The other arm propped his body against the stone wall of the long, winding, underground tunnel he had dropped into. This tunnel was intended to be used by the Russian operatives should anything go awry. It was also the planned escape route for Demetri to be taken after the charges were set in the secret Russian lab, a mission in the works from the American Special Forces for several years, a mission that had gone horribly wrong.

Struggling to traverse the long, sewer-like tunnel in his condition, every throb of pain he felt in his body sent a mental image of the person and object that had caused it flashing through his mind. At each opportune moment, he spat his own blood in the face of his captors.

He wasn't sure how long he'd been held captive, but it was of little consequence now, with the ignorant act of one overconfident captor getting too close. What was likely months of built-up rage, aggression and resentment exploded in seconds on a single person who wanted to gloat.

From that moment, Demetri could not recall exactly what had happened. He'd been trained from day one in the Special Forces to tolerate pain, and he'd separated his mind from his body throughout his captivity, a difficult skill to implement but necessary for survival. But he had been doing it for so long that when he finally managed to escape, it was as if his body had acted alone. His cell for god-knows-how-long was littered with blood and Russian bodies that had been massacred in the most brutal fashion.

He barely remembered setting the charges his captors had failed to discover at the time of his capture, and how he quickly dropped into the tunnels he was now racing through, racing to reach the daylight he had been deprived of for so long—but more importantly to achieve a safe distance from the charges he had activated after his escape, set to go off in moments.

Even with a clear goal in mind, a burning thought in the back of his mind, something he could not pinpoint, distracted him. It was almost as if there were something more, something he had done to regret but couldn't remember. Each step would cause pain but quickly relieved him of this burning thought and forced him to soldier on. He looked back occasionally and noticed a small trail of his own blood highlighting his path. This trail could easily be followed—if the lab he was escaping from was not about to be blown to hell!

After what felt like hours of running a gauntlet of memories and pain, Demetri finally reached the end of the tunnel. A steel ladder led to a sealed metal panel on the ceiling with a metal wheel protruding from the entrance in the absence of a lock and doorknob. He reached up to the ladder with both hands, releasing the pressure on his stomach, and attempted to pull himself up on a lower bar with the help of one of his legs. However, a quick shot of pain through his entire body, generating mostly from the stab wound by his ribcage, caused him to quickly let go of the ladder and return his hand and arm to the wound.

Angry with himself, he looked down to the soil he had been following for so long. "Really, Demetri? After everything you've just been through, you're going to let a little pain prevent you from making your escape?" Mocking his own impish approach to the pain seemed to grant the resolve he needed to climb the ladder and open the hatch.

Only pushing open the hatch a small amount, he peeked his head out of the crack to view the surroundings. A rushing cold filled the tunnel as snow and wind blew through the opening, almost causing Demetri to lose his footing, but he held strong. Several snow-covered rocks almost completely surrounded the hatch, but from what Demetri could see, not a soul was in sight.

He pushed the hatch open all the way and pulled himself out of the tunnel. Examining his surroundings even further, he spotted a town in the far distance. The blowing snow didn't impede his vision. No visible roads led to the town, though it seemed to be bustling with life, considering the lights and chimney smoke he saw, something like a small cottage community in the mountains of Siberia.

His thoughts raced. *Is that where the lab was? Under that village?* His concern was immediately processed in his brain. Although his mission was to reach the very lab where he'd been held captive, he hadn't reached his destination. If that was where the lab was situated, that entire town was in danger.

He suddenly felt a large tremor in the ground below him, and a distant explosion erupted right beneath the village. He realized he had doomed the poor inhabitants. The chain reaction of explosions was like an erupting volcano.

The only thing louder to Demetri's ears were the distant screams of women and children in the village, a nightmare to his emotions.

The sudden flash of light coming from the tunnel quickly snapped him out of his daze as he scrambled to shut the hatch before the impending explosive force could snake its way out. Just as he shut it, the force from the tunnels burst through the hatch, tossing Demetri like a cork through the air. He landed on a nearby rock, rendering him unconscious.

*

"I think he's coming to!" A familiar female voice echoed through Demetri's head as he slowly opened his eyes. The blurred image of two soldiers in winter military gear covered in snow stood before him. It was difficult to see in the heavy snowfall that had overrun the area and thrown nearly an inch of snow over Demetri's lower extremities. His immediate reaction was that of a scurrying rat that had been discovered by a predator.

The soldier who had been leaning over him lightly pulled him back as she pulled down the scarf covering her face. "Decan! It's okay! It's us!"

Finally catching a glimpse of the female, he could somewhat recognize her using his mission code name; it was one of his team mates, Elise. She was a hardened woman, yet in this moment, a look of happiness covered her face. Tears streamed down her cheeks. "You'll be all right, sir; we've got you covered."

Demetri turned his attention to the second familiar voice, a soldier who had also removed his scarf, revealing Nate's face. This seemed to alleviate a great amount of the anxiety that had shot through his mind. His breathing slowed, and he lay relaxed against the rock, facing the burning village in the distance. He quickly swallowed his emotions incurred from seeing the village of innocent people he had just destroyed moments ago and prepared himself for the questions that were sure to follow.

"Are you all right?" The concern on Elise's face was coupled with the cracked tone of her voice. This was his Special Forces team. He expected them to ask him for his report, not ensure he was okay first. Had he trained them improperly? Or had he trained them too well?

"I'm fine, Spire." Demetri replied, using her code name. "What are you all doing here?" Demetri's question was rhetorical; he knew the answer, though he didn't want to hear it.

"Looking for you, sir." Nate answered Demetri's question knowing it was rhetorical. Their working relationship had graduated far beyond the need for words; their verbal conversations were more for the others' sake. "The village to the east of here has been burned to the ground. Women, children and men alike. There are no means of communication anywhere in the town that we could find. We have already called for extraction to this location with Panther and Artemis deployed on the outskirts with sensors active in a ten-mile radius; no hostile chatter. So we will be out of here without incident in three minutes. What happened here?"

Elise quickly came to Demetri's defence. "Ghost, we shouldn't be grilling him right now. He's been in captivity for nearly six months. We need to get him into friendly territory. We shouldn't be having this conversation here."

"He was originally sent here to do a job, and it's not unreasonable to ensure it was completed. Otherwise we are required to do so in his stead. We have the team here now. What is the situation report, sir?"

Nate's tone may have seemed crass, but Demetri understood its intention. Nate was doing it out of concern for Demetri. He knew

Demetri's first concern was to confirm task completion. He was simply helping put Demetri's thoughts in order.

Nate continued. "Your contact was to meet you in Novosibirsk. That is where we lost contact with you. What do you remember?"

For a moment, Demetri's steely resolve waned, but he grimaced in pain as he sat up to address the team, holding his abdomen, which was now professionally bandaged and likely sterilized. The contact … the contact he originally came to Russia to meet, he repeated in his mind. He could remember now; that was the burning thought in the back of his mind. "He's dead."

The stone-faced look on Nate disappeared hearing those words and turned into one of sheer apprehension. "Dead?"

Demetri's expression did not change. He understood the apprehension. Demetri had been sent to Russia to coordinate with their Russian mole in regard to the location of a secret military facility that had been dealing in experimental weaponry. He had no idea how advanced the technology was when he was taken to the facility. As well, he was not taken under the circumstances he intended. "It was a ruse. The contact was Spetsnaz, and he was part of the ploy the entire time. The moment I got the chance for my escape, I broke his neck."

The empathetic look from Nate was apparent to Demetri, though he didn't acknowledge it. He knew why Nate would feel such empathy for him with the experience he had just been through. Perhaps Demetri should have felt more emotional about the entire experience, but his heart seemed to have gone cold on the subject.

"What did they want?" Nate asked.

Demetri closed his eyes, cringing. He had so effectively separated his mind from the pain of interrogation that he actually had difficulty remembering what it was they were trying to extract from him. He remembered mention of the Ultimate Fighting

American (UFA) project. It was a top-secret project that only the American Special Task Force was supposed to know about. That's why he remembered the question; it raised the question of how they already knew of it. They were probing for details, this project in its early stages, a project Demetri and the other four members of his team had volunteered for. As such, they were given intimate details of the process and the risks involved. They were aware of the secret lab's location in the deserts near Las Vegas, where they were to report when the testing stages began. This was to be their last field assignment before reporting back for project testing.

The operation was based on intelligence the Russians were conducting the same project and were further along in this lab. The destruction of this lab would set the Russians back a decade at least, and with the use of the charges using stolen Japanese technology to detonate, any backfire from the event would be directed toward the Japanese. The Japanese had always been interested in gathering the latest tech from around the world, so it would not be a far stretch for the Russians to blame them.

A scientist named Ken Saracen was responsible for acquiring the Japanese technology by means of an old acquaintance from the University of Toronto Science and Technology (U of TST). It made for great advances in American technology with very little applied research. It would stand to reason that the entire design behind the Russian's plot involving Demetri was to try to gather proof as to the mission they knew Demetri was assigned and show it to the Japanese. And Demetri knew exactly how they would know so much about him.

He was set up—by someone he trusted. He explained the Russians already had information regarding the UFA project, America's first serious attempt at a super-soldier serum for mass production, information he had not given them. He left a lot of information out, but at this time, he thought it better they didn't know, at least until he had more conclusive evidence of his theory. He would first have to discuss the potential mole with his superiors. He trusted his team—but after this experience, it would be hard to trust anyone.

Nate held a hand to his ear and turned his head as if receiving a communication, and then looked back at Demetri. "One minute, Decan. Can you stand?"

"Yes." Demetri placed his hands on the ground to push himself to his feet, but stopped immediately as he looked, wide-eyed, a small figure in the near distance running toward them.

The others heard the footsteps and turned to face the approaching runner. Elise and Nate reached for their waist holsters to draw weapons if necessary. Elise knelt on one knee next to Demetri in a protective stance.

The small body slowed its approach as it reached visual range. It was no taller than three feet, dressed in a thick red snowsuit and rubber boots and a thick, wool winter hat likely hand-knit. It was a young boy. His face had small water crystals slowly freezing on his cheeks and chin. It was obvious he had been crying, and he looked in fear at the three faces of these oddly dressed strangers near his home.

Nate and Elise loosened their stances as the child turned and ran without a word.

"What are you doing?" Demetri barked at his cohorts, seeing their lax reaction.

"It's a child. I'm not chasing him," Nate said dismissively, not taking his eyes off the boy.

"You aren't wearing your masks! He's seen your faces! He needs to be eliminated!" Demetri's voice was deep and commanding, not something Nate and Elise were used to hearing. They knew he could give a command when need be, but this was borderline scary. Demetri seemed adamant about killing this child with no compelling reason yet seemed convinced the child was a threat.

"It's a *child*, Decan. We've killed enough innocents on this mission as it is. What authority figure would stage a manhunt based on a child's description? This was an antiterror mission, and the targets have been eliminated." Nate looked at Demetri and indicated the direction of the burned village, confused as to Demetri's illogical reasoning, and then calmly turned back to the direction of the child. "Besides, you were in their custody for two months. It's far too late to hide your face." Nate never took his eyes off the child as he ran, likely thinking along the same lines as Demetri.

Demetri's face suddenly went from commanding to rage as he glared across the field at the running boy. His mind drifted, telling himself the child would endanger the lives of this mission and his team. He rationalized there was no convincing his team why this needed to be done, and they wouldn't believe him.

Demetri reached over to Elise's sidearm and drew her weapon. The metal dragged against the leather of the holster as Demetri pulled the gun, getting everyone's attention. But they turned only in time to see Demetri holding the gun in the direction of the boy, and with an emotionless expression, he pulled the trigger.

Chapter 1

A WORLD IN TURMOIL

I N THE YEAR 2015, THE United States had been a world superpower for 70 years; it had come out of World War II as a global power and never looked back. During its tenure as superpower, it had survived countless wars and conflicts: Vietnam, Iraq, Iran, the Caribbean Revolution and the Siberian Conflict, to name a few. While the United States had no problems winning the war, they could never fully win the peace. For 30 years, they had fought against organizations that threatened American security; but for every victory they struck, another conflict would spark.

The United States seemed to be caught trying to launch a conventional war against an enemy without conventions. They would flush out the terrorist groups and revolutionaries that opposed them only to have the survivors start again elsewhere. The worst part was that with the factitious nature of global politics in conjunction with their own increasingly right-wing views, their opponents never ran out of places for their ideals to take route. The Chairmen of the Joint Chiefs summed it up when he said, "It's like trying to kill a bird with a sledgehammer. You can shatter his nest, but the remains give him more with which to rebuild."

In order to ensure that the nations that were torn apart by American conflicts would stabilize and not turn back into "nests," the US military had to become more and more of an occupying force. This resulted in more of the American economy needing to support the armed forces, thus deepening its crippling recession. The United States was now caught in a bind: if they pulled out as occupiers, a wave of hostility and violence would crash down on US soil. If they continued to try to stabilize conflict zones, America would experience a recession that would make the Great Depression seem like a broken piggy bank.

In this respect, they had one saving grace: Canada. Canada had always been the United States' strongest trading partner (and vice versa); one could not survive without the other. Even though Canada was suffering from the same recession, the two nations' combined economies kept them both strong for the time.

With the world governments now looking to help only themselves, the bond between Canada and the United States strengthened in trade and technology. However, even this close bond was not enough. Canada still kept out of the majority of American conflicts, and despite the urging of their southern neighbours, they would not intervene lest its economy too would fall, dooming both the United States and Canada. What America needed now was a way to consolidate its military and reduce the resources required to continue their operation abroad. Military intelligence was working around the clock to find a solution to this increasingly serious situation.

*

While the United States continued its endeavour to relieve itself from the recession, the rest of the world was far from idle. In 2015, the nations of Europe found themselves struggling with the internal strife created by the many revolutionaries and separatist groups that had plagued them for years. These groups had grown far bolder than in the past by watching America's enemies continually foil the world's last superpower efforts to destroy them. This newfound zeal led to open armed resistance throughout the Balkans, Eastern Europe and Ireland, traditional breeding grounds for such activity. However, the newborn boldness felt within these movements led to uprising in areas that had only had mild insurrections in the past; Southern France, Spain and Southern Germany were now riddled with several independent movements. Though these separatists, revolutionaries and terrorist groups in Europe were far from organized, unlike America's adversaries, the collective effect was to cause the removal of the European nations as a force on the global map. Faced with what was dubbed "a continental crisis against peace and stability," the European Union, primarily a financial/trade alliance, became more and more of a joint defence initiative against the numerous insurrections against its member nations. It was decided that with the natural progression of the European Union paired with the continuing trend of "super-nationalism" (nationalism on a continental scale), the term "union" no longer applied.

In early 2016, in a move that completely altered the face of global politics, Europe collectively backed out of NATO, effectively ending the organization, and founded the Alliance to Preserve European Sphere of Security and Influence, commonly referred to as the European Alliance (EA). With the newfound alliance pledging to end its internal strife and strengthening its position in the world with the "Europe First Initiative," America found itself in even more dire need of allied trade and military resources.

With the waning of United States' superpower status and the new European Alliance's stance becoming more and more isolationist, a power vacuum developed on the world stage. Global markets became increasingly vacant as the world powers began to picket themselves off in their own internal affairs.

In the absence of any major or federally backed competition, one nation—Japan—began to take steps to monopolize the market. Though the Japanese had a longstanding history of being dependant on outside resources, one market in which they prevailed was technology. In the now segregated stage of world politics, technology was like currency.

The stock of global alliances was shown in the technological advancements they could offer as well as their willingness to use said technology to achieve their stated gains. While the bulk of the remaining independent nations with wealth became increasing dependant on Japanese technology, the EA and the United States both avoided this.

As part of the Europe First Initiative, the EA refused to allow the bulk of its technology to come from outside sources and attempted to compete with the Japanese tech market with mild success. The United States likewise resisted Japanese technology, as America's tech market was one of the few remaining areas of its floundering economy that held any semblance of stability.

Despite these two key areas of resistance, Japan generated immense wealth and power by cornering the Asian and Pacific tech markets as well as making astonishing gains in South America and Russia. Although Japan's newfound technological dominance quickly made it a power to be reckoned with, its people did not remain blind to the benefits of a strong multinational alliance like that of the EA and the cooperation between the United States and Canada.

American influence in the 20th century had had a lasting effect on Japan, and the two had once been strong trade partners. Now with the United States trying desperately to bolster its own market by refusing outside resources, the popular belief in Japan was that the American way was failing and Japan should strive to generate its own global influence. A wave of nationalism gradually swept over

Japan, and in late 2018, a wave of federal elections led to 85 percent of the Japanese government being made up of ultranationalist politicians. With the power generated by their tech market, the Japanese government began to take steps to submit its influence on the surrounding nations.

At first this was done legitimately. Several of the Pacific Island states that had longstanding protection and relations with the United States were eager to align themselves with an ascending power due to America's declining power. By mid-2019, this trend had reached the point that many of the remaining nations that were resistant to Japanese influence were brought to heel simply as it was no longer economically feasible to resist. By the end of 2028, Japan had dominance over the entire Pacific Island north of Australia, all of Southeast Asian to the border of India and even parts of the Russian pacific coast, which had long been considered independent since the Siberian Conflict in 2014.

In early 2021, Japan formally announced the creation of the Pacific Coalition (PC), an alliance that on the surface seemed to draw many similarities to the EA. The world population seemed to take little interest in this, as most were either dependant on Japanese technology or too involved in their own affairs to care. On top of these factors, the populations that fell under the borders of this new coalition were more than willing to support an alliance with the technological powerhouse that Japan had become. Behind the closed doors of the United States, EA and few remaining unaligned nations, it was generally understood that this was not a multinational organization but many nations willingly bowing to Japans economical and technological power. Japan's influence seemed to be rising in leaps and bounds with little or no outside encouragement or interference. However, this period of unbridled success seemed to come to an end in mid-2021 as China, Japan's only rival in Eastern Asian, refused to recognize the legitimacy of the Pacific Coalition.

There were many claims as to why China decided to oppose the PC; some said it was the competing nationalism of China's government; others claimed it was the Chinese economy being unable to compete with Japan. The truth was, Japanese technological advancement showed no sign of halting, and China was looking to nip its competition in the bud before its technology was turned over to the PC's military use.

Unfortunately, unbeknownst to the world, they were too late.

With the now unshakeable sense of super-nationalism within the PC and the equally stubborn nationalism of China, diplomatic talks between the two powers broke down within two weeks of China's refusal to recognize the PC. China's military was highly feared due to its strive to modernize its massive forces since the late 20th century. China was now the sleeping dragon that had been America in late 1941. The PC military, on the other hand, had been built up to what appeared to be more of a security force, with the old Japanese Self Defence Force as its nucleus. The nations that had now become the PC did not commit their military to the PC as of yet, and the PC military was therefore a largely unproven force. The Chinese military command decided that what little resistance the PC could offer would be easily swept aside with a pre-emptive strike, leaving the rest of the PC nations to recognize China as the dominant power in the east.

In October 2022, in monitoring stations and military command posts around the world, sirens roared to life as China launched what it called "Operation Eclipse." Multiple intercontinental ballistic missiles (ICBMs) were launched throughout China, as military command posts around the world monitored the situation. Military analysis around the world came to the consensus that if the PC and China went to war, China would win handily over the dwarfed PC armed forces.

Now with China launching a surprise attack directed at PC military bases, the outcome seemed all but predetermined. The world watched satellite feeds and computerized tracking programs as a hundred non-nuclear, high-explosive MIRV missiles arced toward their intended targets.

In the central command, the Chinese military waited to order their ground forces forward upon the first sign of detonation. All those watching these events unfold were shocked that the target areas had almost no activity—no panicked evacuation, no high-speed interceptors and no running for shelter. The Chinese command was already celebrating, having achieved a complete surprise attack, when a strange message showed up on their monitors:

TARGETING TELEMETRY
WTS-0874 MIRV VEHICLE
TARGET: PC AIR DEFENCE COMMAND, FUCHU, TOKYO
MIRV MODULE SEPARATION IN 5 ... 4 ... 3 ... 2
ERROR, ERROR, ERROR
INBOUND OVERRIDE SIGNAL FROM CENTCOM CONFIRMED
NEW TARGET ACQUISITION CONFIRMED
RELAYING SECONDARY TARGETS TO:
WTS-2435, WTS-2481, WTS-2711, WTS-2716
ALL MIRV VEHICLES CONFIRM SEPARATION
DETONATION IMMINENT

The Chinese at central command were baffled; they had sent no commands for their weapons to acquire new targets.

As the optimism they were experiencing faded into confusion, they watched four of their missiles release their numerous warheads, which detonated in a line over the East and South China seas. The explosions were perfectly timed and spaced to destroy the entire wave of oncoming missiles. In fewer than five seconds, the entire missile attack was destroyed.

Frantic commands were already being given for a secondary launch and for ground forces to attack when static came over the screens in a high-pitched whine. As the gathered generals and attendant recovered from the sudden shock and came to their senses, they watched in horror as a final message scrolled across the single operating screen:

TARGETING TELEMETRY
WTS-0874 CONFIRMS SECONDARY TARGETS DESTROYED
PRIMARY TARGET CONFIRMED
TARGET: CHINESE MILITARY CENTRAL COMMAND; BEIJING MILITARY REGION
SEPARATION CONFIRMED
DETONATION IMMINENT
TEXT RELAY SENT
MESSAGE READS: "THE DRAGON HAS WOKEN ... ONLY TO BE CONSUMED BY THE RISING SUN"

The other world leaders watched in shock as multiple detonations tore apart the Chinese central command. The last transmission sent from China's military command attempted to call off the ground offensive and warn that the surprise had failed. The only thing the Chinese units in the field heard was the hailing of an incoming message—and then static.

The recall order failed to reach the Chinese units in the field before they reached their assigned targets. Field commanders knew the missiles had failed, but they were still confident in victory over what they considered an outnumbered and inexperienced enemy. Military commanders and world leaders watched as the full might of the Chinese military juggernaut rolled toward their intended targets, while in the PC headquarters, military commanders now unleashed their trump card.

Across the axis of the Chinese advance, groups of hidden soldiers and subterranean defence platforms rose up from their positions. A collective gasp released from all who watched the battle unfold as the defence platforms opened fire—not with shells or missiles but lasers. Searing beams of energy scythed through the strongest Chinese armour like wheat in the field long before the tanks were in range to return fire. Chinese field commanders screamed orders to close in and fire on the enemy, as every second another tank was lost. When the few surviving Chinese vehicles and troops finally reached their targets, they faced a hail of lead from PC troops.

The defending fire had a rate that was twice as accurate at one and a half times the range, with a rate of fire three times as fast as the best Chinese support weapons. In less than an hour, the opening offensive of the War of Pacific Ascension was over. The Chinese forces suffered nearly 90 percent casualties.

The PC realized battles were not merely won by weapons but with information. The Japanese had already launched mass infiltration into the Chinese diplomatic channels at the beginning of their spread of influence and came to the realization that China would resist them. China would even go to war to preserve their independence. Armed with this information, the PC began covert military research and arming in mid-2019. However, they knew that if they began open war with China at the time, there was a chance other world nations would rally to the Chinese cause, viewing the Japanese as a new violent superpower bent on conquest.

With their infiltrators in place, the newfound Pacific Coalition only needed to steer the Chinese military into an unfounded sense of superiority. These agents would cleverly lead the Chinese government to believe military intervention would be quick and easy, thus permanently securing China's position as the dominant nation in Asia and the Pacific.

By launching their pre-emptive strike, China had played directly into the PC's hands. The appalling losses of Operation Eclipse resulted in a massive retreat of Chinese forces from the heavily urbanized eastern seaboard as the technologically armed PC military went on the offensive. The Chinese forces were in complete disarray as the hacked Chinese MIRV took out the central command in the opening seconds of the war. Any pockets of resistance that the retreating enemy offered were brushed aside in a flurry of lead and lasers.

As the world's military leaders scrambled to find a way to counter the Japanese technology, the PC forces continued to upgrade, and soon even their infantry were capable of wielding laser weaponry as well as highly integrated battlefield technologies. By the dawn of the new decade, the remnant of China had no choice but to hope for peace. The war that global military advisors said China would win in no more than two years was won by the Pacific Coalition in only four months, and it left the PC a global superpower that controlled more than a third of the world population.

Unbeknownst to the world were the repercussions this conflict would have on the other side of the Pacific, an opposition that would change the face of war forever.

Chapter 2

RECESSION

"I T IS NOW OFFICIAL. THE United States of America has declared a state of emergency." The words of a CTV news anchor spread through the common area of one University of Toronto Science and Technology (U of TST) dorm, effectively sending chills through the on-looking group of students huddled around the TV. The U of TST, a satellite university of the University of Toronto, was touted as the best university worldwide for its cutting-edge programs in science and technology, with a revered quality faculty. It was probably best known in the field of academia as having the best gene-aug (gene augmentation) program in the world.

The students gathered in the dorm B-26 were from every program imaginable, but all had a common interest in the declining state of their southern neighbours. The whole group was growing in size by the minute as more students heard the commotion and headed to the lounge. They watched and listened in utter disbelief at the dire situation in America, puzzled about the urgency.

The glow of the TV was the only source of light in the small lounge. Couches and chairs were uncomfortably filled with students; some sat cross-legged on the floor while others stood on tables behind the crowd in order to see the expressions of the anchorman while he reluctantly delivered the news. Not a single word was spoken amongst them for fear they would miss some vital tidbit from the report. Some of the students began to hold onto one another, some thinking about the possible repercussions such a declaration could have on them and their way of life, others out of sheer empathy. The gasps of astonishment were quickly silenced as the anchorman continued.

"At seven o'clock this evening, President Jonathan Morris officially declared the economic recession in the United States to be a state of emergency for the country. The president has issued a statement regarding his plan to help America free itself from this crisis. Though not much information has been given to the public regarding exactly what is involved, he assures Americans that this state of emergency will be short-lived."

"Short-lived? What kind of assurance is that? It's a state of emergency, not a cold," a young voice projected amidst the anchorman's broadcast in response.

Several students briefly glance at the young student standing with folded arms against the doorframe. His tucked-in black dress shirt and black dress pants were wrinkled from weeks of wear, with no obvious sign of washing or ironing, a stereotype of seventh-year students who had been away from home since they were seventeen. His unkempt appearance was furthered by his short black hair standing in tufts, as though he had just lifted his head from a pillow, and he sported several days' worth of a five-o'clock shadow. He was obviously past the point of caring much about his appearance. He focused solely on his studies as they consumed his every waking moment and had essentially become his life's work. He was recognized, although not for his athletic ability (his slender, lean build was a dead giveaway to that) but for his unbridled intelligence in the bioengineering field.

Richard Ceress was the top student in the gene augmentation doctorate course that had only been offered at the U of TST for the last decade. Not only was Richard top in his class, he was also three years junior to most of the other graduates of the program. Richard's genius had brought him to the program when he was barely 15. He experienced discomfort socializing with his peers, initially due to the age difference and gap in intelligence, but even now at the age of 22, it was no different.

It was often assumed he would reverse paralysis or cure autism or any one of many ailments that still plagued society. It was often stated he had the personality of a birch tree. But Richard didn't think of himself in that way. He was simply practical and didn't have time for inane chitchat or generally anything that was not thought provoking or at the very least productive to his studies. He simply chose to keep to himself, to his studies. In his mind, he needed to use his intelligence for the betterment of the human race. Therefore he strictly avoided social situations with university and college students to prevent himself from being reminded of their many faults, failings, and general lack of possible productive contribution to future society.

He was not as selfish or arrogant as people would believe him to be, but it didn't matter to most; that was the persona he displayed, and that was how he would be judged. His comments were often ignored by the general masses; he made them often and as a result sounded conceited. Most of the time, he was simply right, and no one wanted to acknowledge they didn't think of it first. This time was no different. After seeing who had made the "short-lived" comment, the rest of the lounge easily dismissed it as background noise and continued their focus on the anchorman.

It quickly became apparent to Richard that the anchorman was lacking detailed information regarding the crisis, which caused Richard to instantly lose interest. With one light shake of his head and a deep breath, he uncrossed his arms and walked back down the hall to his dorm room. There he could be much more productive with his time and focus on his studies.

The short walk was all but a quiet one. The echo of the anchorman from CTV could be heard streaming out of every room he passed. This announcement was obviously hitting the students hard; for those students from America, it was that much worse. Which made sense—they had family there. So what did it all mean? Were citizens there losing their jobs, their homes? Was this a modern-day equivalent of martial law? It mattered little to him, as he felt it had no direct impact on his studies. He also had trouble feeling sorry for what he saw as their self-inflicted crisis.

When he finally reached what he hoped would be the sanctity of his own dorm room, to his dismay he heard the very same broadcast from the TV inside. He saw his roommate, Jayden, sitting cross-legged on his own bed, arm outstretched with remote in hand and jaw hung open, yet stiff as a board, as if paralyzed by the image.

Richard momentarily stared in shock when he saw his roommate aghast watching the broadcast. Jayden had been watching the sports broadcast when Richard left; the annoying banter of the announcers was the entire reason he left the room to begin with in order to try to get a moment to think.

Jayden was your typical jock: popular with the guys, even more so with the ladies. He always wore T-shirts with campy logos splattered on the front, and jeans that were ripped from playing tackle football behind the dorms every night. His U of TST T-shirt clung to his defined, muscular but not bulky six-feet one-inch frame. Jayden definitely owned the body of an athlete who spent countless hours in the gym. Gel slicked his short, dirty-blond hair into spikes, and the scent of a tub of cologne from the latest commercial claiming to be "the ultimate babe magnet" filled the room. He was a student at U of TST studying communications technology on a football scholarship. Richard was always baffled that Jayden maintained a 3.4 GPA with his less-than-dedicated school lifestyle, even more so that the school handed out scholarships to football quarterbacks. However, he was probably the closest thing to a friend Richard Ceress actually had, though even then their relationship was cordial at best. Richard continually regretted the university's preposterous propensity to assign random roommates. The only saving grace was that Richard spent half his life in the lab and the other half in classes.

He shut the door and made his way over to the TV. "Can we shut this off? There's no new information; it's all speculation at this point. It's just a waste of time to watch now."

"What?" Jayden, having been woken up from some sort of daze, took a moment to comprehend what his roommate had just said. He clicked off the TV and tossed the remote onto his virtually unused desk near his bed. "Hey, it's pretty serious down there. It looks like somebody pressed the panic button. They're going all crazy on everyone. I didn't realize the recession had gotten so bad!"

"You think this state of emergency is because of the recession?" Richard turned to Jayden with one raised eyebrow as if questioning his sincerity in the ridiculous statement he had made. But the glare was short-lived; his face became stern as he addressed Jayden's ineptitude on the subject. "Please, America's been in a recession for nearly twenty years now. You think after twenty years they finally decide to declare it a state of emergency? Mark my words; there's something brewing on the Pacific Coast. After what the Pacific Coalition did to China, there's no doubt in my mind that America believes they're next. And if the PC is smart, they'll realize the same thing. It's only a matter of who will strike first. America is just getting ready for the inevitable."

"Seriously?" Jayden's usually calm and collected demeanour escaped him at the moment, his eyes wide with interest and a hint of fear, head tilted like a curious child's. Tiny facial muscles flinched along his strong angular jaw line, and his usual cocky, confident expression turned to serious concern. "You honestly believe that? Like actual real war, like Pearl Harbor and shit?"

"Yes." Richard's stern look became a more solemn expression. "I think there's a war coming to America." At that moment, Richard looked every bit the lecturing professor. It was something he wished for, if only for the fact he felt it would force others to finally be compelled to listen to his opinions and take them as fact—which of course they were.

The room was silent for a few moments after Richard's grim statement but was suddenly broken by boisterous laughter bellowing out of Jayden as he fell back against the pillows on his bed.

Richard gave him a vindictive glare as Jayden commented between bouts of laughter. "Yeah, right. They tried that before. Does the word Hiroshima ring any bells with you?"

The simple-mindedness of his roommate and Hollywood movie brainwashing was astonishing. "Don't be so naïve!" Richard's tone was much more serious in response to being openly mocked. "An arrogant boast like that is exactly why they're such a susceptible target. It's also what crushed China. They didn't realize it either, until it was too late."

Jayden's laughter subsided as he caught his breath and leaned up to face Richard, still having trouble hiding the disbelieving smirks. "Well. Even if they did, all of the other countries would just come to their aid anyway."

"Forget it." Visibly frustrated, Richard sat at his desk and began sifting through papers scattered across it. Besides the fact the rest of the world seemed to be only considering themselves lately or the fact America probably had as many enemies as allies at this point, his friend—and he applied the term loosely—would never grasp the complexities and realities of the situation. He'd rather line up at midnight somewhere to buy a game and go home and play war with his buddies online, believing the real thing to be just as easy.

"Are you studying again? Give it a rest, dude. You just wrote your finals like a week ago and you're done with classes, aren't you? Rich, seriously, man—you need to calm down and relax. You get so wound up and uptight about things like this. You go to the extreme of what *could* happen when there's no way it would ever come to that." Jayden closed his eyes and lay back with his hands behind his head, supremely satisfied with his "all is right with the world because that's just how it is" attitude.

Richard focused on his thesis paper in front of him and gave Jayden a less enthusiastic response. "We'll see, and I've asked you before not to call me Rich. If anything, call me Ceress at least … pronounced 'Seress', not 'Caress', thank you! And by the way, I'm working on my dissertation."

Eyes suddenly opening with excitement, Jayden sat up and faced Richard with newfound vigour. "I know what you need. You need a good night out, to go out and meet people. You know, real people in the flesh. They are much more exciting and fun to be around than books. There's a party in the frat down the road where we can drop in. Come on, what do you say, Rich?" Jayden smirked as he said it, the extra emphasis on *Rich* this time. "Besides, Ceress sounds so formal. You'll never get anywhere in life acting like some stuck-up official or something."

"I've no interest in attending a function that consists of nothing but drunken frat boys."

Laughing softly, Jayden slowly shook an open hand in front of him to dismiss Richard's observation. "No, no, no. Is that what you think it is? You've got it all wrong. It's much better than that!"

Almost showing an interest in what Jayden may have to say, Richard momentarily stopped sifting through the papers and put one arm over the back of his chair. He turned to face Jayden. "Is that so? Then please enlighten me."

"It's going to be full of drunken frat boys *and girls!*" The expression on Jayden's face with his arms open wide as if expecting a hug from a child was one of sheer confidence that the words he had just spoken could not be refuted. Richard's unimpressed look answered Jayden's next question without having to ask it.

"All right, but you're missing out. I don't know why you're studying on your weeks off. Socially hopeless, I tell ya." Jayden picked up to his feet, and with a clap of his hands reached under his bed, pulling out a six pack of beer. He threw it on his broad shoulder with a wave behind him to his roommate. He stepped through the doorway with his familiar swagger, humming a well-known rock song.

Pleasant greetings between him and other members of the dorm in the hall were heard as he shut the door, leaving Richard in his long-awaited and hoped-for silence. But Richard had to admit to himself, even though they had nothing in common except a dorm room, he did like Jayden. Somehow he could see through Jayden's arrogant façade to the loyal friend underneath.

He turned back to his papers with a roll of his eyes and continued to review his notes of the genome scans he had researched to support his thesis on the use of gene-augmentation technology to cure degenerative disease, such as Parkinson's and Alzheimer's. It was true; his final exams were over a week ago, and he was in the midst of his three weeks off before he had to arrange his meetings with his thesis mentor, Dr. Norman. But there was a nagging need for approval in the back of his mind. He had always strived to attain the greatest knowledge possible, but when he was told he was adopted, something changed within him. It was a strange feeling, wanting to make his biological parents as well as his adoptive parents proud. Even though they weren't alive to see him be successful, maybe somehow they would know. He wasn't sure why he entertained such thoughts, but he experienced a feeling of melancholy when he thought of them. A small part of Richard hung on to normal boyhood fancies and dreams.

Then there was the part of him that somewhat wished for something of a normal life. Not that he could complain about his actual life and upbringing. His adopted parents were very good to him. They cared for him and loved him, provided a wonderful home, paid his way through university, which obviously wasn't cheap, and were supportive of him leaving home in Ottawa to go to the most prestigious new program in the country. But after all, it was hard not to find the desire to support a child with a 99 percent grade average and such a desire to learn.

There was an incredible internship being offered to the top students in the gene augmentation department of the Canadian Government, which was dedicated to the development of such technology to cure degenerative disease, the precise reason Richard pursued a career in the field. It would guarantee him a stable career as well as give him the opportunity to use his talents to help people. The candidates would be posted tomorrow; it would determine whether or not he would get an interview. He knew he would need every ounce of knowledge he had in order to make the difference he wanted and be noticed by the recruiter. Even though Richard had always shown an enormous amount of aptitude in learning and developing anything related to science, he had an extreme fear of failure.

At times like these he was glad he was in Canada. He believed he could focus on his desired studies here and stay away from world politics. He had always had a large fear that the kind of research and technology he was learning about would be used for the wrong reasons. He voiced his opinion whenever the words "military use" entered conversations between fellow students or even professors, and he would make it very clear about his stalwart stance against it. Even still, he knew it was inevitable.

Jayden was right though; these kinds of subjects and focusing too much on classes and grades when he couldn't hope to control them would always get Richard worked up. Even so, after only an hour of reviewing his notes, they started to become monotonous, and his eyes were getting heavy. He put the papers neatly away in their appropriate folders and tucked himself comfortably into his bed. It wouldn't take long to fall asleep, and he made sure his last thoughts were a confident reassurance to himself that everything would work out. Maybe he had more in common with Jayden than he would like to admit. After tomorrow, his life would change; he would get the internship and begin to change the world. He was sure of it.

CHAPTER 3

ADOPTION

RICHARD'S SHORTCOMINGS WERE NO REFLECTION of his model adoptive parents, Adam and Isabella Ceress. Adam was a well-read scholar who owned Sundial Publishing, Inc., a large publishing company founded by his grandfather Dominic Ceress. The family also owned The Book Haven, a store to rival the Chapters franchise stores located in his hometown of Ottawa. Isabella was a university graduate who had majored in the fine arts. Her love and passion was painting still-life and nature. Adam's successful business allowed her to pursue her artistic talents in her studio loft at their luxurious and spacious home. After 10 years of marriage and no children (not for lack of wanting or trying), they were fortunate to have Richard enter their lives. But this was not without many obstacles.

They had worked with the Canada Adopts Agency for four years in the hopes of acquiring a child. The adoption of a child has always been a daunting process, what with all the laws in place to protect the biological parents' rights and the rights of the adopted child to maintain contact if they so desire. It becomes complicated and potentially disruptive for adoptive parents to meet the required guidelines without it affecting their day-to-day lives. Less so if they are willing to adopt a child with special needs or an orphan from another country. Isabella and Adam were certainly ideal potential parents, as screened by adoption agencies, and could have many of those opportunities if they so desired. However, they had their own criteria for adoption. Although they were financially well off, they were not snobs regarding their good fortune, but when it came to raising a child, neither of them wanted the extra baggage that came with most of the potential opportunities they were offered.

Adam and Isabella had a good marriage, but as their 10th wedding anniversary approached, Adam knew he had to do something more. Isabella was beginning to lose interest in her creative outlet, her art. She hadn't hosted an art exhibition in her home for more than two years. Adam was concerned that she would lapse into clinical depression as he saw her fighting spirit begin to weaken before his very eyes. Modern medicine assisted in the conception of a child, but after six miscarriages, doctors declared her fragile condition could not support another pregnancy. They had suffered all of this, and now no success with adoption for four years. Adam knew then what he must do to save his precious Isabella, whom he loved so dearly. Nothing would get in his way!

Adam was a model citizen and earned his place in society always doing business "by the book." But he resigned himself to using his influence and wealth to find the right child for them to adopt, and without Isabella's knowledge, he did some research, accessed his connections and paid a considerable sum of money to find the right agency for his needs. His liaison gave him the name of a private company, the J. C. Hope Adoption Agency, and a contact person, Marion DuFour, who would be in charge of their file. Marion DuFour was the only person with whom Adam would communicate. This arrangement worked well.

*

Two months later, three days prior to their wedding anniversary, Adam received a call from Marion at his downtown Ottawa office.

Adam ended his conference call abruptly and anxiously took the other line. "Hello, Marion, Adam here." He tried not to sound impatient, but in his mind he wondered if this could be the call he was waiting for.

"Mr. Ceress, I have very good news," Marion said. "We have the perfect child for you and Isabella. Our agency just acquired his information, and the child is now in our custody at the Children's Residence. He is a beautiful 1-year-old boy."

Adam's heart seemed to race as he thought of what this could mean. He knew it wouldn't be like the other times when he and Isabella had left the agency, yet again disappointed because the match was not suitable to them. Surely this time would be different—a different agency, different people and different circumstances that he controlled. He wanted so much to make Isabella happy.

Without animation or enthusiasm in his voice he said, "That is good news. What's the next step?" He felt that somehow, by keeping his emotions in check, it would ease his disappointment should this not pan out.

"It is as we discussed in our first meeting, Mr. Ceress. I must meet with you privately for you to do the first screening to determine whether you want to tell Mrs. Ceress about this opportunity. This child is a rare find," she stated emphatically. She continued in a softer tone. "When can we meet?"

Adam didn't hesitate. "I can be there within the hour."

"Perfect, Mr. Ceress. I'll have everything ready."

Adam turned off his computer, grabbed his briefcase and rattled off instructions to his executive assistant as his six-foot frame hovered over her desk. "Amanda, please cancel my afternoon appointments, let David know that he will chair this afternoon's executive meeting, forward important messages to my cell ... and I am not available for the rest of the day."

"Yes, Mr. Ceress," Amanda replied, with no questions, only loyal and total dedication to her employer.

Adam wore a look of urgency on his handsome, clean-shaven face. With a short glance back, he noticed Amanda watching him walk briskly down the hall. Hers was a look of respect and admiration, not something Adam wasn't accustomed to from his employees, though it still made him blush ever so slightly. He pensively ran his fingers through his short, sandy-brown hair as he waited for the elevator.

*

When Adam reached his destination thirty minutes later, the J. C. Hope Adoption Agency building on Carling Avenue, he was greeted by the friendly receptionist, who then quickly ushered him into Marion's office.

"Good afternoon, Mr. Ceress. Please have a seat."

"Thank you." Adam sat across from Marion and noticed a folder on her desk with his and Isabella's name on the front.

Marion looked middle-aged but wore a short, modern haircut, dyed black and tipped with auburn highlights. She was professionally dressed in a black business suit and white blouse.

"I'm so pleased you could make it on such short notice. I can assure you it will be worth your while. Our agency has worked diligently to acquire the right match for you and Isabella, as per your specifications. Why don't I just have you read the child's profile, and then we can discuss it further."

Adam welcomed her direct approach. He opened the folder and read Richard's profile. It only contained four sheets of paper: the child's profile and small photo, birth certificate and genome scan, which gave an exact picture of Richard's DNA. Genomes were now a common practice for all health and medical records. He learned that Richard was very healthy with no potential health risks in the future. Adam was relieved when he read those results.

He looked up at Marion. "Why is this file incomplete? He has a biological father. What about relatives? It's blank on this form. I'd also like to see his mother and father's genome scans."

Marion said, "Mr. Ceress, you must understand the circumstances of this adoption. We cannot reveal any more information to you. What you see here is your copy. We will take care of all the legalities and paperwork. What you must know is that this information must be kept confidential for the safety of the child. He must never know of any living relatives. I assure you, he is a wonderful child, perfect for you and Isabella. An opportunity like this may not come again. But you must act in a timely fashion."

Adam's concerns surfaced. Why was the child's safety a concern? What kind of parents and relatives did he have that the sheer knowledge of would put him in danger?

There were so many things wrong with this adoption. Yet as he looked over the file, he couldn't help but think of his wife, and the smile on her face finally having the child she'd always wanted. This child didn't know the circumstances of his family, so why should he be deprived of a wonderful and loving home because of it?

Still, he had to ask. "I don't understand why he cannot know about his living relatives. And this request from his biological mother is baffling! She wants to ensure that the adoptive parents will adopt Richard as their only child?"

"All I can tell you, Mr. Ceress, is that both stipulations were his mother's request in her will. I know it has to do with the well being and safety of this child. I'm sorry, but that's all the information her will allows us to share. Believe me when I say we have never received a request such as this, but under the circumstance, we do intend to honour it. I understand if these circumstances are unacceptable to you, and I apologize if I seem crass. I only want what's best for the child, and I believe a home with you and Isabella is just that."

Her words were oddly of comfort to Adam and did help him make his decision. Though there were still questions in his mind, it was to his understanding the child would have to go to the next of kin or to the province if none were alive. Still, he found a great amount of sympathy for the child. Perhaps Isabella would be able to make a final decision, though he was torn about how he would tell her. He even contemplated not telling her. He knew she would be hurt that he had deceived her if she ever found out, and Adam was an honest man. He was not about to start lying to his wife now, so he decided to tell Isabella the truth. He couldn't hide it from her if they were going to seriously consider this child.

He had little time to think, so when he arrived home early from work, he knew he had to go with the truth—no rehearsed speech. He parked his car in the spacious area near the four-car garage. As he walked through the front door, he felt a sense of hope that his well-intentioned efforts would bring them the happiness they deserved.

He found Isabella in the family room, which overlooked the beautiful gardens of their home. He gazed at her. She was so beautiful—her naturally wavy, shoulder-length brunette hair framing her soft feminine features. The stretch pants and casual T-shirt she wore revealed her slight build and attention to keeping herself trim. For a brief millisecond, Isabella looked up at Adam with despondence and melancholy in her bright blue eyes, as if to say, "You caught me being unhappy," but then quickly reverted to her usual self and her delight in seeing the love of her life.

"Oh, Adam, what a surprise to see you home this time of day! Is everything all right?" She got up from the sofa, embraced her husband and kissed him fondly.

Adam responded with an extra-long hug. "I actually have something important to tell you, my love."

"Is it another attempt to get me to go to Paris for our anniversary? Because I've been thinking, and … Adam, what is it?"

"Sweetheart …" Adam shared his secret with Isabella.

*

He told her how he had found this new agency and how they could find the right child for them. Isabella was not as upset as Adam had anticipated. After her initial objections, she quickly realized Adam's good intentions. If their money could find them a child to love, then so be it! Adam then explained Richard's profile. Isabella too was concerned about the unusual circumstances and stipulations of Richard's adoption. There was little information about his biological parents and none about living relatives. What an unusual request by his mother. However, by this time Isabella was reticent to let any opportunity to adopt a child pass her by, so she persuaded Adam to go at least to meet the child. Adam agreed.

The next day, when they arrived at the agency, Marion was waiting for them in the lobby. She walked Isabella and Adam to the Children's Residence and directed them to a room at the end of a long hallway.

Isabella and Adam peeked through a window to a little playroom where Richard was quietly playing with an abacus type of toy. A young female adult was with him, watching but not interacting with him. He was gliding the little figures from one part of the rail to another in what seemed to be a random pattern. As they walked into the room, Richard looked up at them and smiled. Isabella immediately fell in love with this beautiful child, just a year old, with thick black hair and the most unusual, spectacular green eyes she had ever seen. And a smile that would warm your heart! This was the best anniversary present! Isabella was delirious in her instant love for this child.

The rest was history, all doubts or misgivings dismissed, and Adam and Isabella Ceress became Richard's loving parents. They had agreed to tell Richard when he was old enough to understand that his biological parents were killed in a car accident when he was a baby. It was what the agency had told them happened, and although neither of them truly believed it, they knew the truth, if any, wouldn't be revealed to them. Isabella believed that if she loved the child enough, the subject would never come up anyway. They didn't want to think further on the subject and went ahead with their lives.

Isabella was a doting mother and Adam a supportive father. Richard grew up properly nurtured and loved as an only child. He was easy to love and care for, a very independent child amusing himself for hours on end. He was into print at a very young age and could read pre-kindergarten. He demonstrated an exceptional mathematical mind and an endless inquisitiveness in science and technology. Not only did Richard's inherited genes give him his genius IQ, but Isabella and Adam recognized his exceptionality and provided the environment and opportunities to foster his learning. Isabella made a special effort to give Richard a balanced childhood, including social opportunities with friends and their families, as neither Isabella nor Adam had siblings. These attempts were mildly successful in promoting Richard's social skills with his peers, as in most cases Richard preferred to engage in conversation with the adults or he simply played on his own, interacting very little with his playmates. The only exception to this was Madeleine, who lived two doors down. They seemed to be able to connect at some level, even though they were not always interacting, at least to the eye of an adult. This is what educators termed as parallel play, a stage of socialization all young children experience. It seemed

Richard still preferred this level of interaction through his primary grades in elementary school. However, this behaviour did not in any way deter Richard's natural development. He was a happy child and thrived when he was immersed in some kind of learning.

Richard knew nothing of his biological parents, as Isabella and Adam held their resolve to tell him that he became an orphan due to tragic circumstances of his parents when he was a year old. They explained how adorable he was and how they instantly fell in love with him the first time they met him, so grateful to be able to raise him as their own. Anytime Richard asked who his parent's were, Isabella would try to hold back the tears with a forced smile and tell him they didn't know for sure. It broke her heart to not have the information for him, almost as much as it did every time he asked. But she dismissed it as the actions of an intelligent and inquisitive child.

*

Memories of elementary school and secondary school were a blur to Richard. His intelligence propelled him through the system at an accelerated rate to meet his needs as a student. His parents enrolled him in a private school to ensure he would receive the best possible education. He received many awards and accolades from his teachers. He was like a sponge soaking in every bit of knowledge his brain could process. He was viewed as the "brainy kid" who didn't quite fit into their social circles by his peers, which spoke a lot to his intellect, being in an elite private school. They accepted him for who he was and acknowledged his awkwardness or unwillingness to be part of the group. He was a very likeable guy—just a little eccentric, perhaps?

Richard was ecstatic when he was accepted at U of TST for the gene-aug program. Adam and Isabella were equally as happy but had concerns for Richard being away from home in a university environment at the tender age of 15. However, they collaborated with a student affairs counsellor, who set up a mentoring program for Richard that included special quarters and supervision during his three years of study. An older mature student acted as mentor while adult supervision was provided appropriately. An extra expense for his parents, but they were happy to provide for their very special son.

Thus Richard's first experience at university was very positive and successful. He quickly came under the mentorship of the professor of gene-augmentation at the University, Dr. Gilman. Halfway through his first year at the university he was approached by Dr. Gilman, intrigued by his acceptance papers and unrivalled talent for absorbing information. The two became very close and Dr. Gilman became somewhat of a second father figure to Richard during his University years, helping him with situations even not related to school.

Richard's grades were perfect, 4.0 in every course every semester. Rumours began to spread that he had bribed Dr. Gilman, as that was the only way he could have grades like that. The rumours didn't bother him though; he was there to learn. He did take his time with his dissertation though, almost as if he was waiting for something specific before he submitted it. After seven years, he was finally preparing for the next step in his life.

Chapter 4

THE INTERNSHIP

THE SUN BEAMED BRIGHT AND clear through Richard's dorm window in the morning, as if to symbolize Richard's next step toward his goals. It was early March, and warm days such as this were becoming more and more common, the winters shorter due to global warming.

He looked out the window at students in their spring wear, and despite the grim news many had heard the previous night, most seemed in high spirits. After all, he thought crassly, making fun of them, America wasn't Canada; they were fine—this wouldn't affect them! They would continue going to school, going shopping, partying all weekend; life would go on.

Richard shook his head in disgust. They were between semesters, and most would go home for the summer and return in the fall. A few would remain to take summer classes to advance more quickly. Others sought summer jobs to help support themselves attending a very expensive university program. Still others, the more fortunate, perhaps those with wealthy parents, were planning vacations with their friends after seeing their grades posted on the boards. It was hard not to be happy for them.

Richard, as always, was one of the few with a more emotionless attitude. He left his dorm room in more of a rush than usual, approaching the large crowd milling around the grade boards. His attire rarely changed regardless of the weather: dress pants and dress shirt, often black. Though as a child he was happy and outgoing, as his intelligence grew, so did his distaste for social situations. He knew many mistook it for arrogance when in truth it was simply that his mind was always active, always thinking. He simply didn't have time to speak with people most of the time, unless it was something that would arouse his interest.

The dozens of students making their way to the boards posted on the east wall of the university centre prompted Richard to exercise his patience and silently curse the person who decided to post the internship candidates on the same wall as the grades. He had little—or in his mind successful—experience with social interactions, and he desired none. Especially, as he thoughtfully concluded, since all was obviously going as planned, he wouldn't have to deal with the milling masses anymore. Pushing through a crowd of excited young adults would only provoke situations he wanted to avoid. All he wanted was to confirm he had been chosen for the internship.

The suspense was getting to him. Even after nearly half an hour with the crowd not showing any sign of thinning, it was quickly becoming apparent that if he really wanted to find the answer, he had to make his way through the crowd.

Slowly slinking forward, squeezing through tightly grouped students, he made his way to the front. He was shot numerous dirty looks as he pushed past with no word of apology or excuse. Many grumbled insults under their breath as they grimaced unkindly at him. Richard was oblivious to it all. To him it was not rudeness or arrogance but a purposeful avoidance of normal social cues. He knew people didn't want to talk to him, and he just wanted to see that board. Now that he had made up his mind and had chosen his course, everything else fell away. His goal was everything.

When he finally managed to manoeuvre his way to the boards, his excitement began to show on his face. He could not yet see the internship sheet, but his grades were visible. He scrolled down the school charter for his name, heart pounding and butterflies performing an aerial show in his stomach in anticipation. Why was he so nervous? He had convinced himself there wasn't a chance he would be outdone for the internship. Aside from the fact that he was obviously the best candidate, nobody else showed any interest in it, at least not to his knowledge. Why would they give an internship to someone who didn't want it when there were others who did? Why wouldn't everything fall into place, just as it had again and again?

He shook his head when he realized he was now reading last names starting with D. He was taking too long at the front, and other students were starting to jostle him from behind. His vision had blurred as his concerns and questions filled his mind. He focused again and went back up to the C section and found his name.

Richard Ceress   4.0

A grin formed on Richard's face. He had scored the impossible, a perfect grade, but for him it was expected. His arrogant demeanour remained visible on his face as he glanced over to the posting where the chosen interns would be listed. With what he had just seen, even though expected, reassured him of the outcome. The list was not far from the grades and showed the three candidates whom had been chosen for the prestigious internship.

Three names—and Richard Ceress was not amongst them.

Utter disbelief filled the words he let slip from his lips, the look on his face that of a heartbroken child. "There has to be some mistake."

Students chatted and flowed around him as he stood dumbstruck. Why was there no outcry of protest at this injustice? Why was no one else as stunned as he was? He had the highest grades. He had the most desire for the position. But he was not on the list. This seemed far too unreal to be true. It was obviously a mistake! Richard would just need to speak with Professor Gilman to get the mistake rectified, and everything would be back on track.

With a renewed sense of purpose, Richard made his way back out through the crowd. He wore a stern look as he marched proudly across the courtyard toward his mentor's office. He remembered the professor saying he would be in his office until the early evening to field any questions or concerns regarding the grades. Richard certainly had a few of each that needed addressing.

He hadn't realized it, but he had rolled his sleeves up as he was sweaty and flustered, a feeling he wasn't used to. Richard's thoughts raced, and he felt confused. The wind picked up, as if paying homage to his thoughts ... the old saying of "the winds were changing," or was it "the winds of change"? Richard didn't dwell on it, as he was never very good with that kind of thing. Meanings for him were always literal, not metaphorical.

As he made his way inside, the main lecture halls of the U of TST were empty. It was obvious that most of the students were on holiday. With no classes to attend, many had already left campus to spend time with their families or friends. This prompted Richard to think about his parents, Isabella and Adam, who would be anxiously waiting to hear the news of his internship.

But he had no other plans. The internship was it—no backup. He certainly never considered going back home, but then he had never considered being denied the internship. More than ever, he had to settle this misunderstanding before calling home. Even though Richard was not the best at keeping in touch with his parents, he knew how important this news was to them.

The door to his professor's office was open, just as had been mentioned in the last class. With a dozen things on the tip of his tongue, Richard marched defiantly into the office but quickly stifled his breath when he saw his professor speaking to the dean of the university.

Professor Gilman was a professional man who followed the highest order of etiquette. He always wore a suit and tie when he taught classes, pointing out that for someone in his position; it was a sign of respect to treat each class as a formal affair. So it was an odd sight for Richard to see him in khakis and a slightly worn-out dress shirt with the first few buttons undone. Even his short brown hair was dishevelled when it was normally neatly groomed. Nothing about this image seemed right. Why was nothing as it was supposed to be this day?

Dean Winters had his back to the door, and his body language seemed to suggest he was waiting for a response from the professor. Even without seeing his face, it was easy to tell that the immaculately dressed man in front of the professor's desk was the dean. Not a day went by when that man donned an outfit worth any less than twice a common man's paycheque. He wore perfectly tailored Italian suits and sported a rugged yet somehow clean-looking stubble. His black, slicked-back hairstyle resembled that of a young student on the prowl. It was obvious neither of them had noticed Richard enter the office—a larger space reserved for the director of the gene-augmentation program, whom at the time was Dr. Gilman.

But Richard was on a mission—he had questions that needed answers! They were important questions that were clearly more important than anything either of these two men could be discussing because it wasn't like either of them had just had their whole worlds turned upside down. So he cleared his throat to get their attention.

"Oh, Richard. I'm glad to see you." Dr. Gilman's smile was genuine as always when he addressed Richard. Gilman had always respected him and encouraged him to strive for the top in whatever he pursued.

Richard searched through that simple statement for any lack of sincerity, but finding none he decided it best to be direct. "Dr. Gilman, I have a concern I feel I should bring to your attention." The tone of Richard's voice cut through any pleasantries that would have followed.

Dean Winters, not even facing Richard until now, put an open hand out in front of him to stop Richard before he went any further. "We know what this is about. Please allow us to explain."

Winters motioned with his open hand to one of the chairs in front of Gilman's desk. Richard hesitantly sat, shooting them both an agitated glance. What could they possibly have to explain? Had these two somehow conspired to keep Richard from the internship? Was this some scheme to somehow keep Richard at the university? Because if it was he wouldn't stand for it. He didn't know how, but he just wouldn't stand for this sort of gross negligence.

Gilman sat on the edge on the other side of the desk. He turned toward Richard while holding a document. "We received a special request from the government. It outlines a new project for which they are recruiting a small group of people. This team will consist of no more than seven people from across the continent. They have requested you specifically to participate in this project, Richard." Gilman's words were as sincere as ever, though there was a hint of doubt in his voice that Richard tried to decipher.

He looked at both men, trying to process what was going on before addressing Gilman. He knew he was the most decorated student in the gene-augmentation field, and his doctorate was all but assured after defending his dissertation. But even being in the most prestigious school for this field and receiving the highest accolades, it still seemed odd that his name would specifically come up. "So if this is separate from the internship, what kind of project is it?"

"We aren't privy to that information." The dean spoke harshly, but his anger was not directed toward Richard. It seemed more like he was uncomfortable being denied the information. "I received a call from a staff member who's here in Toronto waiting to interview you. They also sent a letter with a unique insignia on it, with your name, a time and a place listed on it. Nothing else."

Richard's initial excitement about the project was beginning to wane, as he had suspicions as to what this could mean. Why could the dean not know, or the professor, for that matter? Why would Professor Gilman sound so sincere if he didn't know what Richard would be doing? Richard's mind raced, but it did him no good; he needed answers, not more questions.

"This sounds like the kind of thing CSIS would pull." Richard was obviously unimpressed with his own statement and thoroughly suspicious of the Canadian Security Intelligence Service.

"I'm sorry we can't be more help, Richard." Gilman stood up off the edge of the desk and sat in his chair, facing Richard with a more pleasant expression. "However, what I can do is assure you that if you don't take part in this project, there is a spot reserved for you in the internship. You have my word on this."

Gilman's offer made Richard question the seriousness of the government request. What would prompt Gilman to promise an internship placement for Richard if he chose not to take part in the government project? That could only mean Gilman had concerns about what the project entailed. But they weren't privy to that information? They were making some educated assumptions, it seemed. They both knew how Richard felt about using his research and gene-aug technology for military purposes—or rather, his desire for lack of use in the military. Making a soldier's lungs work five times faster through gene-augmentation so he could run longer and faster, for example, didn't even come close to curing Alzheimer's in Richard's mind. And this entire situation had the distinct odour of the Defence Intelligence Agency or NSA. Gilman's offer did put Richard a little more at ease, knowing he wasn't being denied the internship but rather being offered something that could possibly be greater. Either way, it seemed he could still achieve what he strove for.

Still, the lack of information left an uneasy feeling in Richard's gut. He didn't like situations where he wasn't in control. In the lab, Richard was always in control. It fed his feeling of superiority to know what was going to happen, to predict it correctly, to understand precisely everything that was happening.

"Where and when is this interview?" Richard seemed more intrigued by the notion now, though it was obvious he wasn't sure of it.

Gilman handed the letter to him.

Richard examined it, expecting it to have more details. Instead it only had his name at the top with a seven o'clock time, today's date, and the address of a nearby hotel beneath it. A golden insignia was embossed at the top right of the page. The insignia looked like a medal, with five gold radiating Vs conjoined to form an inverted star. They enclosed a gold medallion of the earth. The star thus formed a presidential blue resting upon a wreath of laurel.

Richard looked up to say something to Gilman and Winters, but after looking at them and seeing their twin faces of apprehension, he found it difficult to vocalize his newfound concern, and instead nodded.

Winters forced a small smile and extended his hand to Richard, "The university will pay for a cab ride to the location and back if need be. Just call the on-duty staff at the central information desk. They've been informed and will call the cab for you. Good luck, Mr. Ceress. I know you'll make us proud."

Richard shook their hands as he stood up. He folded the letter and placed it in his pocket. "I'll be sure to be there early." Believing he would be waiting at the location for some time was fine with him. He liked having quiet time to think when an important decision was imminent.

As he left the office, he stopped just outside the door and turned his head. "Keep the internship ready for me."

As he headed down the steps outside the building he heard, "Richard, Richard, wait up." Professor Gilman was following. "I'm sorry about all this. It must be a lot to process and wrap your head around. I was hoping to be able to do this myself, but Winters insisted on talking to you as well. You know how men in charge like to be sometimes? Come on, the coffee shop around the corner should be pretty empty right now. Let's go have a talk."

Richard generally avoided student hangouts on campus except for the cafeteria. He didn't want to deal with the hassle of the crowds, but he would make an exception today as it wasn't going to be busy, plus he really wanted to hear what Gilman had to say.

"Thank you, Professor. That would be nice. I assume you have more insight or advice to offer up about this unusual situation."

"Richard, just call me Gilman. It's what my colleagues call me, and if anything, you'll be on equal footing with me soon—if not perhaps a level above me, as far as where your career appears to be heading. At this rate, if this opportunity goes well for you, which there is really no reason to believe it will not, I'll be sitting in on a lecture you'll be giving about your work and research at all the big upcoming medical conferences and international science conventions. Through your research, you've discovered ways to actually re-grow and increase the working capability of human organs using gene-augmentation. You're going to save lives!"

The two entered the coffee shop. Richard supposed he was going to have to get used to this. Gilman was right. He wasn't really just Richard's professor any more. Depending on how things turned out, they could be considered equals. Intellectually, Richard had the superior IQ and was capable of teaching many of Gilman's classes. But was that what he wanted? Richard couldn't fathom putting up with all the imbecilic students who thought they knew better.

However, Richard had always admired Gilman—the assuredness about him, and his way of making you feel like you were learning even if you already knew the subject matter. He supposed Gilman probably knew it too, which was why the man went into teaching. Gilman was short on research studies though, as it had been years since he had published any of his own papers or findings, which confused Richard. He thought Gilman would have had unlimited ideas, especially when it came to things like curing Alzheimer's. But Gilman never seemed to have an interest in that kind of research and instead focused on passing on to the younger generation what was already established in the field. Perhaps letting them take the next step was part of why he had become a professor in the field.

That kind of life would never do for Richard, dealing with everyone else's problems and questions, trying to make those with smaller minds understand concepts too large and sophisticated for them. His life led down the path of research and laboratories.

"Hello, Delilah, I'll have the usual today—dark roast, black."

"Of course, Doctor." The girl behind the counter seemed only too happy to oblige. Maybe she was one of those perpetual professor-crush students. "And what will your friend be having today? Is he a new professor you're showing around the campus?"

"Well, Richard, what will it be? My treat."

Richard noticed Delilah eyeing him with much interest. He wondered what her interest was. Did she find Richard strikingly handsome, with his chiselled facial features, short black hair and the most extraordinary green eyes, or did she think he was too cheap to pay for his own coffee?

"I'll have a double espresso, thank you." It wasn't the idea of Gilman buying him coffee so much that disconcerted him as it was the twinkle in Delilah's eye as she looked him up and down out of the corner of her eye. If this was the kind of thing he was going to have to deal with going out in the world. Richard was more than happy to spend his time in the lab. She had already spilled Gilman's coffee while trying to pour it into the paper cup. Richard could only imagine the mess she was going to make of his espresso.

They finally made it away from the counter, and Richard could still feel Delilah's eyes on him as they found a seat in a corner booth. Richard's thoughts were momentarily diverted as he recalled all the fuss and attention he received, especially as a child, about his beautiful eyes. He knew and understood the scientific logic for the genomics of his green eyes. Yes, true, green eyes are rare, as they are a mutation, the product of low-to-moderate melanin, which serves to absorb light. The most common areas of the world where the population may have green eyes are West and South Asia, Europe, and North Africa. Richard's genotype was inherited from his natural parents, whom he knew nothing about.

"Richard, listen. I don't know a lot about what's going on here. I know this smells suspiciously of military involvement, and I know your firm stance against what road that type of influence can lead to, but hear me out. The kind of work you're looking to do with your life needs funding, a lot of funding. You're not just going to be able to walk into some company and have the setup you want with a lab and assistants for life. You'll have to find a way to earn that."

"You said yourself I'm going to save lives. The government or charities for curing such diseases should provide the funding.

They should be happy to receive me and listen to what I have to provide." Richard had thought about how he could fund his research before. His research would deal in curing diseases with established charities and government funding, he was under the impression that he would be able to provide his services to those causes. Gilman's words were giving him doubts though.

"See, that's the kind of thing I'm talking about. You have to find a way to change your, well, I have to say, arrogant attitude. I don't personally like at least half of the other professors on this campus, but I learn to at least tolerate them and develop a working relationship because in order to have a successful career, it's a necessary evil, so to speak. You must deal with people in life. You can't just close yourself off from the world with your work as your only friend. People don't have to like you, but they at least have to be able to respect you, tolerate you or need you in some way. And along the way there will be people who not only respect you but also will like you—and believe it or not, you might like them too!"

This was sounding suspiciously like Jayden's speech the other night. Why was everyone trying to lecture him about his failings as an individual, of not fitting perfectly into society, not recognizing others, or acting superior because of his intelligence? Richard just didn't need what everyone else thought was necessary to live in a standard society. It only interfered with getting down to work. And Gilman was wrong. Work wouldn't be his only friend. In a field where he could help others create cures for terminal disease, he would be excited to work with others and hear other opinions on that kind of work. It wasn't the working with others that bothered him, it was working with military personnel.

"Look, you may not like military applications, but they're sometimes necessary. The military generally has the funding to provide for someone like you for the rest of your life as long as they get something out of it. If that means you come up with a serum for them that inoculates their soldiers against certain types of illness or disease, that's a good thing. Just think of this assignment as the first step of your research, and eventually if you do create some sort of breakthrough cure, it could be manufactured and shared with the rest of the world. What if you created an antivirus serum for the cold or flu? That way soldiers on missions wouldn't have to risk the lives of their comrades by holding them back or not being able to perform properly when they need to. That kind of breakthrough would find its way into the global population. You could help wipe out illness on a global scale. You could use your research and knowledge of gene augmentation to predict or prevent the adaptation and mutation of viruses. Can you imagine what that would mean? The good thing about the military is that one, they have a lot of money, and two, they think big. If you're working on a project for them, you have the potential to affect a great number of lives in a positive way. Even if what you're going to end up doing right now is simply a consulting thing, or working with the effects of a certain chemical on a specific sequence of DNA, it can lead to so much more."

"I know you're right, Doctor. I've just always felt that many people in the military have such a narrow-minded focus of pushing for conflict and aggression. I suppose I always just believed that my work with terminal illness and disease would speak for itself, and I would earn funding or a grant from the government. A friend of mine recently gave me a similar message about life and my work. I guess I just need to change my outlook on things to a degree. Doctor, what's wrong?" Richard's tone quickly changed to a concerned, questioning one after looking up at Gilman's face.

"Well, for one thing, I've told you not to call me doctor, and I guess I shouldn't be surprised to hear that you have friends. I've just never seen you interact with anyone in a social setting."

Richard supposed this type of reaction shouldn't surprise him, since he still wasn't really used to the idea of having to deal with people on a friendship basis so much either. "Come on, Gilman," he said, placing a large emphasis on stating his name this time, which made Gilman chuckle a little, "I don't live in a bunker all alone."

At that, Gilman raised his eyebrows and looked down his nose at Richard with a very teacher-to-student look. "Oh no? Well, maybe you don't or maybe you do, and you just poke your head out of the ground every now and then for some air. Look at your takeout cup, Richard."

Richard looked at his cup, astonished to see a name and phone number sharpied across the side: Delilah's phone number. He blinked, and looked again, but it was still there. "Okay, well, maybe you're right then, and I don't come out of my bunker enough, but an intelligent educated person is always learning and always looking to expand his knowledge. I guess there are a few areas where I'm still a little behind. But I've always hated sociology classes, and they don't really count as science anyways. Wouldn't you agree, Gilman?"

At that they both laughed and rose from the booth to leave. Richard really had no interest in Delilah; he honestly couldn't even recall the colour of her hair or eyes—and did she wear glasses? He wasn't sure, and it didn't really matter, but he held onto the cup as they left and then paused momentarily in front of a trash can. He fleetingly wondered, what if he kept Delilah's number and actually called her? Then what? No ... he immediately dismissed the thought and quickly tossed the cup in the trash close to the building where Gilman's office was located, to which Gilman gave him a slightly dissatisfied look.

"Thank you, Gilman, for all your advice. I'll be sure to consider it when making my decision and how I choose to proceed with things."

"You're welcome, Richard. I wish you all the best, and my door will always be open for you to talk or to go grab a coffee and catch up."

They clasped hands once again and went their separate ways.

*

Richard returned to his dorm, void of noise, people and other distractions. He was deep in thought, digesting the recent conversations, weighing his options and using his scientific logic to assess this situation. He could not figure out why, but something bothered him deeply about this offer. Logically it made sense to go to this interview and find out more about the position so he could make an informed decision. *Well*, he thought, *Time to think later. Must call home.*

He grabbed his cell phone, scrolled to his home number and tapped the screen.

"Hello? Richard, darling," the kind, anxious voice of his mother, Isabella, said. "Oh, your dad and I have been waiting anxiously for your call. How are you? Did you get the internship? Of course you did. When will you have to start? I hope you can stay home for one week's visit at least—"

"Hello, Mom," Richard interrupted." I am well, thank you. I didn't exactly get the internship, and I can only stay for a day and half."

"*What?* You didn't exactly get the internship? What does that mean? There must have been an error! Richard, that can't be! There is no one more qualified than you!" Richard heard his mother complain to his father, "Richard didn't get the internship!"

Before Richard could respond, he heard his father say, "Please give me the phone, Isabella, and sit down. Son? Did I understand your mother correctly? What happened?" Adam asked calmly.

"Yes, Dad, you understood Mom correctly, but I didn't get to finish. There's more to it. I have another offer that may even be better, a government project. If I choose not to take it, I'll still have an opportunity for the internship. I have a scheduled interview in two days to find out more about it. It's a little complicated. I'd rather talk to you about it in person."

"Oh, I see, of course, son. We can discuss it when you arrive for your visit. We can't wait to see you. I'll put your mother back on the phone as she has made arrangements for your trip home. See you soon. Hold on; here's your mother."

"Okay, thanks, Dad," Richard replied, relieved his father didn't press for more details.

Adam spoke reassuringly to Isabella, and Richard heard him relay what Richard had just told his father.

"Richard, darling," Isabella said into the phone with excitement. "I have a plane ticket for you and transportation from the university to the airport arranged. I forwarded the information to your phone with contact numbers and confirmations. Your father will pick you up at the Ottawa Airport at 4:05 p.m."

"Thanks, Mom; that's great. I'll have to leave shortly then," Richard replied, appreciative of his mother's organization and her knack for details. She always took care of all his needs.

"Oh, and Richard, I'm planning a wonderful dinner with all of your favourites," she added, "to celebrate your intern … uh"—she paused—"your new position."

"Sounds good, Mom," Richard replied patiently. He knew how excited his mother would be to have him home, even if it was only for a day and a half. He didn't want to take any of that pleasure away from her.

"Well, yes, it'll be wonderful. And one more thing. I invited Madeleine to join us for dinner tonight. Is that all right?"

Richard paused for a moment. Madeline was his only childhood friend. The neighbour girl who was just as intelligent as him, only she pursued a career in law. He was always fond of her and found himself missing their intense conversations while they were both away at university. "Is Madeleine home from Princeton already? Well, of course, that would be excellent."

Richard cringed as he realized what he had just said to his mother. She was always speaking fondly of Madeline to him, clearly wanting them to pursue a romantic relationship. And now to her pleasure, his mother probably detected a slight hint of happiness in Richard's voice. Richard rarely demonstrated his emotions, and now his mother would be even more excited to see the two together again.

"I didn't think you would mind, darling. After all, Madeleine is just like family, and I'm sure you'll want to catch up."

"Absolutely. Look, Mom, I have to get going if I'm going to make that flight." Richard's mind was reeling with random thoughts of home, Mom, Dad, the internship, the interview and now Madeleine. "I'll see you in a few hours." Richard pressed end on his phone.

CHAPTER 5

VISIT HOME

RICHARD DECLINED THE COMPLIMENTARY ALCOHOLIC beverage the friendly flight attendant offered him. "Just a ginger ale, please." Not that he didn't drink alcohol, he just rarely drank it. Right now he wanted to think clearly and hoped to be uninterrupted for the rest of the flight.

He sat back and reclined the seat a few inches and tried to relax. This was a small aircraft designed for businesspeople or perhaps connecting flights to a holiday destination and was relatively comfortable. The flight from Toronto to Ottawa held almost exclusively businessmen and businesswomen quietly working on their electronic devices or just enjoying some quiet time alone in their thoughts. Richard was grateful for the quiet atmosphere. He had about 50 minutes until arrival.

Richard started to go over the events of the day in his mind, trying to sort them out. He was getting frustrated with himself as he couldn't make sense of it. He was suppressing his feelings of anxiety, wanting his logical mind to take over, to no avail.

Finally after three or four minutes of mental anguish, he gave up and let his mind wander. *I'll know more after the interview ... I'll go home and enjoy a short visit ... Mom will make prime rib, Dad will choose the wine ... and Madeleine will be there.* He smiled as he thought of her.

Madeleine Stone was a childhood friend who lived two houses down the very private cul-de-sac of Richard's home. The Ceress residence was located at the end of the cul-de-sac with no neighbours to their left, only a beautifully manicured lawn and lush gardens bordered by natural green space. The whole estate was enclosed by ornate black iron rod fencing with natural stone pillar posts at the four corners of the property. The driveway entrance, although regal in appearance, was welcoming. Two large pillars of natural stone stood on either side of the double-lane driveway with an attached iron gate, which was almost always open. A bronze plaque on the left post read 6 Dorland Lane. The 60-yard entrance led to a circular driveway designed with beautiful interlocked stone with adequate space to park vehicles in front of their four-car garage.

The architectural design of the home was unique in style to reflect the wishes and creativity of Isabella Ceress. Her home was her castle, and Adam gave her free rein to design to her heart's content. She had used her artistic flair to creatively design each room to exude its own personality. Although the Ceress home was filled with valuable furnishings and décor, Isabella managed to give their home a very welcoming feel for their visitors and comfortable feel for their family.

All six estate homes located on Dorland Lane housed families of considerable wealth. Although this was not your typical neighbourhood, Richard and Madeleine grew up together in the typical way. His parents and hers were good friends and good neighbours, often visiting and entertaining in each others' homes. Madeleine's mother, Olivia, and Isabella became good friends and frequently arranged play dates for Madeleine and Richard. They would take them to the parks, museums and many of the rich cultural experiences the capital city of Canada had to offer. Richard's favourite place, even as a very young boy, was the Science Centre.

The homes of this residential area were almost isolated, each within its own large property area enclosed by walls or fences and green space, not ideal for friendly neighbourhood BBQs. You would not see children playing jump rope, or ball hockey on the street. Dorland Lane was very quiet, with no activity save the few vehicles that frequented its path to and from their homes.

Richard and Madeleine were the same age, now 22, starting their schooling at the same time and now each heading for high-stakes careers, Richard in gene-augmentation scientific research and Madeleine in political science and law. Madeleine had a few more years at Princeton before she would be ready to begin her career. As long as Richard could remember, he and Madeleine had played together as young children and got along very well. They conversed in a way Richard felt comfortable with. She was never intrusive or demanding when it came to talking, right from their preschool years through to their teens. They found solace in each other's company. Madeleine just seemed to know when Richard didn't want to talk or recognized when he was in the mood to converse, and then they would have a great conversation about "whatever." She put no demands on him about what was socially acceptable. When they were together, they just "were" ... together ... comfortable. He liked that about Madeleine. She was a true friend, his only friend, for that matter. But that was okay with him, as making friends was never important to him.

Through elementary and high school, Richard and Madeleine kept in touch and talked about their interests, hopes and dreams. She would call him every Saturday night even after he had gone off to university to ask him how it was going, supporting him with anything he needed from a long-distance-friend perspective. He always looked forward to her phone calls; they were his Saturday night break from work and study, until she went off to Princeton, and then the phone calls became less frequent. Her studies kept her busy, and she had more social interactions than Richard, so he dismissed it as her needing to focus on her studies and went on with his life. She would still call from time to time, but it was less regimented, though she made up for it with the length of time they talked. He wasn't upset about it, though he did miss the regular conversations. After all, Richard had his scientific research (to save the world) and Madeleine the governance of the country and current political affairs. They shared many great intellectual conversations with the same ease and comfort they had shared as children playing games and discussing or correcting each other on the rules of the game. Madeleine was the only person to whom Richard would truly listen. He had a deep respect for her and a fondness that often muddled his thoughts.

Memories flooded Richard's mind of him and Madeleine as children playing computer and board games that required logical thinking and strategy. Adam had introduced them to chess at quite a young age, and they both excelled at the game. As they grew into their teens, they played regularly, especially at those times when they didn't feel like chatting (or at least Richard didn't feel like chatting). Although Madeleine tried her best, Richard most often won. He smiled as he pictured Madeleine's frustrated expression when he said, "Checkmate!"

Richard and Madeleine shared every possible topic freely and with no reservation, no barriers and no limits. Except for one topic. Richard would never have known about it ... except for that day, a day he still remembered vividly, a day that conjured up feelings of anger, hurt and despair. The events of that day created a wedge between him and Madeleine, one he didn't understand and she never knew existed.

Richard came home from school that day and found his mother lying in a foetal position on the family room sofa, sobbing uncontrollably. Richard, twelve, barely a teen and already awkward in emotional situations, had never seen his mother so distraught and had no idea what to do. His mother was always in control no matter what the situation, so to see her like this was truly a shock. Something was terribly wrong.

He rushed into the room, threw his knapsack on the floor and knelt beside her. He softly grabbed her shoulders. "Mom, are you all right?" he asked, and then thought, *How stupid is that? Of course she's not all right!* "Mom, what's wrong? Is there anything I can do?" He didn't know what else to say. Before his mother could answer, he said, "I'm calling Dad!"

Isabella made an obvious effort to compose herself and then looked up at him fondly. "Oh, Richard, darling, I'm so sorry that you had to see me like this." She blotted her eyes with a tissue. "I just heard some very unhappy news that upset me, but I'm all right, darling, really."

"Unhappy news? Mom, I've never seen you like this. You're definitely not all right! What's going on?" Richard had an edge to his voice.

"Well, I suppose 'unhappy' isn't the best word to describe it ... perhaps 'tragic' is better."

"Okay, so tragic is the better descriptor? Tell me what it is!" Richard demanded, losing his patience.

"Richard, darling, I love you very much." Isabella sobbed. "I just don't know what—"

Richard interrupted her but softened his tone as he realized he was upsetting her more. "Mom, I know you love me. I'm sorry if I upset you, but what's that got to do with this tragic news?"

"This news will affect you. Richard. I suppose I just don't want to expose you to the ugly side of the world if I can prevent it.

Mothers like to protect their children." She gazed at Richard with love and affection.

"I don't know what this is about, but I'm almost 13. You can't protect me forever. I have to start to grow up and face the world on my own someday. Whatever happened, you can tell me, I can handle it," Richard confidently replied.

Richard could see Isabella suddenly beaming with pride. "You're right, Richard. In some ways, you're too wise for your age! Okay, I'll tell you. Come and sit here beside me."

Richard dutifully did as his mother asked and then waited for her to speak.

After a long pause she softly said, "This tragic news involves Madeleine."

*

"We're approaching the Ottawa airport; please prepare for landing," the airline hostess prompted.

The PA message invaded Richards's thoughts of Madeleine as he denied his overwhelming emotions. He wanted to help Madeleine, ensure a positive future for her. But how could he if she wouldn't talk about it? Then he suddenly thought of his own genomics. He knew nothing about it. It never seemed important before ... but now he realized he needed to know.

*

Adam was waiting for Richard at the arrival gate. When he saw Richard come through the exit to the waiting area, his face lit up and he rushed over toward him, arms extended to embrace him. "How are you, son? So glad to see you. How was the flight?"

Richard reciprocated the hug and realized how much his father meant to him. "I'm good, Dad. The flight was fine, and it's great to be home ... even if it is a short visit."

"Well, we'll make the best of it. Your mother has a lovely meal ready and can't wait to see you. She is so worried about this internship, your other job offer ... you know how she is. She wants everything to be perfect. I have the car parked just outside this entrance. Let's go and you can get me up to speed on the drive home."

"Sounds good, Dad."

Adam sensed Richard was holding something back, just from his posture and facial expression, and the tension in his voice. As they approached Adam's black BMW, he used the automatic door openers and the passenger and driver's doors opened horizontally. The car was running and Adam hit the Auto Home button while the doors quietly closed on both sides. He decided to give Richard his undivided attention and let the car drive itself home.

"Okay, what's bothering you, son? Tell me about this offer."

Richard welcomed the comfort of his dad's car, the feeling of safety when he was in his dad's presence and the knowledge that his father supported and understood him, no matter what the circumstances. He did need to talk to him honestly about this situation. He valued his father's opinion and advice and readily shared the details of the past few hours of his day.

As they approached the entrance to their driveway, Adam concluded his discussion with Richard. "Son, you must trust your instincts. Your instincts are based on what your mind feeds your subconscious. You have an extremely rich and intelligent mind, keener than 99 percent of the population. Use it and trust it. Just don't let your emotions get in the way of good judgment. You are uncertain right now because there are too many unknowns. After your interview, you can make your decision. I know it will be the right one. You will know it too."

"You're right. Thanks for putting it in the right perspective." Richard felt better and more confident.

They approached the front door, and Adam paused before opening it. "Richard, you said Dr. Gilman gave you all this information about this opportunity?"

Richard's mind started to race when his father made this comment. "Yes, but I don't think he was telling me everything he knew."

As they entered the foyer of their lovely home, wonderful smells wafted in from the kitchen.

Isabella rushed to greet Richard and hugged him and kissed his cheek. "Oh, Richard, how wonderful to see you and hold you in my arms again. I've missed you so."

"It's great to be home. I've missed you too—and your wonderful homemade meals. Prime rib tonight?" Richard knew she loved that Richard appreciated her culinary skills.

"Nothing but the best for you, my love! Now let me take a look at you." She held his shoulders with straight arms and looked him up and down.

Richard knew what was coming next, and although this wasn't his favourite part, he allowed his mother's indulgence.

"You look as handsome as ever, but you need to get out of those clothes. They look ready for donation. Check in your room, my love. I went shopping and bought you a new wardrobe for your new position, including suits, casual wear, PJs, socks and underwear. I knew you wouldn't have time to think of this. Most of it is packed already for you in the suitcase and garment bag. I left out black dress pants and a choice of shirts and ties. I'd love you to wear the emerald-green silk shirt—it'll make your eyes look even more gorgeous, but I know how you feel about color. The alternative is a black shirt with a purple pinstripe, also very lovely, perhaps a little more in your comfort zone."

Richard couldn't hold back his comment. "Mom, really. I'm 22 years old, and you still shop for my clothes? I feel like an infant."

Adam gave Richard a stare that brought him back to his manners. "But you're right—I wouldn't have even thought about that. Thank you," he quickly added.

Isabella broke into a huge smile. "Wonderful! Now you have twenty minutes to shower and freshen up before Madeleine arrives. We'll have appetizers and cocktails before dinner in the living room." She scurried into the kitchen to tend to her meal.

Adam retired to the study and Richard went to his room.

Twenty minutes later the front doorbell chimed, and Isabella rushed to answer it. Richard could hear from his room Isabella greeting Madeleine, and then his father's voice doing the same. They adored her and treated her like family. Richard couldn't believe he was feeling a little nervous. Why? He studied his reflection in the mirror and saw a young man in a black and purple pinstriped shirt (he couldn't do the green) about to embark into a new life tomorrow. Exciting, yes, but was there a sacrifice?

He slowly walked out of his room and headed for the foyer. When he saw Madeleine, his heart stopped. She looked so beautiful with her long brunette hair falling loosely on her shoulders in soft, sensuous waves, caressing her neck and back. She wore a red fitted sheath of clingy material reaching modestly just above her knees but clinging beautifully in all the right spots. Her neutral pumps accented her perfect legs with a gold anklet resting neatly on her left ankle. He drank in her vision as if he had never seen her before. She was stunning! A flood of wonderful feelings surged through Richard's body when he realized their eyes were locked. There was an awkward moment of silence, although it probably was only 15 seconds, and the familiarity of her presence became what it always had been.

"Richard!" Madeleine excitedly ran to him, dropping her shawl to the floor as they embraced for what seemed for a very long time, saying nothing. They just "were," like they knew how to be. From that moment on everything was comfortable again, and they chatted incessantly about what was going on in their lives in the past few months.

Isabella was revelling in the enchantment of the evening. The mood was light as they enjoyed small canapé appetizers with a before-dinner cocktail. Roseanne, the housemaid, took care of all the details behind the scenes and serving so Isabella could enjoy her company.

"Mrs. Ceress, would you like to move to the dining room? The roast will be ready to serve in a few minutes," Roseanne quietly asked Isabella as she cleared the appetizer plates.

"Yes, that would be perfect; thank you, Roseanne. Everyone, let us go to the dining room for our first course, Roseanne is ready for us," Isabella requested of the small group.

As they found their places at the table, Richard and Madeline sat across from each other, and Isabella and Adam took their seats at each end of the long mahogany table.

Adam, as tradition demanded, chose the wine, opened the bottle and poured the petit syrah into four glasses. "A toast," he said, holding up his glass, "to the bright future ahead!" They all clinked their glasses.

The dinner conversation was casual and satisfied Isabella's questions and concerns about Richard's new job opportunity. Richard did a good job convincing his mother that all was well and he had things under control.

However, Richard was feeling increasingly agitated about something, and he tried to hide it, but he knew Madeline would be able to tell. "So the sleeping dragon has risen and the United States is fraught with uncertainty with no plan to save the world!" she stated sarcastically.

"The 'sleeping dragon' refers to China, Madeline. I believe you mean the Rising Sun." Richard mocked her, aware she knew the distinction between the two. He knew she was trying to distract him from his thoughts that would always brew in his head at home. Yet he always enjoyed their discussions. She was not as into the gene-augmentation field as he was, but she had an enormous interest in metaphysics, and though she took a more naturopath approach to the science, Richard enjoyed debating about people's "auras" and qi on a scientific level, and made it a point to be as knowledgeable on the subject as possible.

"I see." She laughed. "So the sun has risen then? I hear that parts of the Russian Pacific Coast have now been brought to their heel. Obviously the US is taking it as a threat. I'm curious as to your take on these matters, Richard."

"It's balderdash." He snorted. "The US has been stuck in a conventional war on another continent against an enemy without conventions. Now the threat of a conventional war is on the opposite coast, and it's a national emergency. Maybe if they just stayed in their own country, there would be no conflict." Richard's bitter tone was not subtle; everyone knew his distaste for military actions in general.

"While I agree with you in part, Richard," Madeline began, "if the United States didn't get involved in the Siberian Conflict, we would have had a much larger terror on our hands."

"Are you referring to the so-called terrorist attacks on the Siberian villages? There is no way the United States would get involved because of terrorist attacks in a remote country."

Madeline raised an eyebrow and tilted her head. "Oh really? So Vietnam was going to take over the world?" she said, clearly trying to provoke him.

"Don't be ridiculous." Richard rolled his eyes. "That was to prevent a communist takeover in the containment strategy. Siberia reeked of US special ops involvement, and if Japan really did have operations in Siberia, there was obviously something there."

"Then why didn't the EA get involved?"

Richard actually had to think about that. The EA, or European Alliance, was created for this specific purpose. Why didn't they get involved in the Siberian Conflict?

She continued, interrupting his thoughts. "It's because they wanted Japan to become the target. Two major powers at each other's throats would strengthen their position at no cost. They knew China would take advantage and invade Japan. They just didn't think Japan would be ready for it. Sheer desire is no match for superior technology, it would seem."

Richard grinned at that statement. "A concept I hope to live by."

Madeline laughed, and Richard couldn't help but join her in the chuckle. A poor joke to be sure, but Richard knew Madeline would take it as such.

Isabella and Adam continued their observation of the two, a knowing smile all but apparent on Isabella's face as Adam's furrowed brow showed his futile attempt to understand why these two enjoyed such conversations.

"Well, with parents like these, you will have no trouble living your dreams." Madeline raised a glass to Isabella and Adam. She respected them and made it a point to show them.

Richard was suddenly reminded of the other issue ruminating in his gut. Although he was only on his third drink, the wine was beginning to affect him as he was a social drinker at best, so without thinking he blurted, "Why haven't you ever told me about my real parents? I am a gene-aug expert, and I don't even know who the hell I am!" Richard stared straight ahead into space to avoid the look on his parents' faces. He didn't understand his emotions, or why he was so angry.

Isabella dropped her dessert spoon onto the table in shock. She slowly got up, excused herself and left the room, making her way to the study.

Madeleine immediately piped in before Adam had a chance to say anything. "Richard, why don't we leave this topic for later this evening, after I've gone home? It is not a good topic for the dinner table," she said firmly but kindly.

"Yes, good advice, Madeleine. Richard, you upset your mother. We'll discuss this later. Zip it!" Richard had no intention of hurting his parents' feelings, but he had to learn about tact.

Adam got up from his seat, said, "Excuse me for a moment," and went to check on Isabella.

After a few moments of silence, Madeline turned to Richard. "Walk me outside. We need to talk."

*

"You acted like an idiot." Madeline chastised Richard once the door closed on the front porch. "Your parents are wonderful people who love you and would do anything for you. They've raised you as their own—they are your real parents. That's what real parents do! You should never speak to them with such disrespect."

"Well, I just want answers. Don't you think it odd that they have told me nothing about my biological parents? They were killed in a car accident? That's all they know?"

"Yes, it's unusual. But I'm sure there's a good reason. Your parents would never lie to you, Richard. They love you." Madeleine looked down at the porch as if her words brought pain she did not wish to face.

Richard immediately knew what she was thinking. His rigid body relaxed and his face softened. He could see Madeleine was forcing those thoughts out of her mind.

She looked back at him.

Showing concern, Richard reached his hand out to hers and grasped it gently. "I'm sorry. I didn't mean to upset you."

"I know." She smiled, still looking down at the porch. "I can't imagine what it must be like for an inquisitive mind such as yours to not have answers to these important questions."

Richard let go of her hand and slowly sat on the top step of. "I can't explain it." He shrugged. "I know how good I've got it. I know my parents love me and would give me the world if they could. And yet I can't help but wonder who my birth parents were. Why did they go through so much trouble to make sure I was an only child with no contact to any related family? Were they ashamed of me? Was I a mistake?"

Only Madeline knew the emotions Richard began to show, and it was rare he opened up even to her. Maybe it was the wine, or the guilt from upsetting his mother, but 22 years of concerns were beginning to spill out of him.

Madeline sat next to him and took his hand, covering it with hers. "If that were true, why would they go through so much effort to ensure you went to a loving family and were safe from what they saw as danger?" She tilted her head in an obvious attempt to look Richard in the eyes. "Your birth parents obviously loved you, just as your real parents do."

The use of the word "real" in this situation made Richard cringe for a moment, but only a moment. As the word sunk in, the fidelity of his parents was becoming more and more obvious. He let out a sigh and turned his head with a forced grin toward Madeline. A form of apology he would always offer, as it would seem they had these conversations nearly every time they were together around his parents. Something about Madeline always brought out the curios nature looming in the back of his mind.

"I understand you want to find out about your heritage. Let me help you do that without putting your parents through the worst agony you can imagine. I have many contacts. If you'll allow it, I'll talk to your parents after you leave as the starting point. I have a feeling they don't have all the information or they would have told you. I'll do the search for you so your parents won't have to be involved."

Richard sighed and nodded." You're right, Madeleine, I am an idiot. Thanks for pointing that out. That's a good plan though. I can always rely on you."

Madeleine smiled back at Richard. "We're a team, Richard, always. Now let's get back to our dessert." She stood and outreached a hand. He allowed her to help him up and joined her back inside, returning to their seats.

When Isabella and Adam returned to the table, Richard made a sincere apology and the evening continued as if the incident had never happened. Everyone played his or her part in understanding what had happened. Thanks to Madeleine, relationships were saved with minimal damage.

The subject was not revisited after Madeleine left. She and Richard had time to discuss their game plan after dinner, when Richard's parents gave them time alone in the living room. They hugged each other at length when they said their good-byes that evening, each fearful of the length of time before they would see each other again. He would catch the late flight back to Toronto that night, to prepare his mind for what would come the next day. Yet his mind would not let him think of anything but Madeline. He knew he had to succeed; he had to complete his research and find a way to cure degenerative disease … for Madeline.

Chapter 6

INTERVIEW

RICHARD WANTED TO HAVE THE university call the cab rather early. He was getting anxious waiting. After waking in his dorm room, he wasted no time with his regular morning routine, and then wandered around the campus, soaking in everything around him. He had planned to leave the university anyway since he was done with his training and education, but this opportunity, so to speak, was fuelling his desire, as opposed to the internship. This was it! This could allow him to pursue anything in this field. With the resources provided by a government facility, he would be able to complete his research and possibly eliminate the threat of felt feeling odd about this line of thinking and quickly suppressed his emotions. He made his way to the reception desk and asked the attendant to call the cab for him, explaining the prearranged destination and fare arrangement. Soon after, Richard sat in the cab on the way to who knew where, thinking about what his future might hold.

After a 40-minute drive, the car pulled up to their destination. "All right, sir, the ride has been charged to the university account, so don't worry about payment," the cab driver pleasantly said with a warm smile.

The statement snapped Richard out of his reverie. "Thank you." He vacated the cab but then turned back around, handing the driver a five-dollar bill. He assumed the U of TST most likely wasn't covering a tip. This was one of those times he tried to do the socially acceptable thing—act more like a regular person, he supposed, although most of the time he didn't care what people thought of him or if they liked him.

He mind wandered to post-interview. What if he turned this opportunity down and had to take a cab back to the university? No sense in it being an uncomfortable ride all the way back because of his attitude.

He straightened his freshly ironed black dress shirt, suit coat and pants. It was an odd feeling for him; he usually didn't bother to iron clothes but always kept one black suit and one black dress shirt for a special occasion, something his mother insisted upon, for which he was grateful. It was a rare occurrence for him to attempt to make a good impression on someone. Whatever misgivings he had about this meeting, this was still a very important opportunity.

Richard looked up at the Chateau Renaissance Hotel in awe. He had to bend his neck backward in order to see the extent and full height of the impressive building. Chateau Renaissance was one of the most prestigious and largest hotels in Toronto. It had meeting halls, conference rooms, luxurious banquet halls, ballrooms and more than 600 guest rooms. From what Richard had heard, the average low-end room at this hotel was priced at more than $900 per night. To put forth that kind of money for a simple interview could mean so many things. Nevertheless, Richard intended to reserve judgment regarding the situation and the people involved until after the interview. So he stood up straight and walked proudly through the front doors.

The lobby immediately invited his thoughts to drift into a tropical paradise, and since this hotel was in the northern hemisphere of the world, that was an impressive feat. A large stone waterfall, laced and decorated with what appeared to be authentic tropical greenery, stood in the center of the lobby. The soothing sound of the water flowing into itself was enough to calm even the most irritated driver from the cluttered trip through the city. Chirping birds created a calm ambience, although he couldn't see any birds. Richard thought it was likely a sound board of some kind. The whole perimeter and area of the lobby was enclosed by a large glass dome that let the daylight and beautiful sunshine flow into the hotel.

Richard stood in the lobby for an interminable amount of time watching the well-dressed guests go about their day as though this kind of environment was expected. He was standing there gazing with his jaw open in awe of his surroundings. *So much for not looking impressed*, he quickly reminded himself as he shook his head.

A pleasant but unfamiliar voice beckoned from across the lobby. "Ah, Mr. Ceress, we've been expecting you."

Richard looked in the direction of the voice, noticing a young lady in the administrative Chateau Renaissance uniform walking toward him. He did not recognize her at all, yet she knew his name. If the company interviewing him was trying to make him feel comfortable and not uneasy, they had failed. Given the fact that this may be a military endeavour, they most likely enjoyed making candidates uncomfortable and probably even viewed it as a test.

The attendant approached him confidently with a smile. Her three-inch-high pumps further accentuated her imposing five feet ten inches. She was impeccably groomed. Her form-fitting indigo suit hugged her feminine curves and was highlighted with a contrasting, stark white blouse with a sharp angled collar. The blouse collar sat primly and perfectly on her suit jacket collar with an appropriate business-attire open V-neck. The style revealed her neck and tanned skin to her collarbone.

Richard made his way toward her, making sure to be aware of his own posture as he approached. A smug look was plastered on his face. "I didn't know I was wearing a name tag," he replied with dry sarcasm when she was within a few feet of him.

"I apologize, Mr. Ceress. I was told you wouldn't know where to go once you arrived, so I was instructed to be on the lookout for you," she responded officiously.

"Just by a description?" Richard's expression was not impressed.

"I'm good with faces." Her smile was genuine enough to alleviate her from any harsh judgment. She seemed sincere and innocent.

As Richard had a moment to look her up and down, he saw her features more clearly. Her silky, straight black hair fell loosely to her shoulders with shorter layered strands framing her face, a face that had natural beauty, only slightly enhanced by cosmetics. The only visible jewellery she wore was a thick, platinum-coloured link chain around her neck. It appeared to have some kind of locket, barely visible below the neckline of her blouse. She also sported an unusual digital watch on her left wrist. Her hair attractively framed her face, accentuating her blue eyes and lightly glossed lips.

Wow, Richard thought, *an attractive woman, one that men would certainly notice.* He thought of Jayden; she was definitely his type … yet perhaps a little too sophisticated?

"My name is Elise. I've contacted Mr. Candora, who will be interviewing you, but you're two hours early. I was told you likely wouldn't arrive until closer to four."

"I was too excited to wait." The obvious sarcasm in Richard's voice spoke volumes of his social ineptitude and lack of tact; his tone alone was enough for even the front desk clerk to decipher his uneasy feeling about this interview.

"Well, don't worry. Mr. Candora has offered to meet with you early since you're here. He's waiting for you in the Wellington Room. Follow me, please."

"If you don't mind, it was a bit of a drive from the university, if you'll allow me a moment in the washroom first."

"Of course, Mr. Ceress, of course. It's right over there. I'll wait here for you."

"Well, I should hope so."

The puzzled expression on Elise's face reiterated to him that he still had a long way to go with his jokes. Richard did not actually need to use the washroom, although he should probably take the opportunity. Who knew how long this interview was supposed to last? He just did not like being rushed into something on someone else's terms.

He splashed some water on his face and looked at himself in the mirror. He still felt out of place; the marble counters and ivory sink fixtures in this hotel didn't help either, the cost of which could probably pay for at least a semester of his school. This again led him to wondering about the location choice for this interview. Was it military, wasting taxpayers' money, or a very large corporation that just never thought about how their money was spent because they had so much of it? And how did they so quickly rearrange their schedule to suit his early arrival? He was still staring in the mirror and then thought he should get back out there. This lady, Elise, was waiting for him.

Elise smiled as he emerged and waited for him to cross the entry hall. "Are you ready, Mr. Ceress? Right this way then." Not weakening her smile for a moment, she turned and headed down one of the halls underneath a large sign marked Conference Rooms.

Richard reluctantly followed, unintentionally dragging his feet. He was becoming more and more uneasy about the whole situation with each step he took, even more so as he watched her walk. Any onlookers would have likely mistaken his staring for admiration of the figure in front of him or some sort of entrancement. But his gaze was actually one of suspicion—for a woman in high heels, she did not have a very feminine walk. Her hips did not sway much if at all, and she walked with two closed fists swinging at her sides.

Her gait was authoritative, and Richard noticed the much-defined muscles in her calves and thighs. Richard gave his head another quick shake. Now he was being paranoid. He needed to save his intuition for the meeting ahead.

"Enjoying the view back there, Mr. Ceress, are you?" Elise glanced over her shoulder at him with one of those down-her-nose looks women seemed to be famous for. Her piercing steel-blue eyes and pouty glossed lips were enough to unravel any male.

"What? Oh sorry, no not at all … just thinking." Clearly not the right comment, as she turned back with a little snort. Either she didn't believe him and looked down on him because he was lying or was insulted that he wasn't staring.

After walking past several large double doors, they come to one marked Wellington Room. Elise smiled at Richard and knocked lightly on the door.

A very deep voice said, "Come in."

"Good luck," Elise stated as she opened the door and motioned for him to enter. She turned her head quickly to acknowledge someone in the room and then promptly exited. At the moment Elise turned her head, her hair moved slightly, just enough to expose what Richard assumed to be a tiny earpiece.

After that first step into the room, Richard's gut twisted into a pretzel. Sitting at the long rectangular table were several men dressed almost identically to him: dress shirts, but theirs were white, with the top few buttons undone, and dress pants that were a deep uniform black. They each wore a suit jacket as well, except for the man at the head of the table, who had his resting across the back of his chair.

Richard was ready to turn and walk out at that moment, but the sound of the doors closing compelled him to stay, if only out of fear. Besides, hearing them out wouldn't hurt. He focused on the advice he had been given earlier. If they were willing to spend this much money on an interview room, think of the labs and equipment they could afford.

"Please, have a seat, Mr. Ceress," the man at the head of the table said, and motioned to the chair at the other end. His deep and stern voice was one that did not allow for any argument, even though it was said in an inviting way. There was something intimidating about this man, and it was something more than his appearance that created this aura. "I'm glad to see you here so early. I'm Agent Demetri Candora of the North American Special Forces."

"Never heard of it," Richard said with a slightly scornful tone as he looked around the room at the others. All were fashioned with brush cuts or shaved heads, except for the man at the head of the table. His short black hair was well groomed and although clean cut, he had a ruggedness to his appearance. His face was slightly weathered, with signs of fatigue, and his eyes had a severe look that seemed to gaze beyond its subject. It was noticeable, even in his seated position, that he was a big man with massive broad shoulders, bulging biceps and a thick muscular neck that emphasized two shiny silver medallion-like tags hanging from a chain, military dog tags.

"That's because we are damn good at keeping secrets."

"I see." Richard decided to bite his tongue on the issue that this so-called secret was so openly mentioned in his introduction.

"I'll get to the point, Mr. Ceress, and I'll forego personal introductions to the panel here today as their name cards clearly identify them. All you need to know is that each one has a vested interest in this project. We're here because—"

"I'm not interested." The quick and less than tactful rejection from Richard took even the agent by surprise, stopping him mid-sentence. Richard took himself by surprise as well; what was he doing? He was clearly more unsettled and uncomfortable than he had thought.

"You haven't even heard what I have to say."

"I don't need to. I know what you represent, and I know what people like you would want someone with my talents in the gene-aug technology field." Richard was making it very clear with each word of his disinterest in whatever he had to say, dismissing every word the agent said with a simple facial expression.

"I understand your feelings regarding this subject, which is the main reason we're speaking right now. If you turn down my offer that's fine, but I have come a long way to speak with you personally. So please, at least do me the courtesy of hearing me out first." The agent's tone was controlled and without emotion, but still had an underlying intimidating factor that Richard did not want to uncover. So he instead nodded and waited for the agent to continue.

"As you know, the recession has now been declared a national state of emergency in the United States. A large reason for this is because of all the military resources abroad in enemy territories such as Iran, Iraq and Siberia, which has them spread so thin. Also, the war between China and Japan has caused the destruction of vital Pacific Rim trade. Several of the scientists in the biotechnology division under the Joint Chiefs of Staff have proposed a plan that, while costly to develop, would eliminate the need for large occupation forces. They have proposed that it could be possible to increase the potential of an American soldier that would, as I've had it explained to me in simple terms, be the equal of ten normal soldiers. With training and proper development, they estimate this ratio could increase to a near unlimited advantage. This process would likely be in the form of a serum to be injected into the soldier to increase all physical and mental faculties. A 'super soldier', if you will. Biotechnology alone isn't enough. We can splice and combine bio-faculties all we want, but we need Canadian gene-augmentation technology in order to perfect this serum for human use and ensure its safety. It's the only way to modify a person's internal workings to accept and adapt to such a serum."

Richard's defiant expression became even fiercer at this point; hearing what he was going to be asked to do would only solidify his decision further. Any hope he had that he would be working on some disease cure or a simplified delivery method was all gone. This was working directly on warfare and death.

"Are you finished?" The unimpressed, almost angry tone that escaped Richard's lips was clearly not lost on the agent, but he seemed to continue unfazed.

"We need someone of your extensive knowledge in the gene-aug field to ensure that this project launches smoothly and safely. There aren't many your age with this kind of skill. Hell, we wouldn't be here if there were many people at all with your skill, regardless of age. I had my reservations about bringing a 'boy' such as yourself to this project. But the potential we believe you hold in this field could be the key to making this project work. Your help could save lives."

"And how many lives will it cost? You're asking me to help in the creation of a killing machine. No matter how you sugar-coat it, that's what these things would be. One soldier doing the job of ten? In other words, don't die for your country but make sure the other son of a bitch dies for his … right? This is exactly what I was afraid of—ignorant and power-hungry people like you using gene-aug technology for military purposes. This technology should be used for curing cancer, paralysis and other such problems that mankind did not invoke on themselves. And instead of helping these people who do not deserve to suffer an unnatural fate inflicted on them, your intention is to take their chance at survival and give someone else the killing power to take away even more lives just to serve your needs! I have no interest in helping one nation become supreme while innocent people could use the help I have to give. Are we through here?"

The panel of military personnel all looked at Agent Candora for his reaction, and even Richard was a little worried what his reaction would be. He had never stopped to think to whom he was actually saying this; a man of his means could be in charge of a project like this and want people like Richard out of the way. But Richard was determined to keep a stalwart stance; he didn't change his expression as he awaited an answer.

Candora glanced at the panel and spoke to them. "Excuse us for a moment, please."

Without so much as an argumentative glance, each member in the panel stood up and walked out of the room without a word, closing the door, leaving Richard in a slightly more worried state, alone in a small room with this military agent.

Candora stood calmly and walked to the other end of the table to Richard. He pulled out one of the nearby chairs and sat. He reached around the back of his neck with both hands and removed the dog tags, placing them in front of Richard.

Richard saw the name on the dog tags clearly, just one word: Decan.

His eyes quickly went back to the agent as Decan spoke less assertively and more sincerely. "Look, kid, I'm going to level with you. And I'm going to do so as one civilian to another. Forget my job, forget my rank and forget my past. I'm asking you as one human being to another. Please. Help us."

The sincerity Richard had thought this man would never be capable of was shining through now, his eyes almost pleading, the rough and tough exterior all but evaporated, replaced by what seemed to be a desperate man.

Richard furrowed his brow, trying intently to decipher the meaning of what the agent was saying. "I don't understand."

"This project is going to go through one way or another. It's near completion; we had acquired the help of a famous gene-aug scientist, Dr. Norman, several years ago to start it. This project has been in production for nearly seven years. Dr. Norman has nearly perfected the serum but wants to bring in a second gene-aug expert to double check his calculations, as he doesn't want to make any mistakes with something like this. He understands the potential risks involved better than anyone. I agree with him, believe it or not. It was my insistence to them"—he nodded toward the far doors through which the panel had left—"that brought us to you."

"Wait. Dr. Alexander Norman?" Richard's confusion was mounting even more, though his interest was highly piqued. Dr. Alexander Norman was the genius who literally wrote the curriculum for the gene-aug program at the University of Toronto Science and Technology where Richard had trained. He was the reason Richard wanted to attend this particular school. This was the man who, in Richard's opinion, was in many ways the founder of gene augmentation. The man who discovered the key to correcting metabolic deficiencies caused by a missing or defective gene in the human body by manipulating another gene to produce the necessary product. He created the course of gene augmentation to teach it to the world, so others could use this technology and bring its uses to unheard of places.

Richard had to choose his next words carefully; he had made open protests against the use of gene-aug for military use in the past. He had already overstepped his bounds earlier; now that they were alone, this man may not be nearly as forgiving. "Dr. Norman is far more knowledgeable on gene augmentation than I. Everything I learned I have indirectly learned from him. How could I possibly be of assistance? Not to mention the fact that my outlook on the use of gene-aug is less … aggressive than others'."

"Less aggressive, you say?" Candora reached toward the floor into a bag Richard hadn't noticed before and pulled out a large folder. He opened it out, pulling the first clump of paper that was stapled together, and placed it neatly on the table next to him. Stamped across the front was the title "Cancer or Cannons? Cure or Create? The Healing and Destructive Aspect of Gene Augmentation and How Our Government Wants to Use It."

"E ... excuse me?" Richard's jaw dropped. That was the acceptance paper he wrote for the university nearly seven years ago. It was the most controversial piece he had ever written, but it perfectly showcased his opinions and desire to use gene-aug for good purposes only.

"That's your paper, isn't it? As is this one." Candora sifted through all of the pages piled in front of him, countless reports all on similar subjects, naming off their controversial titles to Richard who, much to his dismay, recognized each and every paper. And knew full well that each of those papers contained detailed information on how the military and government would want to use the technology, and how ignorant they are for it.

"Okay, so it's no secret that I don't agree with military applications for gene-aug." He snorted. "Oh, I'm aggressive all right, but that's in my stance to keep this kind of thing out of your hands."

"Yes, you made that abundantly clear within the first 30 seconds you were in this room." Candora grinned.

"So what's this really about? Are you here to shut me up so I don't reveal the secrets of the American military? Are you going to arrest me for speaking my mind? This is how I feel, and I'll spend my life doing everything I can to stop gene-aug from being the downfall of this world when it could be its saving grace!" The words that came out of Richard's mouth surprised even him, his passion for this subject had gotten him in a little bit of trouble on campus before.

But this was a military official he was speaking to. Yet Candora's facial expression didn't change. In fact, there was a slight nod in the sway of his head, as if that was exactly what he wanted to hear.

"That's exactly the point. You have the skills to make this project work; that recommendation is from Dr. Norman himself. But you also have the attitude toward it to make sure it doesn't go too far. If we get some foolhardy kid with something to prove on this project, we're going to create something we can't control, the exact fear you have. If we get someone who's been in the field his whole life, he may look at this as a way to make his legacy and go too far. I don't agree with this project, but if in the end it'll save the nation from recession and even save the lives of people on both sides, I'm willing to do anything to reach that goal. It may not solve the trade problem with the PC, but it could at least convince the nation to pull its large standing forces out of foreign nations. A soldier capable of that kind of power, if controlled, won't have a need to kill people, like you fear. They could simply subdue the enemy and kill only if necessary, keeping a strong presence at a fraction the cost. With that kind of control, we could control casualties on both sides of the field. But we won't get that control if we don't have you on this team."

Richard's brow was no longer furrowed. He knew exactly what this man was implying, and as much as Richard began to hate it, he was starting to understand his point. Worse still, he was beginning to agree. There were so many thoughts racing through Richard's mind now. He could help make sure that this project didn't go too far. Candora was playing it off as using them as foreign occupational forces. But he knew the truth; it was a ploy to prepare for war with the PC. A nation that has been surprisingly ahead of the rest of the world by leaps and bounds with technology, it would be hard to believe they haven't made at least some strides in the same idea the United States was trying to create. Perhaps the safest solution was to pre-empt such an attack. He could ensure that some means of control were put into place, but only if he were part of the design process. The question was, was he really willing to work on the exact project he had protested against for almost his entire life? What if something went wrong in the design? He would then be responsible for everything that went wrong. The conflict in his mind was taking focus; his eyes shut forcefully as he turned his head and shook it from time to time, making his conflicts obvious.

Candora then spoke the words that would make the decision clear to Richard. "They're about to create an attack dog that could potentially wipe out a nation. I'm asking you to hold the leash."

Richard's conflict abruptly ended hearing those words. He slowly looked up as if about to speak, but Candora spoke first.

"The decision is yours. I'm not here to force you to do anything you don't want to do. And after all, I suppose I'm here for relatively selfish reasons. But I wasn't lying when I said I'd do anything to make this project work. You need blood? I'll give blood. You need a test subject? Test on me first. You need a body? I'll die for the cause. You can't complain about a problem if you aren't willing to be part of the solution."

Candora stood up and grabbed his suit jacket from his chair and headed toward the door, picking up his dog tags on the way. He stopped beside Richard, facing the door but obviously addressing him. "There will be a limo downstairs for the next 30 minutes. The driver will ask you where you would like to go. If you say 'home', he will take you back to your dorm and you can go on about your life as you see fit. But if you want to help us, to help me, say 'Ground Zero'. We will acquire your personal belongings from your dorm, inform your family of your new job for the government and take you to the research facility. You will be well paid and given a comfortable life with full benefits. I hope you make the decision that the world will be thanking you for some time from now, and not experiencing the regret firsthand later on. I hope to be working with you, Ceress."

With those last words, Candora left the room, leaving the door open so the echo of ambient noise from the lobby could be faintly heard from the meeting room.

Richard easily tuned out the noise of the people talking to each other over the sounds of the cascading waterfall and chirping birds. Not that it mattered. Richard's mind was blank.

Candora's words resonated through Richard's head. "I'm asking you to hold the leash … You can't complain about a problem if you aren't willing to be part of the solution."

Richard slowly stood up from the table and began making his way to the entrance of the hotel.

The sunlight gleamed off the fresh polish of the limo that was waiting at the front just as Candora said. Richard walked up to the limo as the well-dressed chauffer smiled and opened the door for him.

As Richard sat in the comfortable seat with an emotionless, dazed expression on his face, the chauffer leaned in to the door. "Where to, Mr. Ceress?"

Richard looked down at his hands, visualizing the dirt and blood that was about to stain them, and then looked over to the chauffer. "Ground Zero."

Chapter 7

GROUND ZERO

THE LIMOUSINE WAS INCREDIBLY COMFORTABLE, fully equipped with a TV, an electronic panel, beverages and food. But Richard was preoccupied with his thoughts. The windows were tinted, which for a limousine was not uncommon, but from the inside they were not just tinted but completely blacked out, preventing passengers from seeing outside. It prevented natural light from coming in. Though being stuck under a dim artificial light was a feeling Richard found all too familiar, in this instance it was unnerving.

Clearly the location of this facility was intentionally being kept from Richard. A piece of the secret, Richard supposed, remembering Candora's speech earlier. Which begged the question, what if he had said no to Candora? Sure, the agent sounded sincere and understanding enough, but that could have all been an act, a ploy to convince Richard to join this project. Would they truly allow the information they so openly provided to Richard get out in the open? How far were they willing to go to protect the secret? It already seemed to Richard that they had a less than admirable regard toward human life.

Richard reached for the button on the electronic control panel that read "Chauffeur."

"Yes, Mr. Ceress?" the chauffeur replied through the intercom. "What can I do for you?"

"How far is it to the research station?"

"It'll be a few hours, Mr. Ceress. Please make yourself comfortable and enjoy the refreshments and entertainment system. We'll have a comfort stop in about two hours. I'm here to assist you, accommodate your needs and ensure your safe arrival," the chauffeur politely responded.

"Thanks," Richard replied sarcastically and sat back in his comfortable, plush seat. "Of course he won't give me any details ... a few hours?" He looked at his watch ... 5:16 p.m. He pulled his cell phone out of his pocket and tapped the screen to text Madeleine. He wanted to tell her that he took the job and wouldn't be in touch for a while for security reasons. When he pressed send, it beeped and flashed "no signal." He quickly checked the settings on his phone and his watch only to find both were not transmitting, and they were unable to receive signals. These people obviously meant business. Regretfully he could not speak to his parents or Madeleine, or anyone in the outside world, for that matter. Suddenly he felt a frightening sense of isolation, and the magnitude of his decision began to ring loud and clear. He struggled to suppress his fear and decided not to over-think the situation right now. He opened the fridge and stared at its contents. As he munched on some type of trail mix and sipped on a bottle of water, he started to feel totally relaxed.

*

"We've arrived, Mr. Ceress." The chauffeur's voice over the speaker near Richard's ear interrupted his deep sleep.

What had been said hadn't completely sunk in yet, as Richard slowly opened his eyes and tried to get his bearings. Did he sleep through the entire night? Then the door beside him opened abruptly, and Richard's daze was broken as he stepped out of the limousine.

Standing up and examining his surroundings, he was half-expecting to be bombarded with morning sunlight, though after quickly checking his watch it read 10:07 p.m. It seemed he only slept five hours.

Viewing his surroundings, he found himself inside a large facility illuminated by artificial light. The outside walls had to have reached at least ten stories into the air, ending with what looked like a retractable ceiling. The walls and floors seemed to be made of a sleek metal resembling a thick armour that would be used to protect a tank. There was a large closed garage door behind the limousine made of the same metal, big enough to frame a small house. Richard noticed that this must have been the entrance they used to enter the facility as it was still making a loud cranking sound while it slowly closed.

Parked on either side of the limousine were several modes of transportation—about a dozen large armoured hummers and a helicopter in the far corner. Even with those large vehicles, there was still room for at least a dozen more of the same in this entrance area alone.

"This way please." Even with the chauffeur speaking softly, those three words resonated through the area as if shouted into a canyon. He led Ceress to the double doors on the other side of the room.

Richard concluded that this must be a top-secret location for a US military compound and research station. They had certainly ensured he would have no clues as to its whereabouts. Even knowing the time according to his watch, his sense of direction and time were disjointed.

Entering the next room was like a child wandering into the largest toy store in the world; his attention was immediately diverted. This room, just as large as the entrance, had a central pod filled with dozens upon dozens of different pieces of lab equipment. It seemed to be one large laboratory with incubators, medical supplies, research supplies, chemical testing supplies, computers and electronics, a researcher's delight. Richard immediately recognized a top-of-the-line positron emission tomography scanner with nearly a dozen attached monitor screens, a machine used to examine various body tissues in order to identify certain conditions, a perfect device in use of monitoring augmentation of human tissue and the central nervous system. Richard tried to hide his awe as he continued to examine the equipment more closely; seeing machines and devices from all fields of research in the same room together he couldn't help but think how each could be used to further gene-aug research! It was as if every piece of scientific technology was available in this room alone. The moment he walked in, Richard felt that if there was anything he would need to help him in his research, he would have it.

Outlying the large area were about a dozen closed doors to rooms that surrounded the central pod. Three floors overlooked the common pod area. Each balcony was decorated with a small bit of live foliage. Richard presumed this was a weak attempt at creating a comfortable, almost outdoor work environment, though a bit ignorant in his mind; trying to provide a research group of scientists an outdoor work environment is much like providing a computer lab for an athlete to perform his exercises.

This facility was obviously even much larger than the lab itself. Richard thought, *What else could they possibly need with all this equipment here? What else does this facility house?*

The chauffeur pointed at various doors connected to the first floor of the facility. "The room on the far left is the cafeteria, and beside it on the right is the recreational room. There's a gym on the other side next to the wellness centre, and an infirmary through those doors on the other side, each labelled, as you see. Now follow me to your quarters." The chauffeur's explanation caused Richard to roll his eyes as the chauffeur led Richard up a circular staircase in the right corner of the room. He was so caught up in the excitement to work with all this equipment that he had forgotten about the essential living requirements for human beings.

It seemed as though Richard felt more at home in the main laboratory than in any normal setting he would be provided, but a recreational room, a wellness room? That seemed a little out of place for a facility that was to provide the next Manhattan Project. Perhaps their regard for the comfort of their researchers was a small credit to their intentions. What about visible ventilation to provide much-needed oxygen? This facility was exposing to Richard that aside from being a secret itself, it was holding secrets of its own. Their need for an infirmary was of little comfort to Richard as well. He caught himself glancing into the open door as they passed to see if there were any occupied beds, but it seemed unused.

After being led to his quarters, Richard was again taken aback by the attention paid to the comfort level for their researchers. The room was designed as though it were a luxury hotel. He saw a large king-sized bed, fully equipped kitchen, big-screen TV with two large couches facing it and even a large hot tub in the center of the room.

Even with Richard's awed expression as he looked around the room, the chauffeur still found it pertinent to speak up. "If there's anything missing in here that you'd like, just let General Grey know, and you'll have it within a day."

Richard was in complete shock. Candora had mentioned there would be full benefits, but he didn't realize until now just how far those benefits extended.

"Your personal belongings should be here within the hour. In the meantime, General Grey would like you to join the others in the conference room for introductions and an overview of the project now. After the meeting, you will be shown an excellent Welcome to the Facility video, and I would recommend you check out the TV screen menu with every possible category to familiarize yourself with the functions and design of this facility, as well as its amenities."

"All right. Thank you for your help, Mister …?"

"Nate." The chauffeur tipped his hat politely at Richard and turned to walk out of the room. "I'm afraid we can't take any time for you to familiarize yourself with the facility just yet. The team is awaiting your arrival in the meeting room."

"Very well," Richard responded, following Nate back out the door.

They walked to another one of the doors outlying the laboratory. Nate stood to the side of the door and motioned for Richard to enter. He hesitated a moment, but Nate's genuine smile comforted him.

As Richard approached the open door, a middle-aged man wearing a buttoned-up lab coat walked toward him as if to greet him. He was of average build, not athletic, but obviously a man who took care of his appearance. This was apparent by his clean-shaven head and well-kept facial hair surrounding his mouth. He walked with purpose and quickened his pace as he locked eyes with Richard. His large smile grew as he approached with an open hand outstretched in anticipation. "Dr. Ceress!" The excitement in his voice was that of shock and approval, and the use of the title Doctor when referring to Richard confused him even further.

"I'm sorry, I'm at a loss as to who you are. And don't call me Doctor; I haven't earned that title yet." Richard stopped in his approach of the room, ignoring that extended hand that was yet waiting for Richard to acknowledge it.

The man laughed heartily and motioned to himself with his already utilized hand in response. "Forgive me. I'm just overjoyed to see that you accepted my invitation!"

Richard's addled expression quickly turned to wide-eyed shock as he affirmed to himself who this man was. "Dr. Norman?" he managed to assert through his shock.

The man's smile turned to a grin of amusement. "Please, we'll be colleagues now. Call me Alex." He extended his hand once again, and this time Richard immediately gripped it tightly and shook it rapidly, as a child would his hero—which in this case was not far from the truth. This man was the reason Richard was so passionate for the study of gene augmentation—this man was the inventor of the curriculum and in his mind the founder of gene augmentation. If there was ever to be a cure for mankind's diseases, this was the man who would be responsible for it, a genius, a scholar and, as it turned out, a gentleman as well.

"It's an honour to meet you, sir!"

"The honour is mine, Mr. Ceress. You have no idea what it means to me that you have decided to help us in this endeavour." Alex mentioning the "endeavour" turned Richard's adulation to a sullen and far more serious look as he remembered the real reason he'd been called here.

"I would hope our meeting would have been under better circumstances. I'm afraid when I envisioned myself shaking your hand, it was not with the shadow of a colossal mistake based on our research looming over our heads."

"I understand." Alex met Richard's statement with a sombre expression. "And I apologize for pulling you from your life to assist with a project in which I know you have no interest. Demetri was set on the second gene-aug agent being you, and I was happy to make the recommendation to General Grey as well. You must understand the importance our work has to the rest of the world."

Richard wasn't sure whether the mild contempt that had suddenly surfaced was intentionally directed at Alex, or just a general negative feeling toward the project and his situation. Should he feel any remorse for feeling it at all? All he knew was that he was there for a reason, as much as he hated it.

"We should get started." Richard's limited social experiences were once again apparent as the short-lived adulation for the creator of gene-aug had passed.

"You're right. Please let me introduce you to the rest of the executive development team, and we'll bring you up to speed." Alex conceded the small talk and led Richard into the room.

The room was fairly empty, aside from a smart board on one side of the room as well as a table on the other with water, coffee and an assortment of fruits, not unlike what you would see in a hotel conference room. In the center of the room stood a large wooden rectangular table with twelve chairs around it. The room was decorated tastefully with plants on tables and paintings adorning the walls. If not for the sleek metal walls and ceiling that seemed to be the theme in this facility, the room might have been inviting.

All but five of the twelve chairs were filled. At the head of the table was a man in full military uniform with more medals and badges than Richard could count in a short glance. He was impeccably groomed in every detail, flawless from his short brush-cut brown hair to his perfectly pressed uniform. The man seemed to be grimacing, but from what Richard could tell, it wasn't intentional but seemed more of how his face was actually shaped.

Next to him sat the familiar Agent Candora still in the same dress shirt and pants he had been wearing earlier today, or at least what he thought was earlier that day. He gave Richard a warm smile and nod as their eyes met. The relief in the agent's eyes was far from subtle.

On the other side of the head seat sat Elise, the front desk clerk from the hotel. Though now she was out of the front desk attire of the Chateau Renaissance and in a military uniform, looking quite different with her hair tightly braided to her head without a single strand out of place. Her demeanour was officious and confident as she proudly wore not quite the same number of medals as Agent Candora but enough to be recognizably decorated as an officer. So Richard's instincts were right about her; she just didn't fit the profile of a front desk clerk at a posh hotel! However, even with little or no visible makeup, Elise's stark beauty exuded through her serious facial expression.

Next to her sat a young, very attractive woman who was a complete contrast to Elise. Her delicate heart-shaped face was framed sensually with long strands of straight blonde hair hanging in front of her ears and sitting casually below her shoulders. The rest of her hair was swept up in a fashionable knot at the back of her head with wisps cascading from the knot. Her blue silk blouse emphasized her bright-blue eyes, which were further enhanced by black eye liner and a few black highlighted strands of her hair. Her illuminating smile almost forced him to smile back. The overhead lighting on her fair complexion created a natural glow on her pale silky skin. The subtle tilt of her head as her eyes met Richard's made him feel as though she was trying to read his mind, his body language, assessing him in some way. She was probably some sort of psychologist, Richard concluded. "Those types" were always reading too much into every subtle action and word spoken from everyone they met. Finding out how every person operated was their primary goal. Richard could sense her quiet, demure appearance hid a strength of character needed for this position. Though it began to concern Richard how he was beginning to notice more and more minor details of each person he was meeting. It was not in his character to do so under normal circumstances.

Perhaps he was looking desperately for anything wrong with the scenario he was about to be thrust into.

Immersed in his thoughts, Richard suddenly realized he had been staring at her the entire time, creating an awkward moment for both of them. The glow on her cheeks began to tint a slight rose as she broke eye contact and looked away, her smile now uncomfortable.

On the other side of Candora was an African American man in a tight black T-shirt that seemed only to be tight because of the large muscles underneath it. His well-groomed beard surrounding his mouth made up for the absence of hair on his cleanly shaved head. He grinned and nodded as he looked at Richard. Richard checked the chair behind this man in search of a military jacket that he had probably taken off but saw none. With no medals or dog tags, this man seemed oddly out of place.

Next to him was a young man, whose pale skin was only emphasized by the classic yet slightly dirtied lab coat he wore, and his bold black-framed glasses. His bowl-cut brown hair gave him the look of some grungy guy from the 1990s who couldn't afford a haircut. This was a man Richard could tell belonged here, as his eyelids were open to uneven levels, as if he had no sleeping pattern at all and spent every waking hour staring at computer screens. The yellow tint of his glasses gave affirmation to this, and he could tell they were the kind designed to reduce eyestrain and fatigue from prolonged exposure to digital screens.

At the opposite end of the table, a man who had only turned around slightly to get a visual of who had just entered rested one arm over the back of his chair. He wore a similar lab coat, but his was much cleaner. His brown hair, wrapped in an untidy ponytail, fell just below his shoulders, and the scruff on his face gave the impression he did not enjoy cutting his hair on any part of his body. There were similar medals on his lab coat that were also displayed on the other head's military man's outfit—not as many, but a man wearing a lab coat decorated with medals meant he had done this before. Richard recognized right away that this man would be his greatest obstacle to ensuring this project didn't go too far. The look of disdain on the man's face when Richard entered the room made this abundantly clear. Seeing this caused a small devilish grin to crease Richard's mouth. It amused him that this man likely knew why Richard was brought here, even more so that it upset him.

"Ladies and gentlemen, may I introduce the final member of our development team? This is Richard Ceress, top gene-aug student of seven years and an exceptional bioengineering student. He's going to give me the final assistance I need to complete my end of this project." The majority of the room smiled and nodded in acceptance, aside from the man closest to Richard who had been resting his arm across the back of his chair. He seemed to have quickly lost interest and turned back around.

The man at the head of the table stood up for a moment to address Richard. "Mr. Ceress, I'm happy you decided to join us. Let me introduce you to the people you will be working with on this project. I am General Grey. I'm heading up this project. You've already met Demetri and Elise." He motioned toward them sitting on either side of him. "They will be your direct military supervisors for this project."

Both smiled and nodded at Richard almost in unison.

"This is Corey York. He's a leading expert on muscle building and kinesiology." He motioned toward the mountain of muscle sitting next to Candora. "Next to him is Nathan Wilks, one of the foremost technological software and hardware experts in North America." The young pale man nervously waved and adjusted his yellow-tinted glasses.

"Just in front of you is Blake Saracen. He is head of the biotechnology division for the United States and a direct advisor to the Joint Chiefs of Staff." The longhaired man in the lab coat stood up with an emotionless expression and offered his hand. Richard, wearing the same expression, shook it; both gripped quite hard. There was something about a biotech from the United States that rubbed Richard the wrong way. Blake sat back down.

"You already met Agent Nathan Fosk, behind you." The chauffeur tipped his hat again. "And the final member of our executive team here is Jocelyn Triin. She is our psychological and mental-health expert." He motioned at the smiling young blonde sitting next to Elise. "Everyone, this is Richard Ceress. He is our requested gene-aug expert for this project to assist Dr. Norman."

Everyone gave a calm verbal greeting to Ceress.

"Nice to meet you." Richard's words were kind but somewhat empty. He was focused on the man in the lab coat in front of him who had been ignoring him since they shook hands.

"Have a seat next to Nathan, and I'll go over a few things," General Grey said, and motioned to the open seat.

Richard sat while making it a point not to look at the longhaired man next to him. There was something about him that got under Richard's skin. He couldn't explain it, but he was sure that man was already thinking of a way to get rid of Richard. The way he looked at him when their eyes first met was as though he was staring at a rival. He was certain this man knew the real reason Richard was there. *Good*, he thought. *Knowing he isn't okay with my being here makes me feel better about being here.*

"We're still missing Paul and Anthony, but they already know what's going on and aren't part of official development, so we can start without them," Candora explained as he motioned to two of the open chairs. It was likely an attempt at making it clear that there were twelve chairs in this room for a reason.

"Let me begin by thanking you for agreeing to help with this project. You have no idea yet the good service you are doing for the people of this nation, let alone the world." The general's words did not reassure Richard any further, and they lacked a certain sincerity. However, that could just be due to the manner expected of his status and the rank. Perhaps he had to project a certain image.

"You have all been briefed on what this project entails and why, so please bear with me while I reiterate it for our new member." He directed his gaze to meet Richard's. "We're creating a formula to give one soldier the ability to do the job of many. In accomplishing this, it will allow us to pull the bulk of our occupational forces from foreign countries and save us millions in resources down the road, as well as save the lives of thousands. The codename of this project is 'Valour'. You and Dr. Norman will be given access to everything the rest of the team has been working on for the past several years and any other resources you need in order to perfect the necessary augmentations to finalize this project."

Richard rudely interrupted as the general was about to continue speaking. "Excuse me. How did a group of four experts develop a project of this size?"

The general, taken off guard by the brazen comment made by their rookie member, leaned his head slightly toward Richard in reprehension, but Blake spoke up to answer in his stead. "We have access to all other staff on the other levels of this facility," Blake stated in a less than polite tone. "The people in this room, aside from the two currently on assignment, are the only ones with full access to all the information regarding the project. Everyone else who has access to information or is working on some aspect of this project is only given small pieces of an assignment. In this manner, they have no possible way of putting the information into a coherent project. They have just been given a piece to complete and hand back. The team consists of more than 200 people, each completing key aspects of the project in isolation."

General Grey followed Blake's explanation with a serious tone but returned to his commanding stance. "That being said, I need to make something clear. The reason we put so much effort into making this facility comfortable for the lot of you is because you will not be leaving the facility until after the project is completed and deployed."

Richard looked around the room, seeing a look of worry on most of his new colleagues' faces, perhaps fearing this would deter Richard from the project. Richard stood intent.

"There is no contact to the outside world through these walls. This is both for the secrecy of the project and your safety. Anything you need that we can provide, we will do so for you. We want you to be comfortable here while you work, as you will be here for some time."

General Grey faced Richard. "You've had a long trip to get here, and I'm sure you're tired. Your personal belongings should have arrived by now. Take tonight to get settled in your room, get some rest and you can begin tomorrow."

Richard noticed that Candora's intimidating demeanour was not showing nearly as much now; he seemed more at ease than when they last met. Richard thought he knew why ... as with every glance Candora took at him, it was as if to say thank you.

"I have one order of business I would like to bring up before we are dismissed." Ceress could hardly believe he had spoken up, quickly getting the attention of the entire room. He had something to say. Perhaps it was his lack of social tact that prompted him, or maybe it was his backbone making its first public appearance. But he had to say it and he had to make his feelings clear.

"What is it, Ceress?" General Grey asked, almost intrigued.

"This process is one that will not be rushed—my cooperation depends on this fact. Yes, it will be costly, and it could take many years before tangible results are readily available. But if you do not allow me to follow through in this program to its full conclusion"— Richard took a long look at everyone in the room, focusing mainly on Blake and General Grey before continuing—"you will regret it. This is not a threat, but truth that, if it should come to pass, you will all live to see."

In spite of being somewhat baffled by his cryptic words and clearly mildly annoyed by being talked down to by a juvenile, General Grey grinned. "Very well, Ceress. You have our full support in this matter. Do not let us down."

As Richard stood up and started his way back to his luxury suite in the middle of this science wonderland, his mind raced thinking about what was just said. There was an underlying scheme in those few words the general spoke. There was more to this than he was letting on. He was far too accepting of Richard's statement for there not to be. The question was, how many of the people in this room were actually aware of the full intention of this project? Did he actually have allies in this facility, or was he more alone now than he ever had been before?

"Ceress!" A stern and somewhat spiteful calling of Richard's name broke his train of thought as he turned around to see Blake approaching him as if on a mission. His serious expression as he approached was likely intended to make Richard feel intimidated. It only succeeded in irritating him further and affirming his dislike of this obvious obstacle. "I need to have a word with you."

Richard raised an eyebrow and couldn't help but grin as he responded, "If you're here to tell me you will not allow me to destroy the hard work you've put into this project and to stay out of your way, save your breath. I'm here to make sure that ignorant and power-hungry morons like yourself don't destroy the world for your own personal gain in order to satisfy your own massive ego. If you're here to wish me a good night, then I bid you thanks and see you in the morning." Richard quickly turned his back and opened the door to his room when he felt Blake's breath on the back of his neck.

Blake spoke in a soft ominous tone, "Good luck, Ceress."

Richard slightly turned his head as Blake walked calmly away after speaking those insincere words into his ear. He had made his intentions clear. He wanted power, and he believed this project would grant him or his country an unlimited amount. With no visual concern of containing or controlling a soldier that could easily go AWOL, one thing was becoming ever clearer to Richard now. Keeping this project under control would be infinitely more difficult than he had originally anticipated.

Chapter 8

INHIBITOR

Project Valour: Entry 56; Day 182

It has been nearly six months since Demetri Candora recruited me to join this team of researchers. I have had no contact with the outside world and have wondered how my parents are dealing with that, especially my mom. I miss communicating with Madeleine and hope she is doing well and having some success with our personal research project.

The Valour project was designed to bring the greatest scientific and analytical minds of North America together in order to create a serum that when injected into a subject would increase his physical, mental, metabolic and overall combat ability to heights thought unreachable by a human being. I was told when I was recruited that its purpose was to replace large foreign occupational forces with a small elite group to save both human and monetary resources. Apparently they think me a fool. It is clear this project is meant to prepare for war against the PC, but I have decided to assist with this project so I can ensure its success … and control. It has gone through several iterations since I have joined, none of which were stable enough to be brought to the human testing phase.

One of the major issues I've been dealing with over these months is how to control these super soldiers. If one person is given this much power, it is only a matter of time before it is abused for personal gain. But if the people who create the super soldiers control that power, it could be abused on their end as well. Finding a median between those two extremes has proven extremely difficult, especially since I am trying to arrange that part of the project on my own. The time for human testing is nearly here, and I cannot wait any longer to bring this to the team's attention as it needs to be implemented before we begin human testing.

I believe I have come up with the necessary means of control that will be implemented into the Valour project. I can factor a dissipation cycle into something of an "activation serum" in itself so that depending on the amount of serum injected into the subject, the effects will only last an estimated amount of time. After the initial serum is injected, it would enhance the desired genes but not activate them in the body, so the subject would see no effect. We would then inject the activation serum into the subject to turn on the enhanced genes. The maximum non-lethal dose of this serum would stay in a subject's body for approximately one week, activating the enhanced genes, but once it has been in the body for a certain period of time, it will stop feeding the enhanced genes, and they will turn off. Anything beyond that dosage could result in brain damage, irregular blood flow and ultimately death, as it will be too much for the bloodstream. I can also modify the serum and change the biological coding using gene augmentation so the brain will not register that the serum is actually in the bloodstream. This will prevent the synthetic drug addiction that the subjects would experience. This is the best way I could determine to keep the serum under control.

In conclusion, the subject will only be enhanced for the time under the influence of the activation serum and would not be addicted to it. The only downside could be that they may have trouble controlling their newfound strength and abilities. With the brain synthetically unaware the body is enhanced, it will take much training and practice for a subject to properly control and understand what it would then be capable of. It means even after being enhanced, these subjects would need extensive training.

Research has proven that every human being reacts differently to similar doses of medication. The same will be true of the Valour serum. Therefore, each subject to be injected with any portion of the serum will have to be screened first with a saliva sample to examine his or her DNA. If we do not do this, an improper dose of the serum could cause unwanted side effects, even death.

We have split up the Valour formula into three different serums in order to isolate the different aspects it will enhance. It will allow us to troubleshoot any problems once we get into human testing if we introduce each aspect separately. We separated the serum into specific agility, strength and mental aspects. Each will need to have customized doses depending on the subject and will only enhance already-inherent talents, but should have a uniform result with each individual if measured properly. By my calculations, it will require a great deal of athleticism to survive the initial serum injection. This serum will by no means create a super soldier out of anyone. He or she will have to be fit enough to survive the initial procedure. Because of this, I am recommending that the strength portion of the serum, code named "Vigour," should be the first strain implemented in order to increase the success rate of the second and third aspects.

Time has seemed nonexistent to the members of the special research team. With no natural light in the facility, it's been difficult to tell the difference between night and day, and many work such long hours. Most would simply work and stay awake until their bodies gave out. To me it has felt like just a moment from when we started working on this project. This large metal prison may have been a detriment to most, not having access to the outside world for such a long time. But for the small group of specialists involved, it seems to feel like home. I personally took advantage of the wellness centre—yes, not like me at all! But I was gently coaxed by Dr. Triin to try it. I discovered that the physical effort on my part to keep healthy was minimal. Thanks to scientific developments combined with research of human physiology, machines can do it all for you. I have to admit it does make me feel stronger, more aware and better able to focus on my work.

The project seems to be progressing without too many complications. Several arguments have ensued between Saracen and Dr. York whenever Dr. York shut down Saracen's research regarding certain types of muscle-enhancing chemicals, trying to turn Vigour into a super-steroid rather than a gene-augmentation serum. Dr. York's main concern in most cases was that any subject who received a dose Saracen had suggested would not survive the process.

Dr. Triin has become equally concerned with the mental effects the doses would have on Saracen's subjects. She was working closely with Saracen to find a proper median between too much and not enough. It proved difficult with the kind of chemicals that had to be used in order to gain a significant enough effect to prevent a simulation of a drug overdose in the subject. Dr. Triin's main concern was that in any subject, the effects would mimic those of a drug overdose including confusion, coma and hallucination. Despite the protests, Saracen has stood adamant with the type of chemicals and the dosage he felt were needed. He countered that not using the proper dosage (by his recommendation) to affect physical and mental faculties on a relatively equal level, the mind would not be able to keep up with the body and would overwork itself, ultimately resulting in a stroke. Her objections have been the leading reason we had not yet tested on humans.

Nathan has never voiced any opinions. It is obvious he is not the social type—even less than me! He was handed pieces to be used or modified in the provided technological equipment, and he did so without a word. If something broke, he had it fixed within the hour. Even though I'm sure he had never seen this equipment before, he seemed to know them intricately after the first week.

General Grey is not a hands-on leader for this project in the slightest. He would show up and walk around the facility watching the other researchers do their work from time to time, as well as go into the conference room with Saracen. He rarely spoke to anyone else and has not appeared to have checked up on my work at all. But it has been obvious that during this entire time, the general has been growing increasingly impatient and anxious.

Despite numerous protests and factual evidence against what Saracen would implement in terms of chemicals to the serum, Saracen is not yielding any ground. He is far more concerned with increasing the potential of the subjects to the absolute maximum than with their personal safety. I would be lying to say I was surprised, but it is a hard fact to accept that I can only sway a small portion of this project. It may be an important part, but the safety of the subjects has been pushed to the back of my mind in favour of the safety of this nation as well as others.

As for Saracen, his methods seem narrow-minded and somewhat cold-hearted, but I must admit I cannot argue with the results. The serum is now believed ready for human testing thanks in no small part to Saracen. It has been dismissed to test on animals; they tried to preach animal rights. But we all know the real reason: the American military is acting as an impatient child wanting to play with their new toy.

Though it is quite clear that the first test subject would experience all the predicted negative effects to the extreme, there would be no way to find a solution to this without monitoring firsthand what and how the chemicals will affect the patient's mind and body. This is why I am hesitant to produce the full serum for human testing, as I have a feeling I know who the first test subject is going to be. Everyone has been acting strangely toward me over the past few weeks—avoiding talking with me, or not looking me in the eye when they do. Normally it wouldn't bother me, but it seems out of character for a lot of them. Especially Dr. Triin. Still ... I have to share a backup plan with one person ... someone I can trust ... I hope my instincts are right.

Richard Ceress
Date: Oct 12, 2023

*

RICHARD STOOD FROM HIS DESK as he closed his journal, something he needed to indulge in from time to time to organize his thoughts. He was sure they were monitoring him and would not approve such a document, but they had not said anything or stopped him. Besides, it helped him work, and they needed him at his best.

He pressed the call button on his intercom to summon Demetri, and then, speaking without so much as a greeting, he said, "Demetri, get everyone in the meeting room. I need to speak to them."

They all quickly responded, curious as to what he had to say. They made their way to the meeting room but milled around outside, muttering to each other with curiosity as Richard approached. With all of the talk of prepping the serum for human testing, it was time for Richard to bring forth his primary concern: control.

They entered as a group and waited for Richard's address.

"What is it, Ceress?" Saracen's crossed arms echoed the annoyance in his voice, and an obvious stubborn attitude to whatever Richard was about to say.

But this was no deterrent; it was important for Richard to voice his concern. "We're going to be giving a great deal of power to a single human being. So the biggest challenge now is, how do we—"

"Keep them in line?" Dr. York interrupted sharply in agreement to what Ceress was thinking, and then shot a glance toward Saracen, awaiting a response.

Saracen's facial expression turned from annoyance to scorn as he glared for a moment at Ceress. His expression quickly returned to normal as he addressed the group. "A valid point, one we have all considered in this process. The solution is simple. We implant a chip in the brain stem of every subject, who would receive a debilitating pain throughout his body when going against

orders—and if need be, could kill him with the press of a button."
Saracen spoke confidently, as though it was the ultimate solution.

But the faces of the other team members were mortified by his cold and unbelievable response. Dr. Triin was the first to speak up. "That's inhuman! You're talking about making them slaves in return for this serum! What if there was some sort of malfunction with the serum and the behaviour of the soldier was not intentional—would you kill him? Your solution is barbaric!"

"These people will no longer *be* human when they receive this serum. They will be like wild animals, and we need to treat them and control them as such. Punishment of pain and death is the only way."

"You're a fool." Richard's soft but bold statement to Saracen gained the attention of the entire group.

Saracen glared as if he intended to burn a hole into Richard's head.

Richard said, "You're like a lion tamer who believes his lions are loyal, and not just afraid. What happens when the tamer turns his back? The lion will pounce. Chips can be removed and destroyed. You are not controlling these people; you are giving them reason to hate you when they should be thankful to you. You are talking about giving someone the power of many men, and then slapping them in the face and stating, 'If you don't want me to do it again, then do what I say!' Also keep in mind that we are increasing their mental capabilities as well as their physical, so you're making them smarter. You know, like smart enough to figure out how to remove an annoying chip from their head? Not to mention the fact that we are spending hundreds of millions of dollars creating this serum to put into a human being, whom we then press a button to dispose of because he looked at you the wrong way? If you truly believe that a method like that would work, then not only do you not understand humans, you don't understand science."

"How dare you!" Saracen's arms uncrossed abruptly, making a motion to step toward Richard.

"That's enough!" General Grey's voice was heard from the entrance of the garage as he approached the huddled group.

They were acting casual, like a group of fighting elementary school students who were just caught by the teacher.

Grey added, "Richard's right; we need another method. We've been working on this project long enough, and I expect we'll have different approaches to solving this problem. Does anyone have any suggestions?"

Richard spoke up without taking his eyes off of Saracen and began to speak matter-of-factly. "I do. We're going to make the serum temporary. Create an activation serum for the enhancements so it would only activate the enhanced genes while it was in the system, and only last in their bloodstream for a time. That would mean they would need to keep coming back to us in order to get the boost again, and if they did turn against us, it wouldn't last long and would therefore be manageable over time."

Dr. Triin's obvious concern for the mental health of subjects was often the voice of reason. "Then the problem becomes that we're giving them a drug addiction. We would be ruining the lives of every subject, giving them a lifetime addiction they could never beat. Trials from the alpha subjects in the prototype serum several years ago proved that most of them became addicted to the serum. And that was a mild version of what we have created." She looked sheepishly at Demetri as she spoke, as if guilty bringing up the previous trials, though he seemed to avoid eye contact with her.

They had mentioned the alpha subjects to Richard at the beginning of the project, roughly a dozen men and women who underwent a similar serum created from steroids. It was successful but didn't make the difference intended. The subjects were enhanced, but more so to an Olympic athlete than a super soldier, with a few exceptions not detailed. And there were side effects including addiction, schizophrenia and involuntary spasms. It was the result of using a steroid as the baseline, and the very reason gene augmentation was a better solution.

"Not necessarily addicted. I have a solution to that challenge." Richard seemed to not be paying attention when he spoke while looking away from the group into space. "It's possible to prevent the serum itself from registering in the cerebral cortex of the subject's brain if we augment it to have something similar to a computer firewall. It would still allow for the serum to pass through but would do so without registering in the brain. The subject would feel if the effects activate and wear off but would otherwise not feel any endorphins or dependence that would result from an addictive substance."

"So it will prevent the dependence on the serum, and they would still realize when it wears off?" Dr. Triin looked at Richard with an impressed smile. "Couldn't that be dangerous though? Passing through the cerebral cortex like that would mean they would not know what they are fully capable of, which could put them and anyone around them in danger. They would not know what their body is fully capable of doing."

"It would take training. They would not immediately be aware of it; you're right about that. But that's why they would simply have to engage in extensive self-training and awareness in a supervised controlled environment like the training pod in our facility. They would quickly learn their limitations and capabilities safely before accidentally ripping a man's hand off in a handshake, for example. We'd equip each soldier with a self-monitoring device the size of a small pencil, which would read accurate levels of serum in the bloodstream by simply holding it directly over the heart." Richard went over his suggestion in his mind as he spoke, and kept thinking that this might be a perfect solution for both parties.

"This solution allows a balance of power for the subject, without their power going too far or being misused. It also ensures their safety and control. After all, the supply of serum could be quickly cut off the moment they have no more use for it. All we have to do is give them a set amount of the activation serum or find the proper means to distribute it."

Saracen looked over at General Grey in deep thought. Then, after nodding slowly at him, he turned his attention back to Richard. "You really think you can do this?"

"This methodology could be used to help people kick substance addictions and is exactly what gene-aug technology *should* be used for—modifying genes in the brain from registering an otherwise addictive substance. Yes, I can do it." With each passing thought, Richard's confidence in this project grew to new heights. He was actually going to make a difference! He was going to keep this project under control. Even Saracen seemed convinced this was a better option. He had made no objections or comments to Richard's solution.

"Very well; do it. The rest of us will continue to prep the serum for human testing." Saracen nodded to Richard and to General Grey, and then went back to his station and continued his work. General Grey followed him and seemed to quietly scold him on the other side of the room. Richard could not hide the smirk when he saw that.

"Well done, Richard." Dr. Triin's warm smile made Richard's smirk grow even larger. Corey and Nathan also gave similar praise before returning to their work.

Richard's face grew serious again as he addressed Dr. Triin before she walked away. "Dr. Triin, could I speak with you for a moment about the projected effects of this serum on our subjects?" Richard said it loud enough for others to hear. As he approached her, he quietly added "in private" as he gently took her arm and led her to the exit.

Richard noticed General Grey watching them leave the room as he hovered over Saracen in serious conversation.

Richard closed the door and motioned for Dr. Triin to sit on the couch before joining her. Even with the growing confidence he had about this project, he could not let himself get carried away. He was forcing himself to carry through with a contingency plan he had been hatching for some time, something he couldn't keep under his own belt; it would have been too easy to predict coming from him.

Richard believed Dr. Triin's radiant concern for human life seemed the perfect testament to her cooperation with his request.

His words slipped out before he had finished his own thought process. "I wanted to speak with you about something." He still wasn't sure if he could fully trust her. Her concern for human life and mental health were clear, but he had to know more about her.

"Yes, the projected effects of the serum," she replied.

"I know your concern for the welfare of these soldiers, so I'd like to hear your thoughts." Richard was in deep thought as he said these words and then suddenly changed the subject. "Oh, by the way, Dr. Triin—"

"Please call me Jocelyn," she interrupted.

"Jocelyn." He paused. Six months, and this was the first time she'd ever offered he refer to her by first name. Was it because this was the first conversation they'd had alone? Or did it take this long for her to become comfortable with him? "I've been meaning to tell you that I appreciate your convincing me to use the wellness center. I have been taking advantage of it and have found myself much stronger mentally and physically, just as you had said."

"That's great. It is an amazing system."

Richard seemed distracted. "Come to think of it, let's go use it now and we can compare our projections." He wanted to get Jocelyn to a place where their conversation would not likely be "bugged."

"We can go for a walk in the simulated walking or jogging room, a walk on the beach, in a quiet forest—you pick!"

Jocelyn was a little confused by his suggestion but politely said, "Sure, we can do that."

They stood up, left Richard's quarters and headed toward the wellness centre.

*

Inside the walking simulation room they began their walk in an atmosphere of a quiet Canadian forest, with a soft breeze blowing through the trees, birds chirping and sunlight streaming on their pathway.

"I'm all ears."

Her innocent smile caused Richard to stutter his thoughts. Was he really willing to put this woman in danger for the plan he had come up with? A plan he not only was unsure would work, but one that could put his life at stake if Jocelyn decided to take it to General Grey—or worse, Saracen.

"Your feelings toward the health of others have already likely saved numerous lives with your words alone. It's a trait that not many people share, and even less so in a situation like this."

"T-thank you." Jocelyn blushed.

"I need to ask you a favour."

"A favour?" Dr. Triin's cheeks returned to their normal color as she leaned in to hear what Richard had to say.

"Even with how well things seem to be going with this project, I can't shake the feeling that somewhere down the line someone's going to take it too far. We can't let this serum get out of control or it will lead to more wars and even greater ruin to this world."

"Well, I agree. But once we're done here, that's it, there's nothing further we can do. We won't have access to this equipment anymore."

"I know. This is why we need to prepare for it now." Richard looked down at his hands, which were starting to tremble. He did not want to ask someone so good-hearted as Dr. Triin what he was going to ask, but he could trust none of the other members of the research team. Still … he had to be sure. "What I'm about to tell you is just between us. Promise me you won't share this information."

"But Richard, I—"

"Promise me." Richard's interruption was not as rude as it was pleaded.

"I promise." Dr. Triin looked worried.

"Along with the augmentation I'm going to set up for the cerebral cortex of the subjects, I'm going to include something of a safeguard setting. A certain combination of chemicals surged into the bloodstream through the veins will trigger this safeguard in the cortex of any subject. The reaction it will immediately have is to push all the 'activation serum' to filter out of the stream through any open wound on the subject. If there are no open wounds on the body, it may purge out of the eyes, ears and nose. It may seem slightly barbaric, but if I manage to augment it correctly, it will be a sure solution to the serum, and I couldn't think of another way to implement it. It'll cause the enhanced genes to shut off and return a super soldier to his original status. I have a feeling at some point we may need something like this as a safeguard. But too many people here know my stance on this subject and will be watching me too closely for me to formulate it myself."

Richard took a deep breath and looked Dr. Triin in the eyes. "I'd like to give you the formula so you can create it here, and keep it safe in case it's ever needed." He tried to sound as sincere as possible, though he was still unsure he was doing the right thing.

"An antibody? But—"

"Please, Jocelyn. I don't know who else to trust with this. We both know this serum will be unstable. Help me solve the problem before it starts." Richard had never sounded so sincere in all his life; he did not know how it sounded to her, but it made him feel better to put his trust into someone else for once. Even if it was slightly unfair.

"All right, Richard. If you trust me that much, I'll do you the same courtesy."

Her soft voice calmed Richard as he spoke with a sigh of relief. "Thank you."

"The problem still remains though of finding a suitable volunteer for human testing."

"No," he said bluntly. "We need someone in this for the right reasons and willing to give anything to help. And we already have a volunteer."

CHAPTER 9

ALPHA STAGE

THE LABORATORY WAS HUMMING WITH life the evening of the first human test. It seemed as though every machine in the whole room was running at full capacity just in case the test went awry. The entire team was huddled around a large metal examination table as Saracen and Richard prepared the serum, carefully transferring a rather small dose into a syringe. There was an obvious differentiated role contrast of the team members clearly depicted by their attire. The scientists and technicians wore white lab coats, and the rest wore full military fatigue uniforms as per policy.

As Saracen flicked the tip of the syringe a few times to ensure there were no air bubbles, Richard turned to the small crowd. "All right, everything is ready. Let's begin."

"I think I was caller thirteen, Richard." Demetri stepped forward with fake excitement and turned to high five Dr. York with a laugh.

"Are you sure you want to do this?" General Grey asked out of concern for one of his own.

"Damn right I do. If it's not me, then it would be someone with less experience, less knowledge and less control. Besides, this is the first time this stuff is going to be tested. It likely will not end perfectly. And what kind of a leader would I be if I sent one of my men to do something that not even I was willing to do?"

Richard smiled at Demetri's words. His respect for this man was growing daily. He could think of no one better to be the first test subject, which was why he was so worried.

"You're one of my best and most trusted, Demetri. I wouldn't normally allow someone like you to be a test subject. But by god, if this works, I'll be even more proud to have you by my side." General Grey spoke proudly as he nodded at Demetri and firmly shook his hand.

"It's time, Demetri," Richard stated grimly, causing any background chatter in the lab to cease entirely.

"Right." Demetri stepped toward the examination table. He took off his military jacket and shirt, hanging them neatly on a nearby chair back. Even though his muscular build was evident in his uniform, now with his shirt off and his defined muscles displayed, it would have been a physiotherapist's dream. The definition of his powerful steel-like muscles created an almost unnatural frame. Two round pectorals atop an immaculately defined six-pack seemed to fit perfectly with the large ripped arms surrounding them. He was not a large man, but it looked as though he bench-pressed a bull every morning.

Demetri lay down on the exam table with his arms at his sides. Dr. York approached him and strapped him to the table with various leather restraints located at the appropriate places for his limbs, waist, chest and head. Demetri couldn't turn his head anymore but moved his eyes in an attempt to address Richard. "Is this really necessary?"

"I'm sorry, Demetri, but it's for your safety—and ours," Richard responded with a hint of concern before turning away to avoid eye contact.

"What exactly am I going to feel?" Demetri's question, though one of fear, did not seem to be said with any less resolve.

After Dr. York finished strapping him to the table, Richard leaned over Demetri to make it easier for him to see Richard. "There will be three stages. The first will be the serum, codenamed 'Vigour'; you will feel each of these stages flowing up your arm through your veins to your heart. Vigour will seep slightly through your veins into your muscle tissue, which will dramatically begin to strengthen it. It will reach each muscle in this way and be at its peak performance once it reaches your heart and begins circulating fully through the bloodstream.

"Your body will be physically strong enough to accept the next two stages. Second, we will inject the serum codenamed 'Keen' into your brainstem, increasing your mental capacity roughly five-fold as suggested by the alpha subjects, which will increase your problem solving, reflexes, creativity and every brain function, including heightened senses.

"In the third and final step, we will inject the serum codenamed 'Gait' into your heart. This will put it into the bloodstream faster as to synergize with Vigour more efficiently. As Vigour strengthens the muscles, Gait will ensure they remain loose and dexterous, working together to improve the speed in which your muscles can move and react, including the precision of steps. I should mention, to alleviate any concerns, that I have already adjusted the Keen serum so it will slightly augment your cerebral cortex. That is my special portion of the serum to prevent your brain from registering that the serum is in your body. You won't feel much different physically at the end of the process when the serum has taken effect, perhaps a little more alert and aware. But it will quickly subside until we inject the activation serum to turn on the newly enhanced genes. Even then you will not know what you are truly capable of doing until you can adjust mentally and train yourself to read your body signals. You will discover new attributes and skills as time progresses. The results are limitless, dependent on your particular body type, DNA structure and brain capacity or intellect. Although this is an enhancement serum, the effects of the serum can be as individual as each individual soldier. It will be much safer for you and for us this way, and it should also help reduce the pain level quite a bit. Speaking of which, I should warn you, this is going to hurt ... a lot."

Demetri stared blankly back at Richard as he processed everything that was just said to him. "You know, you could have lied to me and said I wouldn't feel a thing." Demetri's grin caused Richard to grin a bit too, and even momentarily made him feel a little less worried about the results. Demetri, after all, was in peak physical condition. He had the highest probability of survival out of everyone present in the room because of it. Besides, better the testing start with Demetri, rather than someone Richard knew would misuse the abilities.

"After the activation serum is injected, it should run its course through your body in about a week. So don't get too used to what you can do; it will begin to fade after the sixth day. I have calculated the proper dosage amount of each serum to accomplish this using the results of your saliva sample. Saracen will inject each one in the correct intervals to create the most efficient collaboration of the serums." Richard was almost trying to reassure Demetri that it was only temporary.

"So then we can do it all over again. Sounds like fun." The hint of sarcasm in Demetri's voice almost sounded like doubt. But seeing the grin still on Demetri's face, Richard realized he was just trying to lighten the mood with his dry humour.

"Quite right." Richard was forcing a grin now. He had a great deal of respect for this man, which amongst people in his circle, was a rare thing.

Dr. Triin began attaching pulse monitors to Demetri's head, chest and arms. "We'll be monitoring your brain waves, heart rate and blood pressure throughout the procedure, Agent Candora. But I must warn you, this is for research purposes only. Once the serum is in, we will not be able to stop it." Dr. Triin looked into Demetri's eyes as she placed the final wire on his chest, almost to silently say, "I'm sorry."

"Juice me up, woman." Demetri's grin turned into a grimace as Richard inserted a needle into the base of his neck, trying to catch Demetri off guard to ease the blow. Though seeing the grimace on Demetri's face, it was clear Richard had failed. For safety, Demetri's head was strapped tightly to the table, so all Demetri could move were his facial muscles.

"All right, we're all set." Richard took a few steps back from the table.

Dr. York came up to the table with a large bite guard, and offered it to Demetri's mouth. "Here, buddy, this'll help." Dr. York nodded at Demetri as he placed the guard into his mouth. Demetri bit down as if to test it, and then smiled a thank you to Dr. York.

Saracen approached the table with the prepared syringe in hand. "Are you ready?" he asked emotionlessly.

"Give me the damn thing already." Demetri closed his eyes and looked to be bracing himself for what was to come.

Saracen searched Demetri's arm for a vein; finding one, he inserted the syringe into it, and injected the first serum into Demetri's bloodstream. "The Vigour serum has been fully injected into the subject. Wait for one minute and proceed with the other two injections."

Saracen's suddenly commanding voice sent an eerie chill down Richard's spine. Regardless, he had a job to do—flip the switch near the injection site at the back of Demetri's head to begin injecting the Keen serum. At precisely one minute, Richard flipped the switch.

Without missing a beat 30 seconds later, Dr. York injected a long syringe directly into Demetri's chest as his body convulsed with pain.

Dr. Triin had closed her eyes and turned away the moment she saw the pain Demetri was experiencing. After all the serum was injected, the scientists removed the needles and took a step back from the table to look at the status screens, waiting and praying.

It wasn't long before the visible effects beyond reaction to pain began to take place. Demetri's blood pressure began to rise, his brain waves became erratic and his pulse mimicked the chorus of "Flight of the Bumblebee."

"His blood pressure is 160 over 110 and rising!" Dr. Triin yelled with grave concern. The whole table shook as Demetri convulsed violently. The look of concern was on everyone's face, save for Saracen and General Grey, who looked on out of sheer interest.

Demetri's cries of pain were muffled by the mouth guard. It was evident he was experiencing what had to be an excruciating amount of pain, yet he only let out a grunt on occasion. The man's willpower and stamina seemed incredible.

As the convulsing continued, the veins throughout Demetri's body began to protrude. Everyone could see nearly every vein in Demetri's body clearly pulsating as the serum seemed to be taking effect. His heartbeat began to slow after almost five minutes of random convulsions, which seemed to become more rhythmic shortly after. Now Demetri's body convulsed along with his pulse rate. Each time his heart beat, his entire body convulsed along with it, and the veins extruded at the same time before briefly going back to normal. Demetri let out a pained grunt after each one.

Nearly half an hour passed with those regular rhythmic convulsions in sync with Demetri's heartbeat. With each passing beat, the violence and intensity slowly diminished until finally they stopped. Demetri's pulse and blood pressure returned to normal.

A uniform sigh of relief filled the room as the researchers began to examine in detail what changes had taken place. Dr. York was the first to speak up. "His muscle size grew slightly; it doesn't look like anything significant. Actually, the muscles in his left arm seem to be the only ones that show any noticeable signs of modification, and even then they are minor at best. That's the arm you inserted the serum into."

"I told you we should have inserted it directly into his heart!" Saracen accusingly addressed Richard.

"We insert Vigour into his heart and his chance of survival would drop dramatically. Besides, we're perfecting the serum first. We don't need him to feel the full effects of it until we know it's safe." Richard spoke to Saracen while not facing him. Richard didn't believe statements like that deserved his full attention and were simply dismissed.

"Yes, well done; we're seeing the dramatic increase to the strength in his left hand! God help whatever poor bloke challenges him to a thumb wrestling match!" Saracen was obviously frustrated, though with Demetri safe, Richard couldn't care less what Saracen had to say.

"Well, that may not be entirely true," Dr. York interrupted almost in defence of Richard. "I said any *noticeable* signs of modification. This serum is supposed to affect his muscle structure on a molecular level, isn't it? I've never dealt with something like that before, so I wouldn't recognize the change."

"So you think the changes still took effect?" Saracen's anger seemed to subside slightly at the prospect.

"It's possible." Dr. York looked over at the unconscious subject on the table. "But we have to wait and see."

"Nothing looks different to me." General Grey made a distant observation of the subject.

"That's what I'm saying!" Saracen snapped. "I'm telling you we would have had much more of a visible result if we had just injected

Vigour into his heart. Now there will be an imbalance in his left arm, and that's even if there is any change in the rest of him at all!" He directed his anger toward Richard. It was apparent who he blamed for the botched test.

"You could have killed him!" Richard was showing emotion he rarely expressed at this point; Saracen seemed to have hit a nerve. "Are you so willing to just throw somebody's life away for your tests? I think *you* should be the one on the table next! Then I won't mind stuffing it into your heart at all, if we can even find the damn thing! Do you not remember, or perhaps you weren't present when we projected that the physical side effects would not likely be apparent immediately?"

"That's enough!" General Grey was asserting his authority to Saracen, and he shot the same glare at Richard.

"I'm sorry, sir, but we may have just wasted a week's worth of testing because we didn't inject Vigour directly into the heart. It would have evenly distributed it throughout the body, and faster too. Now we have to wait for the serum to subside to do it again. And this week will be pointless as there have been no significant changes! He's barely any different!" Saracen was obviously frustrated but seemed to calm down hearing Dr. Triin's voice from across the room.

"You're wrong." Dr. Triin spoke sadly as she viewed the screen monitoring his brainwaves. "His brain algorithms have been completely modified. They are nowhere near the same as they were before."

"Meaning what exactly?" General Grey was now showing obvious signs of concern. Dr. Triin looked over to the group, directing her gaze more specifically at Richard, who could see the beginning of tears in her eyes as she spoke.

"Meaning we may have just killed Demetri Candora."

CHAPTER 10

UNDESIRED RESULTS

"WHAT DO YOU MEAN, KILLED him?" General Grey's anger resonated throughout the entire laboratory. He directed his assault directly at Dr. Triin, who had unfortunately been the bearer of bad news.

"I mean this serum has completely warped his brain," she stated in a panic, motioning to the monitor in front of her. "His brainwaves have been completely altered! He won't be the same person—that's *if* he even wakes up!" Her response was far more agitated than anyone would expect from her. She was truly upset.

Richard's expression quickly went from fear and concern to wonderment as he received the diagnosis from Dr. Triin. He analyzed the computer she had been monitoring to see the results for himself. "It's a separate brainwave."

"Meaning what exactly?" General Grey snorted to Richard, who had not realized that he had spoken his thought out loud. Richard glanced toward General Grey and immediately back to the monitor, almost ignoring the general but responding to the question nonetheless.

"Meaning he's not literally dead, just figuratively—his persona has been completely modified. Or more accurately, he has a second one." He proceeded to analyze the monitor as he continued his explanation. "The serum seems to have activated every part of his brain, perhaps permanently." Richard's concern seemed to be returning in force.

Saracen smiled ferociously as though he had just seen the death of his archrival. "It worked!" Shoving Richard aside, Saracen began typing on the corresponding keyboard with newfound vigilance. "The serum worked! His brain could be calculating both consciously and subconsciously, so while he is consciously deciding how to react to any situation, his brain is already determining every possible outcome." Saracen excitedly dragged his finger across the lines on the monitor as if trying to make sense of the outcome. "This man's brain is now one of the greatest weapons in the world!"

"Are you insane?" Richard could not bite his tongue any longer listening to Saracen. "This man has likely become the most dangerous weapon in the world! Every single thought that goes into his head will be for a purpose, one that none of us could ever comprehend, and you want to *mass produce* this effect? Get this man to the isolation room. He needs to be restrained and isolated while this serum runs its course. We cannot have him walking around freely with the potential to do anything harmful in the week he's under the influence of the serum—if he even wakes up."

Richard ran his hand roughly through his hair, displaying his obvious frustration as he stormed out of the lab, not entirely sure where he was going. Were his calculations off? The serum should not have breached into the brainstem like it did. The whole point of his part in this project was to prevent that from happening. The subject shouldn't be able to exploit his full potential. Richard had accurately formulated that part of the serum. Did he fail? Had his entire purpose here been for naught? Could he still fix it? Or was he just incapable of doing so?

"Richard!" A woman's voice broke his train of thought. He turned around to face Dr. Triin, who had followed him out of the lab.

"Are you okay?" She reached out to touch his arm.

Her touch reminded Richard of Madeline for a moment, but he was far too upset to respond or even react to the physical contact. He looked back at her, his lip slightly quivering. "I failed, Jocelyn. I thought my calculations were perfect. I thought I had a solution to my concerns … I thought I was right …"

With Richard's concession of failure, his gaze dropped to the floor, unable to look anyone in the eye, least of all Jocelyn, one of the few people involved in this operation for whom he still held any respect. In his mind, he just killed one of the few people in this world who truly understood his beliefs and was even helping him achieve his aspirations. After all, this was the only chance he would have had to put any kind of stop to the madness he was helping create. And Demetri, his ally in this endeavour, appeared not to be able to help his cause in his current state.

"Wait a minute …" Richard cut himself off from his thoughts as his facial expression turned from sadness to concern, and then looked toward Dr. Triin.

"What is it, Richard?" She leaned her head forward while tilting her left ear slightly more toward him, as if expecting him to whisper his next words.

"Never mind." Thoughts of an intentional sabotage were spinning through his head, but he couldn't voice his thoughts, not now. Richard was already looking past Dr. Triin and saw that Saracen and Dr. York had placed Demetri on a gurney and were wheeling him out of the room. That stopped Richard from saying what he was going to say, as he didn't want anyone but Dr. Triin to hear it. Now that he was thinking more about it, maybe he shouldn't say it at all. After all, if he was wrong, it would mean he would lose all opportunity to fix what was broken. On the other hand, if he was right …

"Heads up." Richard gently placed his hand on Dr. Triin's shoulder and directed her to step aside and make room for the gurney carrying his injured friend. "Friend" was a word Richard rarely used, yet he had just caught himself feeling that way about Demetri. Maybe that was why he was feeling so strongly about what had happened. It was distracting him from the potentially larger problem at hand, that his serum didn't work as designed. But he couldn't ignore his emotions; he was concerned about his friend.

"Excuse me." Richard turned from Dr. Triin and began following the gurney to the lab's isolation room, opening the door for Dr. York and Saracen.

As Dr. York and Saracen brought Demetri to the bed in the center of the observation room, they began securing him tightly with straps and shackles for his wrists and ankles. All monitors were attached to Demetri and the computers to analyze the data.

Richard stared down at the man with whom he realized he had so little in common; however, their common bond was strong. They had the same goal for this project. Richard had to make sure Demetri was going to be all right, he had to have his ally with him, his comrade ... his friend.

"You shouldn't be in here, Ceress." Saracen sneered at Richard as he turned the gurney to face the door again.

"The man is concerned, Doc. What's the harm in letting him stay with his friend?" Dr. York defended Richard's presence, knowing the relationship he had since Demetri recruited him.

"Ceress said himself that Agent Candora could be dangerous when he wakes up. Besides, he should be packing his bags after the blunder that put Candora in this position to begin with." Saracen was once again "subtly" expressing his desire to remove Richard from the operation.

"If I'm so useless, then you'll lose nothing if he wakes up and kills me," Richard retorted with increasing hostility. "Whereas if you were to remain here when he woke in a rage, what a devastating blow it would be to all of us if he were to choke the life out of you!"

Everyone in the room turned to look at Richard. They wanted to confirm that the statement seeping with sarcasm had actually come from the socially inept student they had recruited. Richard's expression remained stern, though it was clear the sarcasm was fully intended. It was a timely opportunity to begin developing a strong personality.

Dr. York covered his mouth, with his hand pretending to groom his beard in order to hide the mischievous smile he couldn't hold back.

"Excuse me!" Saracen's hateful demeanour had progressed to hot rage. As he began to storm toward Richard, Dr. York managed to intervene in time to stop Saracen with one of his massive forearms.

"Time to go, Saracen." Dr. York took the gurney out of the room as Saracen continued to stare down Richard. The deep rumble of Dr. York's voice seemed to shake Saracen from what was likely going to be a hateful rant. Surprisingly, Saracen seemed to listen to Dr. York and promptly left the room without another word or even glance toward Richard.

Following Dr. York's lead out the door, Saracen grasped the doorknob on the way out and slammed the door. Richard stood silently next to Dr. Triin, who had been quiet through the whole confrontation.

Utter befuddlement overtook Richard on the events that had just occurred. Since when did Saracen take orders from Dr. York? Wasn't he an advisor to the Joint Chiefs? He backed off so easily when Dr. York said so. Richard already knew Saracen hated him. It was nothing new to hear hateful comments from him. But he had done so in front of Dr. York before, so why was this time different? Was it because Saracen actually had respect for the fact that Richard was upset about what happened to his friend? No, Saracen didn't care about Richard or Demetri, let alone their feelings. So why …

"How are you holding up, Richard?" Dr. Triin's sweet and innocent voice once again snapped Richard out of the train of thought that his brain had a tendency to board after a conversation with Saracen. He turned his head to her and smiled almost triumphantly. "I'm better now that he's gone." Richard kept his smile as he pulled up two swivel chairs from the monitoring area of the room next to the bed, motioning for Dr. Triin to sit on one as he sat on the other.

Dr. Triin was happy to oblige with a smile, eager to engage in a conversation with the socially elusive university intern who had been a last-minute addition to the team.

"I'd like to pick your brain if I could, Dr. ... Jocelyn." Richard corrected himself as Dr. Triin had requested on several occasions.

"By all means, Richard. I'd be happy to answer any questions you may have," she replied, stifling a giggle that only proved to confuse Richard. He looked around to see if anyone was around checking on Demetri's progress. No one was about at the moment, so he took the opportunity.

"How did you come to work on this project?" Richard paused for a moment to gather his thoughts. There was something about her that was out of place in this operation; she was ... innocent. Or at least that was the persona she let the world see. Richard needed to know more about her in order to make a judgment as to what her real intentions were in this project. "I'm sorry, let me clarify what I'm asking and why. This project is using the best and brightest minds in North America to create what can only be construed as a killing machine. I apologize if that is blunt, but this is the American government we're talking about, and you know full well how they intend to use these soldiers. So knowing this, my question to you is, why would you agree to something this volatile when your hands are, for lack of a better term ... clean?"

Dr. Triin shifted uncomfortably in her chair for a moment. "That's a fair question ... I guess I could ask you the same. It tells me you haven't read my books." She smiled gently. "I suppose you could say I'm somewhat of a famous author on the subject of the effect of drugs on people and their families. I also have refined the process and best practices for improved mental health and related topics and subjects. Prescription or otherwise, there are literally thousands of addictive substances circulating in the world, and I wanted to make sure everyone can access assistance to face their difficult challenges. I was approached as you were by Demetri. I assume I was chosen because of my experience in the medical field dealing with drug addicts. I was the primary therapist to help many people break their addiction and return to a regular frame of mind and positive lifestyle. It was most likely the celebrities that I assisted in their substance abuse problems that led to getting my name circulating in these circles."

Her gaze left Richard and turned toward Demetri, who was unconscious on the bed. "Demetri was up front with me about this project, and I struggled with the whole concept. I do not agree with it, but if there isn't a specialist in my field on hand to assist with the mental safety and development of these subjects, then their mental stability would not just be a danger to themselves but to the rest of the world. While I don't relish the fact of being part of what's likely going to be considered genetic weapon creation, I refuse to stand by and do nothing when I know I can make a difference."

"I understand completely." Richard nodded slightly. Suddenly he stopped, furrowing his brow as something struck his mind. "Wait. Demetri just outright told you the whole project before recruiting you?"

Richard's confusion was riddled with concern. Demetri did the same for Richard. How could he get away with just telling it to everyone he wanted to recruit? Would he have killed anyone who refused? Did he already kill some who did refuse? How could he be so open with a secret project? It didn't make sense, but Richard buried his true concern so as not to worry Dr. Triin with his theories. But he was sure of it—something wasn't adding up.

"I admit, I did find it a little intimidating that he was so open about it. It was almost as if he would have killed me to prevent me from telling anyone about it if I refused." She laughed. "But you have to remember the kind of person Demetri is. He wouldn't ask someone to involve themselves in such an undertaking without being straight and upfront with them. He is not that type of person. He is not going to lie or sugar coat what they are doing. He wants you to make the decision for yourself, not because of what you think he will do, not because of what you think the government will do, but because it is what you want to do. Truth be told, it was his honesty that convinced me to join this project. His honesty, and his sincerity." Her smile faded as she continued to look at Demetri. "I will feel a lot less comfortable here without him walking around." She shifted uncomfortably again in her chair, avoiding eye contact with Richard.

"Don't worry, Jocelyn. I'm quite sure I miscalculated the dosage and made it slightly too intense for his DNA composition. But I can take measurements of his new altered DNA and create something of a counter-serum to fix whatever problem was created. It's the whole reason I wanted to get into gene augmentation to begin with, to solve health problems in a person's DNA. And his body will heal itself in good time. We are close though, so it'll only be a few more weeks before we can approve the serum for true field-testing. He seems to be resting comfortably now with no adverse effects at this point."

Dr. Triin turned to Richard with a raised brow. "Richard, you don't have two more weeks!"

"The serum obviously works. It just seems I need to recalculate the dosage variant for the host DNA." Richard was speaking very matter-of-factly, as though he was giving her good news. After all, it meant the project was nearing completion.

Then it dawned on him what she had just said. "What do you mean I don't have two weeks?"

"I'm sorry ... we were ordered not to tell you." A look of intense shame overcame her face.

"Tell me what?" Richard tilted his head, with hardly a clue what information he could be missing.

Dr. Triin leaned in to Richard and spoke in a lower register. "The Pacific Coalition invaded the West Coast two weeks ago. General Grey had ordered the requisition of a dozen field agents to be injected with Valour at that time to assist in the defence. Demetri's testing was a precaution they were taking to view any side effects from the serum and find a solution to them for use in the field, if any." She put her head in her hands before she continued. "The PC technology has been decimating the American forces. Nothing in the army, navy, marines or air force can stand up to it. People are dying! They had to do something! If nothing was done, the PC would just advance inland with little resistance. Ready or not, the Valour serum has been deployed for military use. Richard, I wanted to tell you! General Grey ordered all of us to keep it to ourselves. He said it would endanger the project and its subjects if we were to tell you."

She turned to him with tears streaming down her face, "I'm so sorry ..."

Chapter 11

BETRAYAL

"I WARNED THEM. I WARNED them!" Richard was nearly screaming as he stormed through the hallways from the lab's observation room, where he left Demetri and Jocelyn. He marched straight down the stairs, making his way toward what had come to be known as the Situation Room, where General Grey and Dr. Saracen would spend most of their days with the doors closed. Richard had always assumed it was so they could stay apprised of world events and the politics that they had left behind in order to work on this project.

But now thoughts of a tactical command room flashed through Richard's mind. No wonder they had been spending all their time in there instead of helping prepare for the "test" subject. General Grey was already overseeing the creation and deployment of a dozen of these super soldiers. This meant they did it without providing the proper doses. Richard was the only one who knew the formula, and even the test for Demetri seemed flawed. He already had to recalculate. This General Grey had likely just sent a dozen good men to their deaths!

Richard's pace didn't slow down as he reached for the large metal double doors, and with a forceful push forward with his arms he crashed through the doors to face General Grey and

Dr. Saracen. The room was a large circular conference room. A large, black, round metal table took up most of the room, with a holographic-globe device sitting in the center of the table currently displaying an overhead view of what looked to be California. Fires, smoke and debris encompassed a path about halfway through the state, though it seemed to be avoiding population centers and taking the shortest route toward Nevada. No sounds were currently emanating from the device, making it easy for the general and Saracen to hear Richard crashing through the doors, making a beeline to their seated positions.

"What is it, Ceress? We're busy."

General Grey's dismissive greeting only infuriated Richard more. At this point his face was turning red with anger. "*What is it?* You deployed the serum! You deployed the serum before it was ready! You *deployed* the serum before it was even tested! Do you have any idea what you've done!" The emotion Richard was expressing was unlike anything he had ever experienced. He was enraged. He was brought here to stop an untested super soldier from being unleashed, and they did it without him. Why did they even bother bringing him here if they weren't going to heed his advice or use his research?

"We're at war, boy! I'm not going to hold back our greatest weapon to fight off the PC just because some kid fresh out of a learning box tells me it's not ready! Would you rather we just sit back and get taken over? Innocent people getting killed because your fruit punch isn't quite mixed yet? This isn't a game, and I'm not here to play with you. You were brought here for a simple purpose— to make this serum work—so step back and let me do my part of the project—to protect this country!" General Grey was now beginning to show the same signs of anger Richard was displaying.

"I was brought here to make the serum safe! Not just for use on the subjects, but for use in the field! I told you we need to test on a willing subject before moving forward to work out the dosage calculations. If you don't acquire that information from a subject before injection, the results could be fatal. Or worse, they could become a loose cannon in the field and not be able to distinguish between friend and foe. And you deploy them anyway without even telling me? Not only that, you purposely hid it from me! We have a military more than capable of defending its shores. You are using this invasion as an excuse to release an untested weapon. A real tactician would have weighed all options instead of picking the one he thought would be easiest." Richard began to calm himself so he could collect his thoughts. He wanted to express his concerns in a more intelligent way than simply screaming profanities, like he constantly witnessed Jayden doing at local sporting events.

General Grey turned to face Richard. "A real tactician knows when an asset needs to be deployed and not held in testing stages. We still conducted the human test like you requested. It will give us the heads up on any complications we will need to deal with in the near future with our deployed subjects, if any. Besides, these ten soldiers just assisted our forces to send the entire PC army back to the ocean. I would say that is a pretty successful test, wouldn't you? An army of nearly ten thousand highly equipped elite PC soldiers was driven back to the ocean after encountering our ten super soldiers. They saw what our troops were capable of and fell back, no extreme measures were needed. Even though our coastal defences failed to sink the invading vessels, these subjects have won a great victory for us!"

"You can't roll the dice with people's lives! You aren't just toying with their lives but the lives of American civilians too! How many of your own people did you endanger sending these untested weapons into the field? There is more at stake here than—" Richard stopped himself mid-sentence as he replayed what General Grey had just said in his mind and compared it to what Dr. Triin had told him. "Did you say ten soldiers?" Richard was certain Dr. Triin had said a dozen.

"Two of the subjects did not survive the process." The cold response from Saracen only made the statement that much more despicable. He clearly didn't care, and perhaps worse, he didn't care if Richard knew that.

Richard felt bile churning in his stomach that wanted to surface all over Saracen. He leaned over and placed his hands on one of the black metal chairs lining the massive table and breathed deeply. His head spun. His body wanted to faint, but he couldn't; he had too much to think about all at once. Two dead subjects. Were those deaths on his hands? Were the deaths of all the American citizens in the invasion? Did he not do enough to prevent this project from going the distance without his consent? Did he take too long to come up with the necessary formulas that caused these soldiers' deaths? Did he fail the American people by allowing these wild dogs to rampage through their home?

Richard shook his head and placed one hand on his forehead to steady it. No. This was not his fault. They did this. He glared at Saracen and General Grey, his eyes narrowing as if trying to see through them. Then his eyes suddenly widened. *Just because some kid fresh out of a learning box tells me it's not ready.* What? Some kid out of a learning box? Richard's expression was now that of a rabbit who had just caught a glimpse of a hungry wolf. General Grey wasn't listening to his proposals, his research or his suggestions. The general hadn't brought Richard here to work on the project at all.

A loud crackling was suddenly heard from the holographic globe, and a voice scrambled by radio signals came over the com device in the screen. "General, UF Alpha Squad has been recovered. There is no pulse on any of the soldiers. They're dead, sir."

General Grey turned back to the table and yelled at the holographic globe. "What do you mean, dead? You said they successfully completed the mission and were recovered!"

"Yes, sir. There are no visible injuries. Their hearts just stopped beating."

"Bring them back here! We need to find out what happened and why!" General Grey was visibly frustrated, and he slowly turned his head to burn a hole into Richard with his eyes as the radio voice acknowledged the order and broke communication.

Richard's look was far smugger now. Trying to put the death of the soldiers out of his mind, he gathered his thoughts and felt obliged to explain the situation to the general. "Your soldiers did not have a high enough dosage. The serum extremely increased their physical capability, but they were unaware of their limitations due to lack of training. The adrenaline in a body that could handle near fifty times the normal amount would still be rushing through their bodies from the battle. But it would seem you didn't give them enough of the activation serum, and it likely wore off before the body's blood pressure could stabilize. Their bodies would lock up in a full body seizure, unable to handle it, and their arteries probably burst from the rush of blood. Congratulations, general. You just stopped the first wave of an invasion. You showed the ace up your sleeve before it was ready to be played. And all it cost you was twelve brave soldiers and all of your morals." Richard felt like fake applause was in order but under the circumstances decided it would not be a good idea.

"You'd better pray I don't find any kind of tampering in the blood samples of those soldiers, Ceress. If I do, I'll bury you in the desert and arrest your foster parents for the aggravation." The general's comments were sinister, but somehow Richard could tell that behind the seemingly childish metaphor there was some truth to his words.

"That will be all, Ceress. You are confined to quarters until the test results are in from the UF Alpha squad." As if disciplining a child, Saracen's scolding tone didn't intimidate Richard, but he complied, leaving the room and closing the doors with a small smirk on his face.

That didn't excuse the fact that there were innocent people sacrificed in this blatant defiance of Richard's will upon this project. He was feeling less and less like he had any actual power over the project. If this were true, then Demetri likely wasn't aware Richard had no real control, and that meant what was happening to him could be completely intentional, an attempt on his life to keep him from helping Richard complete his goal. Richard's pace quickened with this realization as he made his way to Demetri's quarters, hoping that he had been transferred there from the observation room.

He saw Dr. Triin approaching him, a look of concern on her face. "Are you okay? What can I do?" Her concern was genuine, of this Richard was certain. Being around Jayden when he constantly lied to women gave Richard a sense of how women respond to men, he thought. He felt he recognized sincerity or sarcasm. Was Dr. Triin innocent in this too? If she was, there was only thing she could do for Richard.

He reached out and hugged her tightly. If it were anyone else, Dr. Triin would have taken this as a cheap excuse to get her close, but there was more to it as Richard leaned into her ear and whispered, "Get out. Get out of here, as quickly as you can. It's not safe. The project is finished, just hide in the back of one of the hummers and wait for it to leave. You need to get the antibody out of here. We're going to need it."

He let her go and walked past her toward Demetri's quarters. He knew he was leaving her in a state of shock and confusion, unsure of whether to heed his warning or enquire from others as to why he would be going to that extreme.

Closing the, Richard made his way to the bed where Demetri had been resting and pulled up a chair before his proverbial mind blew. He looked down at Demetri's sleep-induced peaceful face and then down at his own hands, which he had subconsciously clenched with his elbows resting on his jittering knees. He was nervous, anxious and angry. There were so many emotions coursing through his body right now that he was having trouble distinguishing them all, not knowing how to react. He decided to ask the only man who could help him, even if that person couldn't respond.

"Demetri." Richard's head was lowered as if ashamed of what he was about to say. "I need help. I'm scared. I don't know who else to turn to. I don't think I was required to complete this project. But if that's true, why did they agree to bring me on? There's more to this project than what I'm seeing. What am I missing? Why was I brought here if not to help with the project?" Richard paused a moment as if expecting a response. Lowering his head and rubbing his neck, he attempted to relieve some of the tension building in his brain.

He paced the room while he continued his one-sided conversation. "I don't know what I'm supposed to do, Demetri. Am I stuck here? Should I try to leave? If I wasn't needed in the first place, then why would I need to stay?" Richard began concerning himself even more. "Or rather, why would they let me leave if they brought me for a purpose that hasn't been revealed yet?" He quickly moved back toward the chair and sat down, looking straight at Demetri's face as if confronting him. "I came here to stop the very thing that just happened. Does that mean I failed? Or can I still succeed? They have already seen what happens if they don't listen to me, so maybe now they'll actually take my advice."

He nodded at Demetri, acknowledging the disagreement Demetri would have likely had to that statement. "Yeah, you're right. When pigs fly, as they say. So what's the next move? There's more going on here than they'll ever tell me. I can't work on a project without knowing the full story. Nor can I work on a project where nearly the entire team is lying to me. Did you lie to me too? I'm sure there are hundreds of things I don't know about you. All I want to know is, are you really the man you said you were? Are you here trying to stop the exact same thing I'm trying to stop? Can I trust you?"

He leaned forward and reached out to grasp Demetri's hand. Upon nearing his hand, roughly a centimetre from Demetri, Richard felt an invisible force preventing him from actually touching it. Fascinated, Richard pushed harder against this invisible force, causing the hand to sink deeper into the blanket that it was resting atop, even though Richard was not actually touching Demetri.

A grin came across Richard's face as he watched this phenomenon occur. "Full qi materialization and reinforcement. I didn't calculate this … I didn't know this was possible. There was no proven science behind a person's natural aura."

He smiled as he remembered the numerous arguments he'd had with Madeline, trying to scientifically disprove any possibility of a person's natural aura materializing. "But it seems as though the serum has not only given yours a more materialized form, it will actually protect you. Madeline was right. With proper training, you might be able to control it even better. I wonder how strong it really is. It's likely relevant to one's own willpower."

Richard's grin grew to a smile. "It also means you're alive, my friend, and will recover shortly. Your aura would not be so prominent if you were in dire straights." With renewed faith in what needed to be done next, Richard lay back in his chair and rested his eyes. "When you wake up, we'll deal with all that needs to be dealt with."

With a smile on his face and faith back in his soul, Richard was finally able to relax, and noticed a folder next the Demetri's bed that seemed somewhat out of place. He took it and read the label out loud. "Demetri Candora, Psychological Evaluation."

Did Dr. Triin leave this here for Richard to read on purpose? Intrigued, Richard opened the folder and began to delve into Demetri's psyche, in hopes of learning more about his friend, before drifting off into an exhausted sleep.

Chapter 12

ESCAPE

T HE LOUD NOISE OF THE door forcefully slammed opened jarred Richard awake from his lax position on the recliner chair in Demetri's quarters. The lights in the room were still on, and he squinted, trying to adjust. It proved irrelevant to see clearly at the moment as the sound of the shuffling of multiple people across the floor found him and quickly lifted him from his chair. Before he could even think, he was pushed onto the cold floor with both hands being held behind his back by two very strong men. An unfamiliar male voice began to speak in a commanding manner as Richard felt the cold steel of what felt like handcuffs being clamped onto his wrists.

"Richard Ceress, you are under arrest for high treason against the United States of America. You will be held in military custody until your court date has been arranged." The man continued his speech as a cloth bag was put over Richard's head, blocking any chance of seeing his accusers as he was lifted back to his feet and forced to walk forward. "You have no right to an attorney, you have no right to a phone call, and you will be lucky if we let you eat, you son of a—"

A loud snapping noise echoed throughout the room, not unlike the sound of a large switch being turned off. This interrupted their immediate plan, stopping the group in its tracks. No words were spoken, and then Richard felt a jerk on his arms to stop him from moving forward. "What's going on?" Richard's plea was as desperate as a child's. He was scared before, but he was terrified now.

"Quiet!" The commanding voice was lined with its own concern now. "What the hell just happened? Who cut the power?"

A quiet crackling could be heard coming from in front of Richard, and though he couldn't discern what exactly was being said, he was sure his captor was speaking through some sort of communicative device.

The conversation was cut short as a series of grunts and what Richard could only decipher to be thuds of bodies falling awkwardly to the floor began to radiate around him. In the commotion, he felt the grip on his arms let go, and seconds after the commotion had started he felt a hand gripping his wrist. The sound of handcuffs being keyed followed, and Richard's handcuffs were removed.

Richard's fear was causing his body to shake. Did they say treason? What had he done that could be construed as treason? He did nothing but help the project succeed. It wasn't his fault the field agents died—or was it? He heard footsteps quickly moving toward the front of his body as someone pulled the bag off his head, giving him vision of a fully recovered Demetri standing in front of him.

Richard was still in the same room, though closer to the door. The regular lights had been shut off, and he was now standing in dim red lighting amongst ten motionless, well-equipped American soldiers scattered across the floor.

"Demetri! You're okay!" Richard's relief was sincere, but Demetri had a serious look on his face that immediately told Richard he meant business.

"Did you have anything to do with this?" Demetri's voice seemed deeper than before, and slightly more menacing. The fear had been struck back into Richard, especially as he was unsure what Demetri was asking of him.

"Anything to do with what?"

"Did you have anything to do with this!" Demetri shot his face toward Richard as he asked a second time with renewed aggression.

"I don't know what you are talking about!" Richard's response was that of sheer fear. He honestly had no idea what Demetri was referring to. But one thing he was sure of—if Demetri didn't get the answer he wanted, Richard would be in a great deal of trouble.

Demetri glared deeply into Richard's eyes for a few moments, giving a slight nod, as if the answer Richard provided was satisfactory. "Come on. We need to get out of here." Demetri quickly moved toward the door but pressed his back up against the wall next to it, peeking around the corner.

"Demetri, what's going on?"

As if to answer Richard's question, a large explosion burst from the garage entrance of the facility, pieces of metal flying in every direction. Demetri leapt to Richard, forcing him to the ground to protect him from any shrapnel. The garage door now had a gaping hole with the sound from the outer area screeching through. Gunfire was accompanied by explosions and cries of pain from people in the path of either! Richard couldn't see what was going on out there, but he no longer wanted to.

"The PC is attacking the facility. We can't let them have you. We need to get you out of here. We're going to need you, Richard."

"How do you know it's the PC?"

"I heard it over the soldier's com-link before I snapped his neck." Demetri's response sent a chill down Richard's spine. Snapped his neck? Was that necessary? Richard had no love for someone arresting him, but did he really deserve to die? Not that Richard was about to question it with the mindset Demetri seemed to have. And how did he hear the com-link message when Richard could barely hear it? It seemed the serum had even more side effects of which Richard was unaware. Demetri was right. They would need Richard—more than they knew.

But how did the PC find this facility? How did they gain access so quickly? Weren't they just thrown back into the sea? This attack made little sense to Richard, and he couldn't think clearly with the noise and thought it best to turn to the experienced soldier for a course of action.

"So what do we do?" Richard tried to make it clear he would work with Demetri in whatever plan he had.

Demetri stood up and looked out the door toward the gunfire. Appearing to see what he was looking for, he reached back to pick Richard up and bring him to the door. Richard was amazed at the ease at which Demetri accomplished this move. He could barely see through the smoke that had filled this dimly lit facility. All he could see were flashes of what could be gunfire coming from inside the facility firing outward. It was the source of that firing that was the object of Demetri's fixated look. Before looking back to Richard, he motioned with his head toward that object as he pulled Richard with him for a few steps. "Come on!"

Running down what should be a familiar corridor for Richard was proving difficult without any kind of vision through the smoke and dim red lighting. The distant sound of battle was drawing closer, getting louder. Richard had no choice but to follow Demetri as he navigated this area with ease, but Richard was becoming increasingly nervous and frightened as every explosion and gunshot caused him to flinch and instinctively move closer to the floor as he moved.

When they reached the entrance of the facility, right next to the gaping hole was a man holding a large assault rifle against his shoulder. With his back to the wall he was clearly taking cover, his eyes to the floor, almost as if counting the number of shots being taken on the other side of the wall. There was a definite purpose and pattern every time he stepped out from behind the cover and fired several shots before quickly taking cover again.

As Demetri and Richard took cover behind the same wall, Richard realized he knew the man who was combating the invaders. It was Nate, the limo driver, still in his chauffeur uniform minus the hat, displaying his clean-shaven head. Nate looked anything but clean though, covered in soot with minor lines of fresh blood dripping off his head, many minor cuts likely from the shrapnel. Seeing them approach, Nate nodded, and after taking another step out to fire a few more shots, kneeled down beside them.

"Report!" Demetri yelled.

"They already breached the front. We have maybe a half-dozen soldiers left combating them in the lot. They seemed to have come through the facility from above. We have them at somewhat of a chokepoint above, so only a limited number can get down here at a time, like a slow leak. We won't be able to hold this forever though." Nate seemed to know exactly what to say to Demetri, and how. He could also handle a large gun extremely well for a limo driver.

"Where's Jinx?"

"She was up above when they attacked. My guess is she's still engaging them at the chokepoint to try to prevent more from getting down here, giving us a chance to get you out of here. But if you're able to do so on your own, then we can call for the retreat. I suggest you join the other lab personnel at the exit shaft on the other end of the facility." Nate pointed to the situation room as he mentioned the exit shaft.

"We aren't going with them." Demetri was almost vindictive with his statement, which took Nate by surprise for a moment.

But Nate quickly came up with a response. "If you were to take one of the armoured hummers out there you should be able to make your way out the front. They aren't coming in that way, and I can ensure none of them follow you. But you'll have to go through the hot zone to get there."

"That won't be a problem. I need you to broadcast to the SOUL and initiate directive 13." Demetri was clearly giving an order that Richard was unable to understand, but the look on Nate's face was that of sheer shock, even taking a minute to glance at Richard before responding to Demetri.

"Are you sure?"

Demetri glared at Nate the same way he had just glared at Richard when asking of his involvement. "Did I ask a question, soldier?" The force behind his words made even Richard take a step back.

Taking a deep breath, Nate shook his head. "No, sir. Rendezvous at the local safe house. The team will be there."

Demetri nodded at Nate and put a hand on his shoulder as he stood up. "Be safe, Ghost."

"You too, sir." Nate seemed to take a glance at Richard as he stood up and peeked around the corner to survey the situation. Then he turned back to Demetri. "Make sure you take the second from the left; do *not* go near the others." He held out a single key and placed it in Demetri's hand. "On my mark." He pulled a small device out of his pocket not unlike a smartphone, and then Nate pulled it closer to his chest.

Demetri grabbed Richard's arm, pulling him close. "When he tells us, you are to run right for the passenger seat of the Hummer second from the left. Do not stop, do not even look back. You understand?"

"Y-yes … sir." No idea why he just said sir, perhaps it was a sign of respect. Nevertheless, it got a smirk out of Demetri, so it was acceptable.

"Go!" Nate pressed something on his device, and several charges suddenly went off in the lot, one vehicle after another burst into flames in rapid succession, causing smoke and shrapnel to fill the immediate area.

As Richard ran out into the rubble-littered area, he saw the last two hummers on the right burst into flames, sending several bodies clad in black bodysuits like armour flying through the air. At the same time, Nate stepped out and put a bullet into the head of each and every one of them as they were still in the air. A feat that should be impossible, Richard tried to explain the physics quickly in his head to himself. But no human being could have that much awareness and accuracy … was he an alpha subject?

Black smoke had engulfed the entirety of the entrance. Flashes could be seen from behind the various parked vehicles scattered across the lot, accompanied by countless lifeless bodies. Some were familiar soldiers Richard had seen wandering about the facility, and some were unknown soldiers clad in black, skin-tight armour. A second large hole now could be seen in the far corner ceiling of the lot, just above the exit ramp.

It was at that point that Richard remembered he was not supposed to be looking back, and focused on the Hummer second from the left. He was paying even closer attention to that number now, realizing why Nate insisted on that particular Hummer.

As he sprinted toward the Hummer, a black-clad soldier popped up from behind it. Sighting through the eye slits in his balaclava, the soldier aimed his assault rifle at Richard's chest. As Richard was about to stop, he saw out of the corner of his eye Demetri moving faster than he had seen any human being move. Demetri rushed past him in a flash and drove a knee into the spine of the enemy soldier while grasping the barrel of the gun and forcing it upward before the soldier could even pull the trigger. Spinning the gun over the enemy's shoulder, Demetri held it in one hand and grasped the soldier's chin in the other as he was still reeling back in pain. With one quick twist of his hand, he turned the soldier's neck to the side, farther than god intended, and the body fell lifeless to the ground.

"Get in!" Demetri opened the door and placed the gun inside as he stepped in.

Richard hadn't stopped running the entire time. While hearing the sounds of a battle echoing throughout the facility, he had a newfound agility as he sprinted toward the Hummer. The door shot open for him as Demetri again called for him to enter the vehicle. He then reached out to pull him in. Demetri's immediate haste was quickly justified as a flurry of bullets began deflecting off the reinforced glass and metal of the Hummer, causing a deafening combination of rattling noise as Demetri quickly closed the door behind Richard.

The inside of the Hummer was not unlike a computer with buttons and screens covering every inch of the dashboard. As well there was an array of weapons, combat bags and camouflage uniforms laid in disarray across the massive backseat. The vehicle was very neat and organized, other than the disorganized pile of equipment that looked quite out of place. Nate must have prepared all of this for Demetri or himself, knowing it was going to be used as an escape vehicle.

Demetri inserted the key and pressed on the gas pedal before the car seemed to have even started. Like a jet engine, the Hummer roared to life, leaving a black trail of skid marks and a battlefield laboratory in its wake.

Dozens of shots followed them as they raced up a seemingly never-ending cement corridor that was on a subtle incline. The lights bordering the corridor flickered from power surges, likely from all of the explosions occurring near the generators, creating somewhat of a strobe effect and making it more difficult to drive in a straight line out of the corridor. However, Demetri didn't seem fazed.

After nearly five minutes of a remarkable speed, Richard could no longer see a dark corridor ahead of them. Instead he saw what looked to be a steel wall impeding their path.

Demetri showed no signs of slowing. Approaching the wall faster and faster, Richard felt as though he needed to say something as the adrenaline in Demetri must have gotten the better of him and he was not thinking straight. He leaned toward Demetri with the intention of warning him, but before he could even open his mouth, Demetri reached across the seat with his right hand, placing it firmly over Richard's mouth and pushing him back into his seat.

"Not a word." Demetri's hand went back to grasping the wheel as his face did not flinch from its course. "Brace yourself!"

Richard couldn't watch. He put on his seat belt and bent over, covering his head with his arms to brace himself as Demetri suggested. A few moments later, an enormous crash rattled the entire vehicle, with sparks and clashes of metal scattering all across the vehicle from all sides. The impact caused the Hummer to buckle, slowing its speed dramatically. As the crash subsided, the hummer was not showing signs of speeding back up. Though it was not lack of the vehicle's capability, it seemed Demetri had refrained from pushing it any further at this time. Unbelievable! They had penetrated this wall and were alive to see it!

After a few minutes of driving through a steep incline of a tunnel, Richard raised his head and was greeted by a night sky surrounding a large desert. He glanced behind him to catch a glimpse of a large hole in the ground with broken metal and sand particles still dusting the air.

That explains the lack of windows and sunlight … the facility was underground. No surprise, he thought. It also explained the steep incline of the road leading out.

There were no discernible roads where Demetri was driving, yet it seemed travelled enough that the vehicle had no trouble navigating through the dunes. There were so many questions that Richard had, but he thought it best to heed his early advice and not speak a word yet.

As the minutes rolled on and there were still nothing but dunes decorating the landscape, Richard could not contain his concern anymore. He had to speak. But once again, the moment before he could open his mouth Demetri slammed on the brakes, bringing the vehicle to a steady halt in the sand. He then opened his door and stepped out of the vehicle, walking to the driver's side.

Perplexed, Richard also vacated the vehicle and ran around to the other side of the Hummer to confront Demetri. He positioned himself beside Demetri as he sifted through the equipment in the back of the vehicle, only to further Richard's confusion.

"What are you—" Richard's question was interrupted immediately by a feminine squeal as Demetri pulled a body out from beneath the amalgamation of military equipment. As the slender body was thrown rolling across the sand, Richard recognized the clothing and the hair. It was Jocelyn! Richard hadn't even had time to think of what her fate might have been amongst this chaos.

"Get in," Demetri coldly said to Richard before closing the side door and walking back to the driver's seat.

"What? Are you crazy?" Richard felt a rush of emotion seeing Jocelyn in this situation. Running to her aid, he abruptly ignored Demetri's command and gently took her hands, helping her to her feet and dusting some of the sand from her body.

Jocelyn, reacting to the kindness, looked at her aid in the eyes, now aware it was Richard. Her eyes welled with tears and she wrapped her arms around his neck, burying her face in his shoulder and lightly whispering, "Thank god."

Richard could not help but return the embrace and allowed her the time to calm herself and regain her composure.

Shutting the driver's door as well now, Demetri turned to face the embracing couple with obvious agitation. "This is not a negotiation, Richard. Let's go."

"We can't just leave her here! I'm not leaving her." Richard half-turned his head back toward Demetri almost disrespectfully, avoiding looking him in the eyes, feeling his grip holding Jocelyn tighten ever so slightly.

"We're in a dire situation, Richard. I have a very short list of people I trust. She is not on that list, and therefore I cannot risk bringing her with us. If she truly is innocent in this, then she will not be a target. If she comes with us, however, she will be construed as such by our enemy."

Richard was still in a state of shock. Did the Pacific Coalition know who he was? Was that why they attacked the facility? Were they looking for him? Wouldn't they just want the serum? If that was true, was he willing to put Jocelyn in that sort of danger for his own selfish reasons? Selfish reasons … Richard had just considered protecting the life of another person to be a selfish reason, and a woman at that. Perhaps his mind was beginning to lose its grip on the important information on this subject. Perhaps Demetri was right.

"No," Richard said quietly to himself. "This isn't right." He released his grip on Jocelyn as he turned to Demetri with a defiant look. "Either she comes with us, or I stay with her."

Demetri narrowed his eyes, glaring at Richard and then at Jocelyn, who had taken a position behind Richard, avoiding eye contact with Demetri. "Fine. But not a word from either of you until I say so. Understand?"

Confused but obligated, Richard nodded as Demetri opened the door to the vehicle and entered, shutting it behind him hard enough to shake the large armoured vehicle. Richard was grateful that Demetri changed his mind, as he knew he easily could have thrown Richard into the vehicle and left Jocelyn there if he wanted to.

Richard looked down at his hands. They shook from fear and adrenaline. He immediately put them in his pockets and then looked at Jocelyn. With a calm and almost soothing tone, he said, "Let's go."

As Richard began to make his way back to the vehicle, he felt a light pull on one of his arms as a small dainty hand held it. Jocelyn walked beside him and gently kissed him on the cheek. As her lips met his skin, it sent an odd feeling throughout Richard's body.

A shiver surged through him, a shiver he had never felt before, a warm shiver. As her lips passed by his ear, the light whisper that grazed his face once more initiated that same feeling. He knew then he had done the right thing. This feeling made all the wrong that had happened around him today seem to just fade away, even for a moment.

And all Richard could think was that this feeling was from her slight touch and those two words she whispered: "Thank you."

CHAPTER 13

PREPARATION

S ILENCE WAS THE NATIVE TONGUE within the vehicle for the next
few hours. The dunes passed by, and the sun was beginning
to show itself in the distance, signifying the start of a new day.

Richard could finally see a paved road a stone's throw away.
The rising sun had more meaning to him than just the start of a
new day. There was no doubt that things were changing. Not just
for him but for the entire world.

Questions raced through his mind, and he wanted so badly to
ask Demetri everything that was concerning him. What were his
plans? He was clearly a man with a mission, as he had been since
the day he recruited Richard. If the Pacific Coalition attacked
that facility, they were either after the serum or trying to destroy
the production of it. If they had what they came for, this entire
country as well as the rest of the world would be at an even greater
disadvantage. *If you create a weapon to destroy a monster, what do
you do when the monster takes the weapon? This isn't going to be a
war—it's going to be a massacre.*

The vehicle suddenly surged forward as it transitioned from
sand to pavement. The motion was jarring enough to cause Richard
to shake his head as his train of thought was again interrupted.
The motion from Richard caused Demetri to glance over at him

with his eyes soft yet keeping focused on the road ahead of them. No words were spoken, but Richard could still tell that the glance was one of concern. It was clear Demetri wanted Richard safe. It was clear that Richard was part of Demetri's plan.

While glancing to the side of the road and behind them where they had just travelled for hours in the desert, Richard had one of his concerns slightly alleviated as he could visibly see the wind moving the sand enough to cover up the tracks they had created. They had clearly been in the middle of the desert, but it was also clear there was a path or route established for them to drive. He wasn't sure if he should be afraid of being followed, but now that they were on paved road, it seemed like a moot point.

A long paved road in the middle of the desert had to be on American soil. No deserts in Canada! Richard was trying to gain his bearings with the information he had. Seeing fluorescent lights atop dozens of buildings in the distant morning light bathing an otherwise empty sky gave him the answer: Las Vegas! It made perfect sense. The amount of power required to run a lab the size they were in would raise flags anywhere to enemy spies, except in a place where the amount of power being used was always tremendous night and day. In an otherwise untraceable location in the middle of the desert, it was the perfect hideout; that is, if some fool hadn't ordered the bodies of their ill-issued super soldiers to be brought to their "secret" facility from the very battlefield the enemy was still monitoring. As much as Richard hated to admit it, Saracen was smarter than that. So the question became, did he do it out of frustration in the moment trying to make a point to Richard? Or did he know exactly what would come of that order?

"Welcome to Fabulous Las Vegas, Nevada." Richard wasn't a gambler or a party animal, but something about passing that sign excited him. The shows and active nightlife of this city didn't appeal to him. However, the large crowds to hide within it did.

With a quick glance, a smile found its way to his face as he saw Jocelyn lying across the backseat asleep. Everything on his mind caused the time to fly remarkably fast, forgetting that they had been on the "road" for hours. Upon entering the city, he felt compelled to wake her, though he quickly dismissed the idea as it would break the silence he was told to keep by Demetri. He also wasn't fully aware if this was even their intended destination.

Turning his head toward Demetri, his inquisitive stare was being fully ignored. Did Demetri actually have a plan? He seemed to know where he was going, but in the time that Richard had known Demetri, it was clear he was the type who would never allow his demeanour to show any sign of weakness or turmoil.

As Richard faced forward again, Demetri turned into a large parking garage underneath one of the major hotels, Excalibur. He also noticed a sign at the entrance to this garage stating there was no access to the hotel from within it. This made no sense. They were going into a dead end with no access to the hotel? Were they planning to hide out in a parking garage that likely had cameras at every entrance, exit and every level within it? Maybe Demetri wasn't thinking clearly. Maybe he didn't read the sign at the entrance. At least that's what Richard thought until Demetri pulled into a parking spot on the bottom level.

Turning off the engine, Demetri turned to Richard with an intimidating glare. "All right. I've given you a fighting chance now. You're on your own." The cold statement was reinforced by Demetri's abrupt exit from the vehicle.

Richard leaned toward the open door, trying to catch Demetri before he closed it, speaking with a hint of fear in his voice. "What do you mean we're on our own? You're just leaving us? You said—"

"I know what I said! Now get out of the vehicle! You won't want to use it if you intend to escape." Demetri was not quite yelling, but his raised voice still carried the deep rumble of his intimidating nature.

The commotion had caused Jocelyn to waken. Darting up from her prone state she quickly exited the vehicle for fear of retribution.

Richard, confused, followed suit and exited the vehicle, standing beside Jocelyn as they closed their doors and watched Demetri walking around the vehicle to their side.

Jocelyn turned to Richard with a look of sheer concern. "What's going on?" Her voice broke and crackled with fear.

Demetri grabbed their arms and pulled them along as he walked even deeper into the parking lot. Without much of a choice, Jocelyn and Richard followed reluctantly, their confusion mounting even more at Demetri's actions. Didn't he just say they were on their own?

He led them to a black Dodge Journey; a beep indicated the alarm was deactivated. The doors unlocked as Demetri opened the back door. "Get in."

Demetri looked sternly at Richard and Jocelyn, motioning toward the open door. Now he was contradicting himself. Did he plan to get rid of them? Were they a liability? Then why would he help them escape and take them so far?

"Hurry up!" Demetri's insistence made Jocelyn jump slightly in fear. She stole a quick glance at Richard and then entered the car.

Richard took a moment to glare back at Demetri, and he noticed something soft about his eyes. His demeanour was stern and intimidating, but looking into his eyes, Richard did not feel intimidated. Was he getting more courageous? Or did he still trust Demetri's intentions?

Richard entered the vehicle and sat beside Jocelyn as Demetri closed the door and made his way around to the driver's seat. He produced another set of keys from his pants pocket and started the car, said nothing and began to exit the parking lot.

Richard could not hold his tongue anymore. "What's going on?"

"Sorry. The other vehicle was bugged, and I wanted to give the impression that we weren't going to be together. At least that way we may have a slight advantage, at least for a short time." Demetri's intimidating tone had disappeared, and they seemed to once again be talking to the Demetri that Richard had grown to trust. The difference between the two was … scary. Almost as if they were two completely different people.

"Won't they be able to just check the cameras and see that we got into the same car together?" Richard's concerns were now of safety and details for their successful escape as would be Demetri's. After all, if they were being hunted, neither one of them wanted to be caught.

"No. It's taken care of. The cameras in this complex are live, but they are not recording information. They won't be able to see what happened, only what is happening."

"You knew this would happen, didn't you?" Richard refused to believe this was all spur of the moment. Demetri had this entire thing planned. Now Richard had to know if he was part of this elaborate plan, and what the purpose was.

"I was prepared, Richard. I knew what I was getting into, just as you did. In my profession, you always have an escape plan. Even the greatest bomb shelter will not protect you from an explosion inside the shelter."

Demetri's words took a moment for Richard to process. Was he saying that he didn't trust his own countrymen? If that was the case, why did he agree to help them in the first place?

"Because I intended to know my enemy."

Richard shook his head in confusion—had he said that out loud? "What? I didn't say—"

"But you wanted to know," Demetri interrupted.

If Richard didn't know better, he would have said Demetri had just read his mind. But Demetri obviously knew what Richard wanted to ask.

Before Richard even noticed, they had entered a small rural area just past the Vegas strip. After driving for another half-hour, Demetri pulled into a driveway to a house probably 1600 square feet in size. It was not a fancy house by any means, with a decent size lawn and what looked to be a small backyard. The lawn was trimmed and well kept with a flowerbed decorating the cobblestone pathway from the large double driveway. The house was well kept with spotless windows and immaculate surroundings. This indicated to Richard that it was clearly occupied, with fastidious owners that perhaps used professional services for lawn and garden care.

With the press of a button on a small device attached to the sunscreen of the car, one of the two doors of this double door garage opened for Demetri, allowing him to pull the vehicle inside, and then he shut the door. The other spot in the garage was unoccupied at the time, but even the garage itself was immaculate. A wooden work bench at the side would have insinuated metalworking of some kind was done in here, but there wasn't a single particle of dust or dirt anywhere around the work station. Tools that didn't even look used, almost as if for decoration only, were neatly organized on the wall behind it. Was this Demetri's house?

Demetri exited the vehicle, closing the door, and went straight to the inside entrance door of the house using a key attached to the same keychain as the car keys. He left the door open, likely anticipating that Richard and Jocelyn would follow, though they had not yet left the backseat of the car. Both sat nervously in their newly acquired vehicle, their bodies reacting in the aftermath of a rather traumatic experience. Richard would classify it as a bloodbath, and it still had them shaking. Although it seemed like it was days ago now, the images of explosions, bodies and bloodstains on the floor crept into his mind. Demetri was a seasoned soldier, clearly seeing far worse in his times in the field, but Richard had just left university several months ago. The most violent thing he had seen in his days was when a guy made fun of Jayden's hair or challenged his masculinity. Jayden was very protective of his masculinity, it seemed, and would usually lay out anyone who insulted him. A single punch to the temple, and the opponent was out! It hadn't even occurred to Richard until now how traumatizing this experience would be to a sweet and caring woman like Jocelyn.

Richard reached over to clasp her hands, which were folded in her lap. Her eyes stared at the back of the seat, and she jumped slightly as Richard's hands touched hers, causing him to pull his hand away, fearful he had scared her.

"I'm sorry," Jocelyn muttered as she put one of her hands to her face. The other reached back to Richard and grasped the hand he had just extended to her.

"No reason to be sorry. I apologize if I was forward. I just wanted to make sure you were okay. You have been through a lot, after all." Richard's concerned words elicited a smile from the half of Jocelyn's face he could see as she turned to face him; then she removed her hand from her face.

"Thank you, Richard." She leaned down to look Richard in the eyes that were currently focused on the car seat between them. "Not just for earlier today, but the advice you gave me yesterday. You saved my life."

Richard raised his head again as though those words had fuelled his confidence. He did want her to get out of the facility, but it was never his intention for her to meet up with them and become a target, as was the rest of the team. It was, however, a … happy coincidence. Richard's eyes suddenly widened as he recalled the fate of the other vehicles that were in the laboratory's parking facility, the ones that were being ignited by Nate during the battle.

"I cannot believe my luck! Jocelyn, I'm so sorry! I could have gotten you killed with my advice! I didn't know the other vehicles were set up to be some sort of defensive explosions." Richard had grasped her hand with both of his at this point, assuming the position of a begging man pleading for forgiveness. Jocelyn put her other hand on top of his and stared deep into his glistening green eyes with a smile.

"But it didn't. The other vehicles were locked, so that was the only one I could get into. It all worked out. We're both safe, and we got away. Take the thank you, Richard."

Jocelyn's smile had all but melted Richard, but he still felt guilty for the danger he had put her in. However, her smile and kind words put him on top of the world. "Okay."

"Richard …" Her words took on an inquisitive tone. "What did you mean by 'your' luck?"

Richard felt his face turn red, though he wasn't fully sure why as he turned his head away in an attempt to formulate a response.

"Hey!" Demetri's loud voice echoed throughout the garage, startling Richard and Jocelyn into breaking their hold of each other's hands. They looked through the windshield at a confused Demetri staring at them from the entrance to the house. "You guys coming in or what?" He tilted his head again in confusion before turning around and entering the house again, leaving the door open.

Richard cleared his throat and nodded at Jocelyn awkwardly before exiting the vehicle and entering the house at a pace that rivalled professional speed walkers. He heard the other car door open and close behind him as Jocelyn also made her way inside.

The house was not only fully furnished, it was fully furnished for a family of ten! The living room had four couches that were arranged in a square surrounding a large coffee table, ideal for conversation. The TV was a quaint 19-inch plasma screen set outside the perimeter of the couches in a corner, clearly not the focus of the room. Looking down the hallway between the kitchen and living room were six more rooms, each with their own door. It was obvious Demetri didn't live here alone—if at all. Making his way to the kitchen, Richard found lots of food in the fridge, including fruits, vegetables and fresh-cut meat. It made it seem as though Demetri had been living here the entire time they were in the laboratory.

"Help yourself if you're hungry." Demetri's voice could be heard from down the hallway coming back from one of the unexplored six rooms. "It's all fresh. Make yourself something to eat, but don't get too comfortable. We aren't staying here for long."

"What are we doing here?" Richard asked as he closed the fridge, nearly on a frustrated level. He saw out of the corner of his eye that Jocelyn had made herself comfortable on one of the couches. He subconsciously blocked Demetri's line of sight to her. "On that note, where is 'here' anyway?"

"One of my safe houses. The one we were prepping in case something like this happened. We'll use it as a staging ground to plan our next course of action."

"So you don't know what we're going to do next?" For some reason, that thought made Richard feel slightly better about the situation.

"I have ideas. But I need the rest of the team to report in before I can make an educated decision."

"The rest of the team?" Richard's stomach began to drop again.

"Yes. We're not doing this alone, Richard." Demetri leaned to the side to get a brief line of sight of Jocelyn before narrowing his eyes subtly at Richard. "We're going to need a full team to pull this off."

"Pull what off!?" Richard had grown tired of the innuendos. He wanted an answer this time. "You pull me out of the laboratory after it gets attacked by what you tell me was the Pacific Coalition in the middle of a war with the very country we're trying to create an ultimate weapon for? Now they have control of that facility, we got out safely, and you're telling me we're going to 'pull something off'? I need to know what I'm now involved in. Tell me, what exactly are we pulling off?"

Richard shot his head to the garage door entrance. The sound of it opening from the outside distracted him briefly, as did the sudden knock at the front door seconds after. He looked back at Demetri, expecting a response. Demetri was still looking at the door before slowly meeting Richard's gaze to give him the answer he was waiting for.

"Treason."

CHAPTER 14

THE CALLING

HE WORD "TREASON" REVERBERATED THROUGH Richard's mind and immediately brought anger to the forefront, but only briefly. He quickly rationalized that Demetri was speaking of treason against the people Richard was morally fighting. Perhaps now was the time Richard could take more than just a moral stand on his beliefs, although his belief in Demetri's intentions was beginning to wane. He was reminded of how quickly he had brutally dispatched the American soldiers arresting Richard, and with such little regard for the human lives he had taken. Perhaps it wasn't Demetri's intentions that Richard was beginning to question but more the means by which he was willing to execute them.

It seemed as though Demetri's predominant thoughts were of his survival and the advancement of his own goals without concern or remorse for anything or anyone caught in the crossfire of his crusade. Could Richard truly bring himself to work with such a ruthless persona? Was they even safe traveling with him with such an outtake on the situation? Regardless, at the moment Richard was at the mercy of Demetri and his persona. Perhaps soon, with the arrival of his guests, his intentions would become clear.

After a quick knock, the front door opened to reveal two men dressed in identical black tailored suits buttoned neatly at the waist with a plain red tie highlighting a plain black dress shirt. The perfectly seamed dress pants draped neatly over their black shiny Doc Martens, thus completing the outfit as the most inappropriate attire for such weather in Nevada. The identical outfits were further emphasized by what looked like identical faces on both men, clean cut, their black hair styled forward, their eyes a deep brown. The only discernible features distinguishing the two were odd physical characteristics—their brows and eyes. One's eyes were wide and active, with brows high and arched, rapidly scanning the room and glancing back at Richard and Demetri. The other's eyes were more narrowed, with furrowed brows, precisely glaring directly at Richard, almost as if marking his prey.

Without breaking his gaze on Richard, he pulled a small white medicine bottle out of his jacket pocket and placed two small pills into the palm of his hand.

Demetri spoke to them using words Richard could not understand. "*Mors venit.*"

This caused them both to lock eyes with Demetri.

The two men both stood up straight and lined up beside each other without varying their gaze from Demetri, and with a disconcerting grin from both of them they responded completely in sync with each other in a deep and raspy voice, "*Mors, est hic.*" These men made Richard uncomfortable, and it wasn't their attire, it wasn't the fact that they spoke in sync or the voices they spoke … it was their eyes.

"Sit down," Demetri said in a soft but commanding tone to the two men while motioning with one hand to the couches. "Richard, this is Paul and Anthony. They've been working off-grid for the past few months as a contingency."

They nodded in sync while they made their way to the couches. His introduction to them did not relieve his tension toward them. Nor did the fact that Demetri only introduced Richard to them, not the other way around. And a contingency to what? They sat opposite Jocelyn, and the narrow-eyed twin focused directly on her as he threw the two pills in his hand into his mouth.

Jocelyn seemed nervous, and Richard saw a shiver the men's actions sent down her spine.

The other man scanned the room frantically with his eyes, though his head remained relatively still.

Richard was about to make his way to the couches when he heard a car door shut from the garage, and almost immediately afterward the door swung open with a moderate force behind it. Holding onto the doorknob was the battle-worn Elise in a soiled military uniform. Her usual flowing shoulder-length hair was now a dishevelled mess, as some of the military-style tight braids were loosening from her head and hanging to one side. Her uniform was dusty and dirty right down to her military boots, which seemed to have patches of dried blood on them. A fairly large-calibre handgun was holstered on both hips, both of which looked worn with use, indicating she had done this more than once.

Richard's first look was of concern for her, but the composed face and confident demeanour she displayed spoke volumes of her resolve, and that Richard's assistance or concern was not warranted nor desired.

"Mors venit." Demetri repeated the words he said to the two men.

Elise quickly responded, "*Mortem dormierit.*" It was slightly different from how the others had responded. It was clearly another language, seemingly derived from a form of Latin. Richard began to determine that this was how they acknowledged each other—or to be more precise, ensured they were safe, not followed and not under duress. There could be any number of reasons they would greet each other in this way. This seemed significant, especially since he had not seen Demetri address Elise in this way, and they had greeted each other numerous times in the lab before this.

Elise made her way to the couches and sat on the farthest one from Richard and Demetri, facing them.

Demetri turned to Richard and looked at him for a few moments with a quiet purpose. He spoke softly enough so only he could hear. "Have a seat, Richard. It's time to begin."

The thought of what was about to begin had Richard slightly rattled. But his curiosity was outweighing his fear, and he composed himself bravely in his mind while he walked toward the center of the room and sat next to Jocelyn on the couch across from the unnerving "twins."

Demetri slowly leaned over the couch with his hands resting atop it. He looked back and forth. Even Richard found himself drawn to Demetri's commanding presence.

Without a word, he had the undivided attention of everyone in the room. "The Pacific Coalition has taken the facility." His words were coarse, speaking matter-of-factly rather than with concern or fear. "They obviously know what America was planning. And if they didn't, they do now."

He pushed himself up off the couch as though his upper mass required a feat of strength simply to stand up straight. "But our enemy spreads further than the PC. We have a mole on the Project Valour team."

Richard's face turned pale. A mole? So all the work he had put into this project was being monitored by another faction? In other words, everything he was doing to prevent this from becoming a worldwide epidemic was for naught? The blood that had momentarily lapsed from his face now returned with a vengeance as his face burned red with an emotion that Richard until now had never felt, not in this force. He'd been used? Now a goal was forging its way into Richard's mind. There was no way he would allow his research to be used against him! He had helped create the serum, and he could damn well put a stop to its continued existence.

Richard put his feelings aside for the time being as he was now very interested in what Demetri had to say.

"The three pieces of the serum, Vigour, Gait and Keen, have been sold to the black arms market."

"Sold?" Richard could not keep quiet anymore; his outburst drew the attention of a now slightly annoyed room with the exception of Jocelyn, who had been staring blankly at the floor since Demetri had said the word "sold." "What do you mean, sold? How could this be? And for what purpose?"

"I was hoping you could tell us, Richard." Demetri's tone was not accusatory, which made what he said next harder for Richard to process. "Since it was your bank account that was used to deposit the large sums of money that would appear to be for the three serums."

The blank stare Jocelyn gave the floor turned to utter shock and disappointment as she slowly turned to face Richard.

Richard's eyes watered from the emotional dagger in his heart. His emotions were all trying to force their way through his body at the same time, preventing any of them from surfacing. The clutter of emotions gave Richard somewhat of a pseudo resolve; he knew what he was feeling on the inside, but suddenly, his demeanour became resolute. He sat up and stared directly into Demetri's eyes. He did *not* do this, and his eyes spoke words his lips never could.

"Relax, Richard, you already told me you had nothing to do with it. And I believe you. Besides, it's obviously a setup." Demetri's words were calming to Richard, and he felt his heart slowing its pace as the adrenaline that had surged through him subsided.

Events in the lab were beginning to make more sense. So the arrest was based on the fact that the money had gone into Richard's accounts. What else could they think? Then came the harsh words spoken by Demetri, demanding to know if he had anything to do with it. It was almost as if just by looking deep into Richard's eyes

Demetri could tell if he was lying or not. But Demetri had been unconscious in the lab, so how did he know about bank account setup? It seemed that the more things made sense, the more they seemed to raise even more questions. Perhaps it was best to leave it, at least for now, at the fact that Demetri believed in Richard's innocence.

It was at that moment the front door swung open, this time without a knock preceding it, nor any discernible noises associated with another guest arriving. The entire room, aside from Demetri, suddenly turned their attention to the door. The twins were reaching inside their suit jackets while Elise was reaching to her hips where her guns were holstered, all within milliseconds. They held this stance even when the entering figure was revealed to be Nate, albeit a battle-worn version of him.

His military clothing was torn, and ragged, much like Elise's. A slow stream of blood leaked from one side of his mouth over the already dried blood on his face. He had scratches across his face and hands. Yet the man walked with such purpose as to force even a royal guard to stand aside as he passed.

Demetri greeted him in the same way as the others as he entered, only this time with an undertone of urgency. "Mors venit."

Nate did not slow his approach as he responded, "*Mors evocator.*"

There was a brief tense moment for Richard and Jocelyn as they didn't know what his response meant.

Without further eye contact, Nate flopped onto the couch in front of Demetri and lay back with a sigh of exhaustion, his eyes closed. At that same moment, Elise and the twins relaxed their earlier defensive position.

Demetri did not seem to give him time to relax. "Report!"

With a reluctant grunt, Nate sat back up and reached into his back pocket, pulling out what looked like a palm pilot, though a brand Richard didn't recognize. This tech seemed far too advanced to be a simple device available to civilians but was obviously available to the military.

"Well, you were right. Each piece of the serum was sold off to the black market, and each one was purchased by a different world power." Nate used his fingers to navigate the touch screen device, accessing information. "Vigour was purchased by the Militärischer Abschirmdienst in Germany, Gait by the PCI and Keen by CSIS in Canada."

Canadian Security Intelligence Service? Richard wondered why Canada would purchase the serum when they had the monopoly on gene-augmentation technology in their own Toronto University. And what were they doing on the black market to begin with? Research?

He had to ask, "Who made the purchase from CSIS?"

Nate glared at Richard, seemingly offended that Richard would even ask a question of him. Nate turned his head to Demetri, who in turn gave him a nod. Nate turned his attention back to Richard, and in a tone dripping of reluctance, answered his question while reading from his device, "Professor Robert Gilman."

"What?" Richard's heart could not take many more shocks today. It raced at the mention of his professor's name. "Gilman? That's not possible!"

Nate renewed his annoyed glare toward Richard. "Look, kid, I don't have reasons yet, I just have names." The friendly demeanour Richard had enjoyed from Nate before had all but dissolved. All that remained was a bitter military grunt, one who seemed skilled in the world of intelligence, and a crass one at that!

"Professor Gilman of the Toronto University of Science and Technology. Then that's our first target." Demetri spoke confidently, as though he expected the room to stand at attention and follow orders.

Though the only one who stood was Nate, and it was not at attention, it was in anger. "Excuse me? Our first target? Just what kind of mission are you assigning us? I highly doubt the American government has commissioned us to gather intelligence in Canada when the entire West Coast was recently invaded by Coalition forces!" Nate had thrown his device on the couch in defiance as he gestured in the air the direction of his spoken location. "It may seem like our super soldiers drove them back, but it was far too convenient. The pulled back too quickly. It doesn't make sense. And I guarantee you they weren't scared of those soldiers!"

Demetri reeled slightly back at Nate's comment. "Explain."

Nate took a deep breath, as if about to admit defeat. "There was a soldier during the attack on the facility. Faster, stronger—enhanced."

"An alpha subject?" Elise asked.

Nate shook his head. "No, far stronger. I couldn't hit him. Every shot I took he seemed to evade with the most minimal movement. I couldn't even touch him."

Richard saw the shock on the faces of nearly everyone in the room. They must hold Nate's accuracy in high regard. "So how did you make it out of there then?" Richard asked suspiciously.

Glaring at Richard in aggravation, Nate responded, "Because he wasn't after me. He tossed me aside and proceeded farther into the facility. I saw him enter Demetri's room before I evacuated the facility."

Elise shot a concerned look toward Demetri. "Was he after you?"

"If not him, he was after Richard." Nate turned his attention to Demetri. "I believe it would be a safe assumption to expect this soldier to be on the hunt for us … sir."

Demetri's voice changed in line with his demeanour, which had made an abrupt turn from a charismatic leader to an intimidating commander. "I'm trying to pre-empt a far greater threat than the simple military of a nation. I'm not concerned for myself. We have to prevent this new 'virus' from spreading worldwide."

"So we're just supposed to abandon our country because of the actions of some money-hungry megalomaniac? I'm not going to betray my country just for some righteous crusade against an enemy that has not yet revealed itself!" Nate seemed to be taking a moral stand for his country as well as a physical stance in front of Demetri. "You think that just because you have some kid scientist to work with you that you can stop an epidemic like this from happening? This world will always be at war! Nothing will stop that! The only thing we can control at this very moment is the safety of our country and its people! We have to defend against the immediate threat, not what our enemy could be several years down the road!"

The mention of Richard in Nate's argument encouraged Richard to speak in response. "You're right, Nate." Richard's reserved and calm voice normalized the volume in the room as attention was once again on him. "Humans seem destined to fight each other for the entirety of our existence. The very nature of being human speaks to our stubbornness in our beliefs, and every human on earth will never believe the same thing. Some even go as far as to force our beliefs on others through politics, religion and war. The only way to stop war between humans, is if there were an enemy so great, that the very existence of the entire human race depended on banding together to stop it. Only in the face of utter annihilation would enough of the human race band together and stop war between each other. So even in peace between humans, we would still be at war." Richard's words put a halt to the entire argument for what seemed like minutes as everyone in the room was left in a state of confusion, depression and anxiety.

The silence was soon broken by Nate, who slowly shook his head and turned it back to Demetri. "Great. So barring an unexpected alien invasion, we're destined for war with each other."

"Don't be ridiculous, Nate," Demetri scolded his sarcastic dismissal of Richard's words. "That's not the point he was making. This country does not depend on just us to defend it; it has an army. We have to stop the rest of the world from getting this serum or these wars will do nothing but deplete the very humans of this world you are claiming you want to protect. As soldiers, we do what needs to done!"

"You haven't given us a plan, Demetri. You've preached what our goal should be, but you haven't stated how we're going to go about it. That doesn't inspire much confidence." Nate had calmed down, but it was obvious he was still questioning Demetri.

"I'm still your commander, Nate. Since when do I have to explain myself?"

"Since Siberia!"

The silence that overwhelmed the room was ominous. It seemed the other three members of Demetri's team had even stopped breathing and simply looked in shock and horror at Nate for saying what he did.

Demetri glared angrily, though amidst the burning rage boiling in Demetri's face, Richard swore he could see the makings of a tear forming in his eye.

Neither Jocelyn nor Richard knew the context of Nate's words, but even they could tell he shouldn't have said it.

CHAPTER 15

TRUTH IN LIES

After leaving the living room from the awkward silence following Nate's comment, Demetri had gone to his room to lie down to try to calm himself and force the memories of a murdered child from his mind. As he slowly became aware and began to distinguish reality from memory, he looked up to see that Richard had just entered his room in the safe house. The door was still half-open.

Richard's eyes locked with Demetri's as he slowly closed the door and crossed his arms, leaning up against it. Richard's eyes on him were not as judgmental as they had been over the past day, as he gazed upon the exhausted and heaving body of the rattled Demetri.

Demetri did not break eye contact as he continued an attempt to regain his breath waiting for Richard to say something, feeling very uncomfortable that Richard was seeing him in this vulnerable state.

But when Richard finally spoke, it was not with the words Demetri was expecting. "You do care—don't you?"

The question took Demetri by surprise. So much so that he didn't know how to respond, going over the question in his head, though it quickly became apparent to what Richard was referring. "Do not mistake the demeanour of my actions to be heartless. Everything I do, I do for good reason. I would never take a life if it did not mean saving at least two more. I will not apologize for doing what is necessary." His words were callous, but there was an underlying waver in his voice as he spoke. This could be a social obscurity that would normally be attributed to his current state of mind, but his words just seemed insincere.

"You're lying." Richard did not speak in angst or anger. His words were more matter of fact. He could not help but grin as he spoke, as if pleased with what he had just witnessed. "Dr. Triin shared your psychological profile with me. I know of your inherited … condition."

Demetri's exhaustion visibly turned to apprehension at the mention of his "condition," and his words were borderline hostile. "I'm not sick, Richard."

"I beg to differ. You're using the mainstream definition for 'sick.' Being sick can simply imply you are deeply affected with some unpleasant feeling, such as sorrow. And from what I just witnessed here, your regret for previous actions and cannot deny that you feel as such about something. Even I can see that the subject is one you wish to keep as private as possible. In my observation of your actions over the time I have known you, I began to worry that the things you have done recently were out of malice or sheer disregard for human life. But now I know, you are simply a victim, a victim of your own inner turmoil."

"There is no turmoil, and I'm not a victim. I will not make excuses for my actions. Nor will I ever apologize for them. I have a job to do. It's as simple as that! There are millions of lives that will be in danger if we cannot succeed in our mission, and I will not hesitate to take a life to achieve that goal." Demetri's voice had returned to a monotone, as if reading from a script rather than speaking from the heart.

"I'm not a member of your team, Demetri. You don't have to put on airs for me. I understand what you're doing, and I respect you for it. You make the actions and decisions that are difficult to live with to save your soldiers from it. You seem to me to be the type of leader who will never ask his soldiers to do anything without first doing it himself. Your condition causes you to go too far, and you clearly regret the actions it forces you to commit. It's common with multiple personality disorder. But to save face, you maintain with everyone that your actions are directed and intentional, when in reality, you have no control over them and are often your 'other self'—a strong leader with no regrets is far easier to follow and believe in than one who questions his own actions, and continuously looks back on mistakes. My question is, when did this truly start? It's obvious someone with that condition couldn't have made it this far up into the military. Are you that strong-willed? Or did something happen only recently to trigger the symptoms?"

Demetri's stern look faded. Richard's words pierced his demeanour and reached Demetri on an emotional level.

"I can help. And I can do it without your team knowing. But you have to let me."

Demetri moved his lips as though trying to speak, but no words came out. He had known Richard for several months now, and never did he speak as sincerely toward him as now. Still breathing heavily and holding his chest, he nodded in acknowledgement of Richard's offer, and creased a small smile.

Richard reciprocated the smile, but it quickly faded when it became apparent that Demetri was still reeling from his memories. His skin was slightly paler than normal. It was expected that his skin would lose some color from spending months in an underground facility, but this wasn't a subtle lack of color, it was a complete absence of it.

"Are you feeling okay?"

Demetri continued to breath fairly heavily as he responded, "I feel winded."

"Like you've just run a marathon?"

"No, I've run marathons before, and I wasn't nearly this winded." There was a hint of fear in Demetri's voice with his response.

Richard stood off the door and walked over to the bed, placing his hand on Demetri's chest to feel the heartbeat. It was beating far too fast for someone who had just woken from rest; even the worst nightmares wouldn't cause the heart this much strain.

"Your heart is beating a mile a minute. And your skin is pale, you're short of breath … you're displaying signs of anaemia."

"Anaemia?" Demetri seemed concerned.

"It's when your red blood cell count is less than normal. Though I don't understand how that can be possible. The serum should be strengthening your red blood cells to compensate for the enhanced performance of your vascular muscles. It must be reacting with something in your bloodstream. Have you taken any medication since the procedure?"

Demetri's face quickly turned from concern to stern, almost annoyed. He stood from the bed and attempted to smooth his wrinkled clothing. "I appreciate your concern, Richard. But right now we have more important things to worry about."

"No. Right now your health is my primary concern. I will not be responsible for your death—I need to make sure this serum runs its course through your body without incident."

Now staring at Richard with sheer purpose, Demetri spoke with a serious undertone that caused Richard to shiver. "And I need to make sure I efficiently use this serum before it runs out."

*

An awkward silence followed as the two stubborn men looked at each other, Richard trying to think of what to say. A light knock at the door broke the moment.

The knock caused Richard to jump, startled from his trance.

Demetri responded to the knock with a much friendlier tone. "Come on in."

Jocelyn sheepishly entered the room and quietly closed the door. Nodding at Richard, and then turning her attention to Demetri, she asked, "Are you okay?"

Demetri rolled his eyes whilst shaking his head in derision. "Yes, I'm fine."

"We're all worried about you. You left so abruptly after the comment Nate made. I wanted to make sure you weren't still aggravated."

"I wasn't aggravated. I needed to extricate myself from the conversation before it reached the point of … look, I just needed to lie down to get some rest and straighten my head out. It's been a long few days." Demetri's words seemed sincere on the surface, but Richard could tell he was once again putting on a dominant display for the sake of Dr. Triin, something she would believe. Regardless of his reaction, being a psychologist and understanding Demetri's condition, she would do anything for his benefit.

"I'll go speak to everyone now. We've wasted enough time, and we need to get moving." Demetri arched his back, producing a loud cracking noise before exiting, leaving the door open.

"He wasn't born with multiple personality disorder, was he?" It wasn't so much a question as a statement he was looking to have corroborated.

"No."

Neither of them yet turned their heads away from the door.

She added, "It would seem his experiences in Siberia created it."

"Is he on medication? He seems to have it under control." Richard was trying to find any cause for the possible anaemia Demetri was in all likelihood experiencing.

"Medication would only help emotional symptoms. The underlying problems would still remain. I attempted eye movement desensitization and reprocessing shortly after I was brought onto the project to see if it would help his condition. But it did not have the desired effect."

"What do you mean?"

Jocelyn had now turned her head to Richard and lowered her voice. "Eye movement desensitization and reprocessing involves integrating traumatic experiences into the brain process so as to not hold it back. It would appear those traumatic experiences are the cause of his condition."

Richard turned to meet her gaze. "So it triggered the condition when you treated him? Isn't that part of the therapy?"

"No. Generally it is used to assist with posttraumatic stress disorder. It is intended to assist the brain to process the events so that they do not linger in the brain and continue to vex the host. But instead of processing them, it seems to trigger the subconscious memories to a conscious state."

"It causes him pain?"

"Quite the opposite. Pain causes him." With that cryptic statement, Jocelyn left the room to follow Demetri.

Richard was left in the room pondering the implications of what she had just said.

A loud bellowing from Demetri in the living room broke Richard's train of thought.

"Listen up, everyone!"

Even though he wasn't part of the military team, Richard felt inclined to quickly make his way to the living room at Demetri's beckoning. Almost running down the hall, he reached the living room to see the four team members standing at attention in front of the couches from which they had risen. Jocelyn also stood to one side of Demetri.

Demetri continued on the earlier subject as if nothing had occurred to interrupt their discussion. "There is a conspiracy at work. Someone who had access to those serums has sold them to the most powerful and resourceful nations in the world. It's only a matter of time before they spread even farther across the globe and a national threat becomes global. This was meant to be a defensive measure for the United States and is now being used against us for someone's personal gain. This is an act of war that cannot be allowed to go unpunished. We will not be acting under national orders, and we will not be working with government agencies. We will be on our own. Many, including our own country, will think we're the enemy. But we need to find who sold the serum, who bought the serum and who is using the serum. We need to put a stop to this now! We know an exact location of one of the target serums. Our mission is to secure the serum and apprehend any party responsible for its purchase or distribution. We cannot allow these serums to go worldwide. What we're doing goes against all orders, and I don't think we can trust anyone outside this room."

Demetri took a deep breath and looked at everyone before continuing his speech. "I do not expect you to follow. I know what I'm asking. If you feel you cannot participate, I will not hold it against you. But I know this needs to be done in order to stop a worldwide epidemic of super soldiers. And I will do everything I can to stop it."

An eerie silence encompassed the room as Demetri continued to slowly look around the room to make eye contact with all those within it.

Nate walked around the couch and toward Demetri, a serious expression masking severe apprehension on his face. "Demetri, you know full well that we would stand right beside you in front of the gates of hell if you asked us to." Nate looked behind him at the other three agents still standing tall before turning back toward Demetri, looking at the ground in shame. He clearly was sorry for his earlier comment. His body was apologizing to Demetri better than words could, an act not ignored by Demetri, who nodded in approval, "If you believe in this so strongly ..." Nate lifted his head once again to look Demetri in the eyes. "Then tell me what to do. I'm in."

Elise picked her head up as she spoke to catch the attention of Demetri's eyes. "So am I."

"We never liked our government anyway." Still speaking in sync, the twins responded in kind with the others.

Elise and Nate stifled a laugh at the twins' poor attempt at humour.

Demetri turned to face Jocelyn and Richard, who had taken positions out of the conversation behind him, watching precariously.

Demetri addressed them. "What I'm asking is nothing short of life-changing. You've always preached how you wanted to ensure that gene augmentation was not used for this exact purpose, Richard. I'm giving you the real opportunity now to put a stop to it. Will you help us?"

Demetri's question caused Richard to look away. It wasn't meant to be rude, but he couldn't answer right away; this was a serious undertaking. But Demetri was right. Richard always did want to prevent this from happening; originally he thought it best to control it from the inside and ensure it did not become this epidemic. This seemed like the "real" opportunity to accomplish that goal, as Demetri said. Wait ... the "real" opportunity? That was the wording he used, which piqued something in Richard's mind. Was this his true intention the entire time? He thought back to his interview with Demetri when he was first recruited, and Demetri emphasized that he did not agree with the project. And it was at his own urging as well as Alexander Norman's that Richard had been recruited. Maybe this was what Demetri was planning the entire time. The local safe house, fully stocked with fresh food, the quick response of his team—it all added up. But did that mean he had something to do with the attack on the facility? This was too much information for Richard to process this quickly. The team was staring at him, expecting an answer from himself and Jocelyn. She hadn't spoken a word since addressed either. Perhaps she was having the same conundrum as Richard.

The awkward silence was broken by Nate as he looked at his palm device. "Sorry to tell you, kid. You may not have a choice." He turned the device so Richard could see that the small screen was displaying a news report from CNN. He couldn't hear the sound as it was either muted or being directed to an in-ear device Nate was likely wearing. All he could see was a female news reporter speaking to the camera, with a small display in the corner of the screen with Richard's student identification picture, and the words *Wanted for Treason against America* displayed beneath it.

CHAPTER 16

OPERATION SUNSET

THE AROMA OF FRESH COFFEE brewing from the kitchen roused Richard's senses from an unconscious state. He had fainted from the blow of being accused of treason by the country for which he had put his life on hold. His daze began to fade as he reoriented himself to his surroundings. Elise and Jocelyn stood over him lying on the couch, and he heard Demetri speaking quietly to Nate in the kitchen. He could not make out exactly what the conversation was about, only several words were fully comprehensible. "Toronto" and "bounty" had come up several times, though Richard could not decipher their context.

He sat up in order to see over the couch and make eye contact with either Demetri or Nate to interrupt the conversation. He wanted to be brought up to speed on what he had missed, unsure of how long he was out.

"You all right, Richard?" The kind words came from Demetri as he turned to face the newly roused gene-aug student.

"Yes. My apologies. It would appear the shock was too much for my body to tolerate." Richard remained professional in the wake of a moment of mental weakness—at least in his mind. Richard had never lost consciousness in his life. He was mortified that he had now as he believed he had a stable mindset. He did not like the feeling of having a small gap in his memory in the middle of a crucial event, especially one as serious as this.

Demetri said, "There's no need to apologize. I understand how you must feel. Just know you're not alone; all of us are here to support you. And all of us know that the accusation of treason isn't true."

Although Demetri's words were what you would expect from a leader, the meaning behind what he was saying was sincere enough for Richard's concern to be alleviated, if only temporarily.

Richard looked back toward Jocelyn as if to confirm what Demetri had just said. It was odd to him, but the opinion of these American agents did not seem to matter nearly as much as this one woman whom he had known for just as much if not less time than the others. It was her opinion regarding this accusation that he was truly concerned with; if she didn't believe he was innocent, he would have to do something to prove his innocence.

As if expecting such a look from Richard, Jocelyn smiled and nodded as their eyes met.

Nate walked over toward the couch where Richard had now sat up to address him directly. "I don't mean to seem as though I'm pressuring you, but I want to make sure for all our sakes that you're onboard with us, Ceress." Nate seemed more careful with his words and tone than in previous interactions with Richard.

At first Richard thought it was an accumulated respect for what he may have finally realized Richard was capable of doing. However, he felt a small measure of patronization in his voice, as if talking to a heartbroken child.

Richard decided to take it with a grain of salt and respond as he felt about the subject and not the individual he was speaking to. "When I was brought onto Project Valour, I warned them that if they did not abide by my rules they would regret it ... I'm a man of my word. They have taken the help I offered and are using it in the very way I was trying to prevent. And now they accuse me of being the villain and think this will protect them from my promise? I'm not worried about my reputation, Nate. Their mistake is believing I won't follow through. I'm in."

An approving nod from Demetri and Nate was nearly in sync as they turned to each other and then back to the rest of the group. Demetri's voice had once again changed from concerned friend to voice of authority.

"Then as of this moment, this is an official black operation. Real names and aliases will no longer be used. Code names only. The codename for our good Dr. Triin will be Sage, and for the gene-aug specialist, Akira."

"Akira?" Richard raised an eyebrow at the name he had been given by this military team. He tried to think of what the name meant. It was Japanese, he believed, but could not think of any connection between anything about him and the operation that would warrant it. "Sage" for Jocelyn he believed was quite suitable, as it implied the mind, intelligence and great knowledge.

But "Akira"? "Why Akira?"

Nate shifted on his feet, clearly uncomfortable with the subject, but answered nonetheless. "According to the news report about you, they are claiming you are an undercover Japanese agent sent to infiltrate American military intelligence, and are the reason the Pacific Coalition managed to infiltrate American satellites, bypass the surface ships and submarines, evade AWACS aircraft and breach the coastal defences. They are claiming your real name is Akira. Akira Yamarito."

Too many thoughts shot through Richard's mind at this new information. Now the government was fabricating far too much— there was no way they could fake Richard's entire background, although being adopted did give them some leeway. And how could one person negate all of these disparate points of intelligence? Even for someone as intelligent as Richard, that kind of counterintelligence would be impossible. But in claiming this, did that mean Richard's adoptive parents would be in trouble? Wouldn't the government have to silence them from telling the truth if they were going to fabricate his heritage and origin so egregiously?

"What about my parents? Won't they be in danger?" Richard asked in a panic.

Demetri paused for a moment before answering, which made Richard uneasy. "Not immediately, no. They'll only be used as a pressure point for you if they have trouble apprehending or eliminating you as a threat. The government is used to burying the 'truth', no matter how many people know it."

His worry still lay on his parents, though Demetri's answer did make sense. "Wait a minute. If they're accusing me of all this under the name Akira, why would we make that my code name?"

Demetri looked at Nate. "Please fill him in, Ghost."

"With pleasure." Nate nodded to Demetri and then slowly walked around the couch to face Richard. "You were accused of treason. More specifically, the sale of the Valour serum pieces to different world powers. They then claim you are a Japanese agent whose real name is Akira. I created more than a dozen offshore accounts under various aliases that I have associated with Akira Yamarito. Not only will this fund our operation, but if we are lucky, it will help to draw out some of the buyers when need be. So as we are referring to you as Akira, it will help give the impression that we are responsible for the sale, and therefore the go-to sellers for this market."

"Doesn't that just make me even guiltier? Isn't that what they want?" Richard was trying to poke holes in their logic, though he knew the answer.

Demetri spoke up immediately, expecting this exact question from Richard. "No. They want you to try to prove your innocence. If you embrace this accusation, they lose control over the situation.

It will force them to deal with you instead of focusing on their true goals."

Richard turned behind the couch again in response to Demetri's remark. "And you want them to have to deal with *me?*"

The grin that then creased Demetri's face was so sinister it sent a chill through Richard's spine. "Yes. I do."

"From the sounds of it, that has already worked." Richard sneered, for a moment confusing both Demetri and Nate as to what he was insinuating.

"You're referring to the aforementioned 'bounty hunter', aren't you?" Nate's response was not so much a question as a realization that nearly everything he had tried to keep hidden from Richard had come in the open in a matter of minutes. "There is an underground bounty on both your head and Decan's. Decan's is for a body ... but they want you alive."

Richard shook his head and snorted in derision. "Who's Decan?"

Demetri laughed softly and said, "Decan is a black-ops call sign of a dangerous special-ops agent, a man who for years struck fear into his enemies just at the mention of his name. But there is no meaning behind it; it is simply a shortened combination of his first and last names, to emphasize the absence of fear should his enemies discover who he is. In short—I'm Decan."

Richard was not shocked to hear this, though Demetri's arrogant boast about himself did concern him a little. "To be put in the same league with someone that feared...America really is trying to stop me before I start, aren't they?"

"Actually, Akira," Demetri retorted, "the bounty was placed by the Pacific Coalition. It would appear they resent having a false agent associated with them."

"Great. You weren't kidding when you said we would be the enemy to everyone." Richard noted Demetri's facial expressions, which seemed more put off with this information than before. "You seem upset about this, Dem"—Richard quickly corrected himself, remembering the codename he needs to begin using—"Decan."

Demetri's expression slightly changed upon hearing Richard's fumble, hiding the grin quickly as he explained himself. "I want the attention of those responsible. This will only succeed in irritating us. They will be random agents who have been contracted to fulfill the bounty ... perhaps even some expert agents from the Pacific Coalition payroll."

"So what's the plan?"

"We'll deal with them as they come. As long as we cover our tracks and keep out of the public eye, they won't be able to track us. We just cannot afford to be careless with our steps." Demetri appeared to have addressed the entire room with his last comments as he scanned the room for objections. "It shouldn't too difficult with the war going on."

Richard had completely forgotten there was a war going on. It was an invasion by the Pacific Coalition across America's West Coast. He remembered that the first wave had been fought off by the ill-used Valour subjects. News had suggested no further attempts had been made in the meantime, with no mention of an attack in Nevada. It was becoming clear to Richard that this "invasion" was a ruse to reach the facility. But how did they know it was there? For a populace that was recently attacked, he did not recall seeing any signs of panic in the streets because of it. In fact, he vividly remembered that the regular Vegas shows were still playing across the strip, indicated by the billboards around the city. It was as if citizens had no concerns.

This was American arrogance in Richard's mind, a stereotype with all too much prejudice. "What's the status of the war?"

Demetri shot a glance at Richard and then slowly broke eye contact as he walked toward the window. His stride was slow and purposeful. His hands clasped behind his back, he stopped at the window, the sun highlighting his face, the rough skin noticeably weathered and worn. "The Pacific Coalition withdrew temporarily to their carriers, which are now pulling back across the Pacific after their defeat at the hands of the arrogantly dubbed 'ultimate fighting American soldiers'. It appears after their fall and the attack on the research facility, they need to regroup. They have not made any further move to date. Several Tomahawk antiship missiles have even sunk a few Japanese carriers in their retreat."

"Something doesn't add up." Richard couldn't help but interject his thought on the situation. "The Pacific Coalition is smart. Smart enough to try more tactics against a new enemy before immediately pulling out at the sight of them."

"What are you insinuating?" Nate asked.

"I'm insinuating that the Pacific Coalition wouldn't just back off like that after such a bold move as invading America. Unless they knew what was going to happen." Richard turned to Demetri as he spoke, with an expectant look. He knew Demetri agreed with him.

"He's right. There may be more to this Japanese agent than we're giving credit. There is obviously a correlation between Project Valour and the Pacific Coalition. The timing of everything was too perfect. Not to mention the knowledge they acquired, knowledge that should only have been available to members of the project. This is all the more reason we need to do this on our own."

"Something else doesn't add up." Richard was trying to process this information. "Let me think out loud here ... so there is likely a PC agent somewhere in this project, and the Americans think it's me and have charged me with treason. The Japanese know I am not this agent but want me in their custody for my scientific knowledge of Valour. Do the Americans really believe I am this agent, or is this a huge ploy to get me into their custody if I cry innocence and give myself up to them as I have nothing to hide?"

Richard paused for a moment when a thought flashed through his brain and a sick feeling overcame his gut—now both factions would be interested in his parents. He could only imagine what they were going through right now, knowing of the public allegations made by the Americans … and then there was Madeline. This moment was not the right time to bring up these concerns, but he would address them with Demetri when he could. He had to go forward in understanding the plan at hand.

"So we're taking advantage of this confusion and creating our own misconceptions as a means to an end?" Richard asked.

"A simplified summary, but yes." Demetri watched Richard closely while he was speaking.

"Then what exactly is the plan, Decan?" Richard asked in a patronizing tone, or at least, patronizing to people who weren't familiar with the way Richard asked questions.

Demetri leaned over the couch where Richard was sitting. "We have only one solid lead."

"Gilman." The name ran a movie reel through Richard's head—of all his classes, his lectures, the one-on-one discussions he'd had with him. Gilman was one of the few men Richard had respected professionally in this world. Was it possible that he represented everything Richard opposed? Or was he being set up the same way Richard was? "You intend to apprehend him?"

"No. I'm not going to assume anything. We need to investigate further. Panther, Artemis." Demetri stood from the couch and addressed the twins, who stood at attention at the mention of their names. "We can't let the other leads run cold. I need you to find out more about the other two buyers. I need a traceable location, and I need to know who the *real* seller is."

Motioning and speaking in sync, they both saluted. "Yes, sir." Artemis's eyes were still jumping around the room as Panther's focused directly on Demetri without a single blink.

Demetri turned his attention to Nate and Elise. "Spire, you and Ghost will accompany us to Toronto. We're going to find out more about the transaction between Gilman and the Keen serum. Perhaps he can enlighten us as to who the real seller is."

Elise and Nate saluted Demetri. "Yes, sir!"

"By 'us', I'm assuming you mean me and … Sage too?" Richard sheepishly interrupted the commanding session Demetri was having with his associates, unsure if Demetri still considered Jocelyn part of the group.

Demetri gave a modest glare toward Richard. "Yes, both of you."

"I do have a matter that requires attention as well, Decan." Richard stood and faced Demetri but quickly turned to the rest of the group. "Some of you may have noticed that Decan has been feeling out of breath lately, sluggish and pale. I think there are some irregularities in his body's reaction to the serum. I can deal with these irregularities as I am more than capable and best qualified. However, there is only one other place that I can perform those kinds of tests, as I need the necessary gene-aug equipment."

"The university in Toronto," Elise piped up, forcing a smile.

Demetri grumbled under his breath and renewed his glare toward Richard. "My health is a tertiary concern, Akira."

"No, it's not. The health of this entire team is a primary concern for me," Richard retorted.

"Mine as well," came an almost insulted statement from Elise.

"And me!" Jocelyn had thrown her hat into the ring as well. "No one is an asset to the team if not functioning in a healthy manner."

The grumble that emanated from Demetri was far more audible this time. He didn't speak any further about the subject, but he seemed to have a quiet submission regarding it.

"We will cross the border through Niagara Falls," Decan said.

"You and Akira will have to cross by unconventional means, Decan," Nate interjected. "You may not be wanted in Canada specifically, but this bounty is worldwide. CSIS will likely have been given a copy of Richard's profile. They see you at the border, and you will be sending up red flags to every bounty hunter and intelligence agency in the world. We cannot leave any trace. Even the slightest oversight could jeopardize not only the operation but our lives."

Demetri nodded and continued. "The three of you will cross the border by normal means using the car. I will take Akira and make our way across the border utilizing a point up the river leading to the Canadian side of the falls. If we do it under cover of night, we should be able to cross without incident. They have increased border patrols because of the American invasion, but I do not foresee them covering an entry point along the rapid river and pounding falls that can't be easily traversed in a boat."

"So how will we get across? Are you sure we can do this?" Richard was not trying to be insulting, but his concern stemmed not just for himself but for Demetri as well.

Though Demetri's sneer told him he did not take it as such. "Yes—I'm sure. After crossing, we will rendezvous at the loop right next to Clifton Hill. From there we will make our way to the university. We will decide on a course of action at the university once we survey the surroundings. Any questions?" Demetri looked around the room, waiting for a response.

Having received none, he continued. "Very well, then. Initiate Operation Sunset."

Chapter 17

BORDER CROSSING

HOURS OF DRIVING IN THE black Dodge Journey procured from the Vegas parking garage gave plenty of time for conversation for the five team members. With Artemis and Panther working elsewhere on tracking down the other buyers across the world, the remaining five would begin to make their way to the Canadian border. They had all changed into civilian clothing at the safe house. Richard and Jocelyn left their lab coats behind in exchange for a suitable jacket for the cooler Canadian climate. Demetri wore black pants, a green long-sleeved shirt and black leather casual jacket. Nate wore black pants with a beige shirt and dark brown casual jacket. Elise was a little more stylish in her fitted black pants, a blue, long-sleeved shirt and a feminine black jacket with metallic decorations. She restyled her hair into one elegant French braid down the back of her head. They would blend in well with the general population. Weapons were well concealed inside the vehicle in a special compartment under the backseat floors. They were ready!

Nate sat with Demetri in the passenger seat, which excluded them from most of the dialogue in the back, although they seemed quite content in their silence.

It was an enlightening experience for Richard as it gave him the opportunity to speak with Jocelyn about the two members of Demetri's team. He had never been introduced to them or even spoken to them. Jocelyn had mentioned that she was brought onto this team as the mental-health expert when it was created. Therefore she had access to their entire medical history, information on which Richard desired to be enlightened.

The twins, the elusive Paul and Anthony, were the subjects. They were a pair of men who seemed to be on the far side of quirky. There was more to their story that Richard wanted to know—there was more to this entire team's story that Richard wanted to know. He decided to be bold and ask more about their history, an attempt to strike up conversation. Although it was quickly apparent to be a conversation neither Demetri nor Nate were willing to engage in. Luckily, with Jocelyn sitting between him and Elise in the backseat, it was simple enough to strike up a conversation with her. Richard was fully aware that their conversation would be heard by the entire car, which may have made Jocelyn slightly uncomfortable under the circumstances, though Richard didn't understand why. After all, she was just explaining medical conditions and history of the two members of whom he had no prior knowledge.

"Prototypes?" Richard raised his left eyebrow higher than he thought possible as he confirmed what Jocelyn had told him.

"Yes. 'The Soul' was the twelfth batch of prototypes utilizing the base formula of project Valour. It was the formula Dr. Norman used as a baseline to develop the other serums. It was not nearly completed, nor did it have the design to thin out of the bloodstream, so their changes are permanent, unlike the alpha subject steroid formula they were technically improving. It is likely one of the reasons Demetri survived the process but was unconscious for a while. The body can only handle so many foreign substances at a time." Jocelyn spoke more loudly. Her intention was clearly to project her voice to be heard in the front seat. "It is also why I believe it extremely important to conduct the necessary tests on Demetri to ensure his continued health."

Demetri slowly turned his head to face Jocelyn in the back. With a deadpan look and deep voice, he said "My name is *Decan*, Sage." He then turned back around without another word and continued to stare straight ahead.

"S-sorry," Jocelyn responded as if embarrassed, slinking to an almost foetal position.

Richard darted a glance toward Demetri, quickly realizing it would be completely ineffective. He looked back at Jocelyn and spoke as though Demetri's comment didn't happen. "Were the serums different for each subject?"

Jocelyn did not change her position but did continue the conversation, though with a much more sheepish tone. "Not all the serums, but the dosage and where it was injected were the variables. A high dosage of a modified drug was injected into the brainstems of Panther and Artemis. A high dosage was injected into the hearts of Spire and Ghost. And a moderate dosage was injected into both the heart and the brainstem of Decan."

"A drug was injected into the brainstem?" Richard tilted his head in confusion. If this was based on a steroid formula, the brain stem is the *last* place they would want to inject it.

"The formula was modified in a way that they believed would actually increase the brain capacity of the subject. They were correct." Jocelyn raised her head slightly so her eyes could barely see Demetri's shoulder from under her brow. "Unfortunately, as you would suspect, there were … complications."

Richard didn't even flinch. Obviously there were complications; without further integration with gene augmentation, there was no way a drug could affect the brain on an intellectual level without adverse effects. He may not be a psychologist, but he did consider himself a gene-aug scientist, and he knew what would happen when augmented drugs were injected into the brainstem.

"Their brain function wouldn't stop," he said. "It would have the capacity to process more information, and faster. But it would act similar to an over-stimulated child, unable to focus." Richard thought back to his first encounter with the twins, and how one's eyes constantly moved—as if over-stimulated. It made perfect sense. Though the other, while oddly gazing, seemed focused. The pills! He had taken some pills when Richard first met him. "So those pills—"

"A powerful alternative to methylphenidate." Jocelyn finished Richard's thought, pleased that he had already come to the correct conclusion. "He becomes extremely focused as long as he takes a regular dose. However, he is still capable of an unnatural amount of thought processes and multitasking."

Richard furrowed his brow at the concept. "So if he's taking those pills, why isn't the other? Was he not given the opportunity? Perhaps it was a way of telling the two apart?" His attempt at humour was beyond lost on every passenger. Apparently Richard still had more to learn about how and when to tell a joke.

"He was offered it. But he didn't want it. Unlike his brother, he believed he was more effective the way he was. And as unstable as you may think he is, the two of them have completed missions in hours that Navy SEAL teams were incapable of performing over weeks. The entire team seemed to inherit similar attributes, increased physical strength, speed and reflexes, although Decan showed the greatest improvement in all respects."

Richard felt he knew the answer to this and spoke up proudly. "That's because they distributed the serum evenly between his bloodstream and brain. It wouldn't be nearly as great a shock to either system, and then the serums would be better integrated. The body could adapt better and utilize the distribution better, like a planned power grid."

Jocelyn's nodding confirmed Richard's suspicions. But there were more questions creeping into his mind now. If it was successful with Demetri, then why wouldn't they mass produce it? Because they could do more with it when they discovered gene augmentation. That would mean this was all performed before gene augmentation was a practiced science. "When did this original project take place?"

"Ten years ago." Jocelyn had finally relaxed her position again from her near foetal crouch. She now sat more relaxed on the seat.

"Ten years ... that means—"

"Yes. The university program is based largely on the research and development that occurred during the project's conception," she said, proud once again that she believed she finished Richard's sentence. She smiled, although her smile quickly faded when she saw the sickly look on Richard's face.

He thought he was going to vomit. All that time he was fighting against military use of gene-aug research—and it was military use that the entire program was based on? Was this always the intention? Even in Canada, did they know the entire base of this program was founded on military use and research? Did Gilman know?

The serum ... Gilman supposedly purchased the serum. If not him, then the university or Canadian intelligence did. They *must* know. Was that why they had agreed to send Richard to the American research facility? Was that how they were going to get the contacts necessary to purchase a serum? What was going on?

"Rich—I mean Akira, are you okay?" Jocelyn's soothing voice speaking quietly in Richard's ear snapped him out of his fog.

Realizing he had placed both hands over his face in frustration, he let them rest on his knees and turned to look Jocelyn directly in the eyes.

"Holy shit." An abrupt and rude comment from Nate in the front seat caused both of them to break eye contact and turn their attention forward. Out the front window, they could see the numerous hotels that decorated the landscape on both sides of the United States and Canadian border, a large waterway separating two countries and the one long bridge, the Peace Bridge, the only visible connection between them. The Peace Bridge was jammed with cars trying to enter Canada, lined up nearly a mile past the bridge itself. Regular traffic in Niagara Falls, New York, was known to be hectic, but with the backup of cars trying to escape the inevitable chaos from the war in America, it had simply stalled to a halt. Horns honked on every street and parking lot, and the line into Canada was moving, but at a snail's pace. With the sun setting on the horizon, it seemed this situation would continue for quite some time. In the meantime, life in New York State was unsettled.

"Looks like you two will have plenty of time to make your way across. At this rate, we won't get through until morning." Elise spoke up as she peeked over Demetri's shoulder to see the clutter for herself.

Demetri turned his head toward the mist climbing up from the cliffs of Niagara Falls. "Just let us out here. The further from border authorities we are when we part, the less chance we have of being noticed," Demetri barked.

Richard looked at Jocelyn nervously, though she avoided eye contact. Richard didn't know why. Was she still feeling uncomfortable? Was there something she wasn't telling him? Or perhaps ... she was just worried about him.

Demetri opened his door, stepping back as he vacated the vehicle. "Let's go, Akira." He shut the door, creating an ominous silence in the car as Elise and Jocelyn looked toward Richard, and he back at them. Nate did not say a word, though Richard could see his eyes looking at him through the rear-view mirror with a look of impatience.

Giving a worried look to Jocelyn, Richard turned, opened the back door and exited the vehicle. The second Richard shut the back door, the car drove off at a steady pace. It wasn't long before it made a turn down a street between some buildings and was lost in the sea of cars and concrete.

He turned to Demetri, who was already crossing the street headed toward the American side of the Canadian Falls. They were headed to the parkland and tourist pathways that led to the magnificent view of the falls. Demetri's stride was long and purposeful, clearly assuming Richard was following him as he didn't so much as glance behind him to check.

Richard scrambled slightly on his feet to catch up to Demetri, dodging the few cars that were currently travelling on the side road where they had been dropped off. He struggled to keep up with Demetri. The silence between them became increasingly uncomfortable for Richard as they continued their trek through the city streets. He felt as though it was his duty to say something, though he could not think of any words. Should he share his fear with Demetri? Or would that only aggravate him further?

It was clear something had been changing in Demetri since Project Valour. Perhaps not quite changed yet, but some processing with the integration of serums was having a huge impact on his physical and mental functions. His mannerisms and general demeanour would change at the drop of a hat, which would imply that his physical and mental capabilities vary to extremes in the same way. Richard could not help but think about what happened to Paul and Anthony through the same prototype project. Perhaps the same thing was happening to Demetri but at a slower pace, due to the reduced volume that was originally injected into his brainstem. He needed blood tests, and fast. Perhaps Richard could prevent this change from happening, if he caught it in time and had the proper antibody. It would be too much of a risk to wait for the serum to run its course. It was obvious that whatever effect Valour had on Demetri's system was amplifying or hastening the adverse effects caused by the prototype serum already flowing through his veins.

It was not long before they stood before the raging river leading toward the Canadian side of Niagara Falls. They were positioned at a remote point on the New York side of the river just above Horseshoe Falls, the point where the river narrowed to tumble over the giant cliff. The Canadian side was barely visible, as a thick fog enveloped the area in eerie ghostlike clouds. This was a common phenomena for autumn weather in Canada near bodies of water.

The sun was now set, and moonlight reflected on the glistening waters amongst fog and mist. The spray from the fall, though still at least two football field lengths from them, was still spraying lightly on Richard's face. Something about feeling the water was soothing. It was as if the soft caress of his home country was welcoming him in its misty embrace.

Richard stood beside Demetri as he surveyed the river in a quiet meeting within his own mind. Richard's comfort got the better of him, and he closed his eyes and engaged his senses in his country's embrace.

A few moments later, he noticed Demetri staring directly across the river at the Canadian land. His peaceful comfort quickly changed to fear and anxiety as the power of the raging river and thunderous falls became a dangerous threat, a barrier to their safe destination. A goal, so close yet seemingly unreachable from this venue. The speed of the river was likely stronger than Demetri had originally anticipated, and so close to the edge of the falls! As strong as Demetri had become, it seemed unlikely he would be able to traverse such an obstacle by his own physical means. And Richard could see no boat or flotation device. That was how they were going to get there, wasn't it? A slight feeling of panic surged through Richard. He wanted to ask Demetri the question but noticed Demetri's eyes had almost become glazed over, staring at the land on the other side. It was as if his mind had been so intensely focused on how to reach their intended destination that it had completely removed all conscious thought.

Richard was beginning to worry. He took a step toward Demetri, but the moment Richard was within arm's reach, the glazed look in his eyes disappeared and was replaced with a scowl of determination. In one fluid motion, Demetri threw Richard over his shoulder, turned and began running away from the raging river. He stopped several streets into the empty edge of the city and then turned sharply, facing the river once again. Demetri bent his legs in almost a crouched position and sternly stated, "Hang on."

He took a step back with one leg, while holding Richard firmly and began running at the river at an increasingly remarkable speed. Richard felt as though Demetri was breaching a faster pace than even most cars capable of as the wind flew by his ears almost painfully at the speed they were moving. Then several steps before the river, Demetri suddenly leaped forward into the air with such force that Richard's entire body fell limp as he lay over Demetri's shoulder, anchored close to his body by a powerful arm. The force of the leap was so great that they were launched nearly 200 feet in the air. The shock from the leap left Richard breathless, as his attempt to scream was marred by his lack of oxygen. He could instead only look wide-eyed at the land they were fast approaching from a vertical angle.

Despite the length and height of the leap, it was only seconds before they descended onto the grass of the well-kept lawn decorating the Canadian river border. Richard felt Demetri lift him up from his shoulder to the full extent of Demetri's arms above his head less than a second before hitting the ground. This removed a great deal of the impact that would have slammed Richard's legs into the ground with serious damage due to the velocity of the jump. Demetri's hand then guided Richard's body into a roll so they both landed in a rolling motion, quickly engaging in a fast and rough tumble across the grass and through grass and bushes, finally stopping nearly 200 feet from where they initially landed, ending on a relatively clear path that almost seemed targeted by Demetri's jump.

Richard was still in shock as he lay facedown on the grass of his home country. To his surprise, when he looked up, he saw Demetri already standing, as though he had rolled perfectly to his feet.

Looking down at Richard, Demetri's face slowly lost the intensity that had preceded his inhuman feat of strength and dexterity. Richard's hamstrings were throbbing from the clamp-like grip Demetri had used to carry him across. But it seemed of little consequence from what the proven super soldier had just accomplished.

Clearly impressed with himself, Demetri looked down at Richard, still lying in shock on the ground, a grin creasing his face in amusement.

The look was erased in an instant as he shot a look inland, as a predator would sense prey.

Richard was poised to stand and turn but was instructed otherwise by an authoritative voice that had been accompanied by the sound of a gun being cocked. "Don't move!"

CHAPTER 18

ANONYMITY

"**S**TAY WHERE YOU ARE!" THE commanding male voice yelling at Demetri and Richard was accompanied by a second voice barking similar instructions. A static-filled communication filtered through a radio clipped on their shoulders, though Richard could not make out exactly what they were saying aside from the last two words, "En route."

"Get on your knees and put your hands where we can see them!" The order was clearly directed at Richard still lying facedown on the grass. An order that Richard obeyed, slowly pushing himself off the ground and to his feet. He raised his hands above his head as he reached a standing position and turned to face his aggressors.

Two men held their sidearm pistols firmly in their hands, one aimed at Demetri while the other was on Richard. They were dressed in light rainproof jackets, uniform green, matching their military-issued pants. The jacket was decorated with a Canadian flag on the right shoulder and Canadian Border Control badge on the left. This type of officer was only recently instituted in Canada, but Richard remembered that these men were generally recruited from the military. It was mandatory that these officers had already served in the military a minimum of five years. This was to ensure skilled and confident recruits who would not show any hesitation for action and quick decisions required in this field of patrol.

Although Richard was complying with every request the officers were giving, when Richard turned to look as to whether his counterpart was following suit, he was concerned to see that Demetri had not moved from his hardened stance. His arms were still set firmly at his sides with his fists clenched, and his scowl had not waned for even a second as he responded with the authoritative stance of the two border officers in defiance of their order!

Richard could see in Demetri's eyes what he was thinking. Demetri's posture was like a lion ready to pounce on an unsuspecting antelope. Richard's head shook from side to side as an inaudible protest, hoping to sway his decision. Demetri's thoughts had become clear enough to the officers, as the second one who had been keeping an eye on Richard had now adjusted his sights in an attempt to deter the noncompliant member of the obviously unwelcome party.

Looking at both officers now training their guns on Demetri, Richard saw their hands slightly quivering. These military veterans had trouble pointing a gun at someone? That did not make any sense, as they must have done it a dozen times before, and now at a clear invader of their country! Come to think of it, their response time was far too fast for it to have been reported. They must have seen how Demetri jumped over the river. Because of the heavy fog and rising mist, their vision of this inhuman feat was likely obstructed. But they had seen enough, which would explain their hesitation to engage this "hostile." Richard imagined it would be much like attempting to arrest a man you had just witnessed effortlessly lifting a car over his head.

The two officers were steady nonetheless. They slowly crept forward and repeated their instructions over and over again, each time with more and more urgency. The unwavering stance Demetri had taken was making them increasingly nervous, though they stood strong as they stopped just out of arm's reach.

"I'm not going to tell you again, sir! Get down on your knees with your hands up!" The one officer barked as the other inched forward, neither of them lowering their guard or their firearms.

Demetri closed his eyes as a malicious grin creased his lips. As he opened them and glared at the officers, Richard began to back up, knowing what he was about to do. But before anything could escape Richard's lips, Demetri had reached out with both hands, grasping each officer's firearm, taking one in each hand, and squeezed tightly. The sound of grinding metal creaked through the air. Demetri had completely crushed the barrel of both guns with his bare hands. Demetri's feats of strength and agility were becoming increasingly concerning to Richard, and Demetri acted as though he knew exactly what he was capable of. But how could that be possible?

The immediate shock on the officers' faces only intensified as Demetri's aggression turned to them. With an open hand Demetri struck one of the officers in the throat, using his thumb and forefinger, causing the officer to clutch his neck and gasp desperately for air. As his arm was recoiling from the strike, Demetri spun around, raising his leg into the air. He kicked the other officer across the head with such force, it sent him spinning in a torque motion through the air before slamming into the ground face first.

Without hesitation, before the second officer could recover his breath, Demetri leapt off the ground, grabbing the back of his head with both hands, and in one solid motion pulled his head down as he raised his knee to connect squarely across the bridge of the officer's nose. Yet a man obviously capable of crushing tempered steel, he showed enormous restraint not crushing these men into red paste with his strikes. Why was he using such elaborate movements to deal with men who obviously posed him no threat? Looking more closely, Richard could see a grin cross Demetri's face with each strike. Was he enjoying this?

Landing gracefully on the grass, Demetri resumed his stance with closed fists as he watched the second officer fall backward and hit the ground. Richard looked at the two men, praying the force Demetri had exerted against them was only enough to incapacitate and not kill them. He rushed over to the officers and quickly felt for the pulse of each man, breathing a sigh of relief as they were still alive.

He glared at Demetri, no longer in accusation but relief. "They're alive. We should go before more get here."

Demetri furrowed his brow as a parent would to a child who'd spoken out of turn. "Of course they're still alive. I haven't killed them yet."

"And you aren't going to." Richard stood defiantly. Whether this was Demetri talking or his second personality, there was no way Richard was going to let this happen. There was no excuse good enough for killing these men. This was exactly the kind of abuse of power Richard was worried about super soldiers exercising.

"They cannot be allowed to live, Akira. We're conducting a top-secret mission and are currently being pursued by nearly every superpower in the world. We have the advantage right now. They do not know where we are or where we're headed. If these men are allowed to live and identify us, not only do we lose the advantage, but the entire team will be put in danger and the mission itself could be jeopardized." Demetri's tone was forceful but not condescending. It seemed he understood Richard's stance and even took a position of respect toward him because of it. After all, in his mind what he was saying was simply a matter of fact, in order for the mission to succeed. Richard being new to the scene would understandably not comprehend its necessity.

"No. We're not going down this road." Richard stood between the two fallen bodies and Demetri, even taking a step toward him. "You cannot simply kill innocent people for being an inconvenience to your 'greater' purpose. By doing that, you're justifying the very thing we're fighting against."

"What are you talking about?" Demetri's fists relaxed. He folded his hands behind his back, genuinely listening to what Richard was going to say.

"We're being hunted because we're an inconvenience to the nations we served. I can safely say I personally would not be an immediate threat to these people were I not condemned to the world because of them. The very act they have committed in trying to eliminate me due to my inconvenience has made me their enemy. If you kill these men, you will be the enemy of their families, their friends and the country they serve. And they are the very people you're striving to protect with this operation!"

"We no longer have the luxury of allies!" Demetri stepped toward Richard, standing with his chest nearly touching Richard's chin as he looked down on him, emphasizing the difference in stature between the two men. "We cannot ignore the greater threat simply because it'll make you feel better. We're likely being hunted by a soldier who could possibly be even stronger than I am! These men will die because they were doing their duty for their country. If they are allowed to live, they will jeopardize our mission and will eventually die at the hands of our enemy anyway, along with half the population. So ask yourself, do you want the blood of a dozen soldiers or a million civilians on your hands?"

Richard swayed away from Demetri, as if physically taken aback by his statement. Then he leaned forward to speak to him frankly as he lowered his voice. "If we discard our morals, then we have already failed our mission, not just as soldiers, but as human beings. The world is always seeking villains, Decan. Do not let *us* become one."

Demetri had avoided eye contact with Richard through his entire speech, until his last statement. Something seemed to visually click in Demetri's mind as he glanced back at Richard. The two stared into each other's eyes for what seemed like an eternity. The sound of crickets echoed around them, and the distant sound of the falls crashing against the water below created a peaceful ambience—until the radio from the fallen officer began to chatter more clearly.

"Officer Jensen, what is the situation? Officer Jensen, report!"

They looked at the radio and then back at each other,

"Would you like to call Mrs. Jensen and explain that her husband died for a greater good? Perhaps their kids would understand."

"Let's go." Demetri turned and began running away from the scene, but not going so fast as to outrun Richard.

As Richard took off after him with a confident and triumphant smile, he looked back at the two officers still on the ground unconscious, pleased with the success of his resolve.

*

It wasn't long before they reached the rendezvous point established by their group. There was a long road filled with cars driving by, and dozens of people lined up across the Cliffside gazing at the now colourfully lit up Niagara Falls wonder. Both the Horseshoe Falls on the Canadian side and the falls on the American side were putting on their nightly light show.

A flash of concern crossed Richard's face as he thought of all the people here who may have seen what Demetri did to cross the border. But in hindsight, there was still a heavy fog and it happened so fast, so it was very unlikely. Another factor in their favour was the lights being used to illuminate the falling water, a sheer focus for most onlookers, not to mention the majority of the American populace in this area trying to get as far into Canada as quickly as possible.

Richard turned from his own gazing at the falls to see Demetri sitting on a nearby bench, his breaths rapid and short. Sitting beside him, Richard put a hand on his shoulder. "Thank you."

Demetri turned his head, still breathing heavily. "Don't thank me. Not yet."

"Then when?"

"When the time comes, I'll tell you."

Richard felt a chill creep up his spine when Demetri said that. There was something ominous behind his words, something that gave Richard a bad feeling. But this had to do with a simple thank you, so it should be something to strive for, not fear.

A familiar car pulled up beside the bench, and both passenger side doors opened. Elise exited from the front and then turned quickly to get into the backseat without any acknowledgement of Demetri or Richard. They stood up and entered the car, Demetri in the front and Richard once again in the back. They were greeted by the other three members of their team.

Nate turned to Demetri after he closed the door. "Any problems?"

"No," Demetri stated flatly as he stared straight ahead. "Let's go."

As the car sped off from Clifton Hill, Nate drove down Lundy's Lane and made their way to the QEW highway to Toronto. Richard noticed Elise was entranced by her mobile device. She was frantically navigating through the device, clearly looking for something, her face becoming more and more frustrated.

"What's wrong?" Richard asked.

Without taking her eyes from her device, Elise shook her head in aggravation and responded, "I'm looking for a way to gain access to the lab without being detected. There are no windows in it, and the lab itself is monitored by multiple cameras covering every angle. Disabling the cameras is easy, but with security constantly monitoring them it wouldn't take long for them to physically check what was going on." She faced Richard. "I'm assuming it wouldn't be nearly enough time for what you need to do. How long would you need anyway?"

"I'm not sure." Richard truly wasn't sure, but he knew what he had to do and what equipment he needed. Being limited to a time frame was not his strong suit! "I'll need to take an analysis of the blood and identify the different compounds within his bloodstream. If I can isolate the different pieces of the serum, I'll be able to extract them and diagnose what the problem is and what's causing it. From there I should be able to create an antibody for it."

Elise furrowed her brow at Richard's last comment but shook it off and returned to her device. "That doesn't sound like a short process."

"Actually, isolating the different pieces of the serum won't take long at all with the equipment at the university lab."

Elise's busy hand on her device stopped. "We need to make sure you'll have the time to accomplish all this."

Nate suddenly spoke up from the front seat. "How many guards are on duty at any one time?"

Elise looked back at her device. "Four. With one changing shifts every hour. Meaning if we simply took out all of the guards, we would have less than an hour total to infiltrate the facility, complete the operation and get out before being detected."

"That's more than enough time for me, but if you need more then why don't you post near the security office so you can intercept as many as needed?" Nate asked.

Richard piped in at that suggestion, as he had a fear of his own. "Decan will be incapacitated for the duration of the tests. I'll need one of you with me in case something goes … awry."

Nate turned his head from driving to give Richard a glare. He turned back to face the road, but Richard swore he could hear Nate's eyes roll.

Elise nodded in understanding and continued to search her device for an answer. "I also believe their radios are linked with local police. The police listen to their check-ins with each other and may notice any lack of communication between them." Elise sighed, exasperated. "It would appear our only real option is a distraction to keep them busy at another part of the campus."

"You mean like a fire?" Jocelyn asked.

"No. A fire or large-scale disaster would get their attention, yes, but also local emergency personnel. We need to keep it as discreet as possible. We would need to draw their attention for a more common occurrence."

Jocelyn looked down at her lap in thought. "But what kind of common occurrence would get the attention of all four on-guard officers?"

Thinking back to his earlier days at the campus, Richard recalled hearing about numerous times that all four guards would be engaged at the same location at the same time. He remembered the stories of the officers calling in all of their off-duty staff to help quell the rowdy parties thrown by the less studious students. Remembering these stories, and more importantly the one who would regale him against his will with them, a grin could not help but cross Richard's face as he raised his head. "I have an idea."

CHAPTER 19

BACK TO SCHOOL

"YEAH, BABY! THAT'S HOW IT'S done!" Jayden took off his football helmet and waved it joyously in the air. His cheers could be heard even over the thundering cheers from the crowd in attendance at the football match at the University of Toronto's stadium. Many of the students and fans were in no mood to watch a football game after the war in America had broken out and stayed away. But it was important to some to go about life as usual, at least for the time being. Students knew little else of how to react to the invasion of their neighbour. Many went home, but the American students remained in their dorms, fearing what this war could mean. A good number remained jovial in their student lives and tried to continue their campus life as normal.

The Toronto Inferno were facing their long-time rivals, the Ottawa Warlords, in the first game of the season. It was a great morale booster for the home team to beat its rival in the season opener by more than 20 points. Jayden's team mates on the field lifted him, their star quarterback, on their shoulders as the local crowd's cheers grew louder, and Jayden bid farewell to the opposing team as they left the field in shame. "See ya next time, shit lords!"

The smack talk from the team captain roused the crowd even further. Jayden knew how to play to a crowd, especially his own.

Arrogant as he may have seemed, Jayden still appreciated his team mates. He was high-fiving all of them and pointing at other members who contributed an above-average amount of effort, warranting a heightened cheer with each point of the finger.

After making several laps around the stadium, the triumphant Inferno let Jayden walk on his own two feet to rally back to the locker room for a continued celebration. The crowd's cheering became an echo through the halls underneath the stands as the team began entering the locker room. Jayden took a position outside the door and slapped hands, head butted or chest bumped every single member as they entered the room screaming his name.

As the line of team members began to wane, and the ruckus from inside the locker room was beginning to rival that of the entire crowd in the stadium moments ago, a figure caught Jayden's attention out of the corner of his eye. It was a woman with shoulder-length black hair, slightly dishevelled, but attractively framing her flawless face. Her cheekbones were accentuated by a seductive grin as she looked at Jayden with lust in her eyes. Her hourglass body leaned up against the equipment room door. She sported a white miniskirt and blue halter top, which only brought out her bright blue "come hither" eyes. Her dark-blue fingernails drew his attention as she pointed a single finger at Jayden and beckoned him with it.

Jayden, being the powerhouse with the ladies he believed himself to be, was all but surprised by this scene. As if expected, he turned to the remaining members of his team who had not yet entered the locker room with an arrogant grin. "Well, gents, if you'll excuse me, I must have a meeting with our new ... 'equipment manager.'"

The reverberating vowel that burst from his members nearly shook the walls themselves. "Ohhhhhhhhhhh!"

As Jayden made his way strutting toward his prize, he could hear his name being chanted over and over again behind him. His smirk grew even wider as he reached the woman beckoning him, and she grabbed his jersey, dragging him into the dark equipment room and shutting the door.

"Seven minutes in heaven, eh? My kind of chick." It was an all-too-familiar game Jayden had played with women since his high school party days. It was exactly what he was looking for: quick fun, and then sneak away when he was done. He extended his arms in front of him to try to find his playmate.

The lights flicked on, and Jayden was shocked by what he saw.

Three men and another woman were waiting for him. Two of the men were built like him and were standing on either side of the door. But he recognized the third: his long-lost roommate, Richard, stood in front of him with his usual look of condemnation toward Jayden's actions.

"Rich! Holy shit, good to see you, buddy!" His arms were wide open, expecting a hug from his old roommate, but his mood quickly changed from happy to concerned as he remembered he was surrounded by two other men, and a woman who was now ignoring him as she was changing into a far less-revealing outfit.

"Don't worry about them, Jayden. This is Decan, Ghost and Sage beside me, and the one you are so hopelessly staring at is Spire." Richard tried to set Jayden at ease but was quite sure he hadn't heard a word. He was too entranced watching Elise change in front of him, obviously not bashful at all. She was simply doing a job and couldn't care less about the perverted, lust-filled eyes of a university student. "Jayden!"

Shaking his head out of his trance, Jayden looked at Richard with a smile and eyes that attempted to tell him he had been listening the entire time. "Yes?"

"I need a favour," Richard said bluntly.

"A favour? Hey, wait a minute, what's this I've been hearing anyway? About you being a Japanese agent or something? Who are these guys you're hanging out with? Bodyguards or secret agents … buddyyyy, not the crowd I thought you'd choose. Is your real name even Richard?" With Jayden's words, Richard could see Nate reaching into his jacket, and Elise shaking her head at him as if to call him off an attack.

"Of course my real name is Richard! It's all a lie. A fabrication to make me look like the bad guy, when in fact, they're the ones who are guilty of the exact things they are accusing me of doing."

"Who?"

"That's what we are trying to find out." Richard was speaking mysteriously, trying hard not to give too much away to someone who was known for having a big mouth. But he felt a need to explain himself to Jayden. He was, after all, one of the few friends he had actually made in his life.

"Oh. So are you like … working with the government now? Oh my god!" Jayden's eyes widened with surprise and he suddenly changed the subject, as if seeing a shiny object that had distracted him in the middle of the conversation. "Is that a girl I see standing beside you? Do you have a girlfriend?" The open-mouthed smile covering Jayden's face nearly broke Elise's resolve. She had to cover her mouth and look away to stifle a laugh.

"W-what? N-no!" Richard nervously denied the claim, but Jocelyn's blushing face did not help his case.

"Enough of this!" Demetri stepped from the door and stood between Richard and Jayden. "We don't have time for childish antics."

"Eaaaaasy, bro, just catching up with my buddy Rich. What are you, his bodyguard?" Jayden asked casually.

"If need be."

"Ah, that's why you feel the need to puff your chest in front of me? You going to beat it and growl too? I hear that makes women all hot in special places." Jayden's sarcastic attitude was a scene

Richard had only seen a few times, when other men challenged him either physically or socially. It was one of the impressive things Richard respected about him, a man who would stand his ground no matter what the odds. But right now Jayden was being an idiot!

"Math must not be your major. You're outnumbered, and you're being an instigator," Demetri sneered.

"Math may not have been a major, but I can damn sure count. You guys are all unarmed, and I have one"—Jayden raised one arm and flexed it as hard as he could, and then the other—"two guns!"

Richard knew he had to get to the point quickly. Both men had alpha personalities, and the last thing he wanted was for Demetri to consider Jayden someone "in the way." He could tell Demetri and Nate were not impressed. "You'll want to hear what I have to say, Jayden."

"If it's that you have a girlfriend, I had a feeling you did." Jayden relaxed his arms and looked past Demetri toward Richard and Jocelyn. "So I take it this is Madeline?" Jayden asked coyly.

The look on Richard's face was of sheer confusion; he had never spoken of Madeline to Jayden before. How did he know about her?

"Who's Madeline?" Jocelyn asked shyly, trying not to seem too accusatory toward Richard for not mentioning her.

"She's a childhood friend of mine. I've known her all my life," Richard said directly without concern for potential feelings he may be hurting by saying it in such a way. He turned to Jayden to finish his statement "But I never told you about her."

"Nah, she just sent you a letter a little while back, like maybe a week ago, I think? Don't worry though, I didn't open it. I put it aside for you and was going to actually send it to your parents' place once ... you know ... once I remembered to do it." Jayden shrugged awkwardly and then gritted his teeth, looking at Jocelyn. "So ... guess that's a no, eh? Um ... sorry, bro. To be fair, though, how could I have known you'd become a player working for the government!" Jayden laughed.

Richard rolled his eyes, unsure of what he was talking about. "Look, can we get to the point of why we're here, please?"

"Oh, sure. Sorry, caught up in the moment. I'm just so proud of you!"

"Jayden!"

"Sorry!"

Richard took a few steps forward, even lightly moving Demetri out of the way to face Jayden. "Look, Jayden, my team and I are here to gather some information to help clear my name, and I need your help."

"Hey, sure, I'd love to help you buddy. Not sure what I can do to help?" Jayden seemed intrigued with the idea of doing some kind of secret mission job!

"The first thing is, you cannot question why, you must just do!" Richard wasn't sure if he was going about this properly as he threw Demetri a questioning glance.

"Okay ... ya got me. What do you want me to do?"

"I need you to throw a party. A big party."

The look on Jayden's face was shock. "Really? A party? This will help you?" His face then changed to mimicking that of a child who had just opened the Christmas present he had wanted all his life. His eyes went wide, and a bigger smile could not be painted onto his face. "Oh, hell, yeah! Not just any party! *The* party!" Jayden clapped his hands in excitement and hugged Richard as Richard hugged back awkwardly. "Dude, this is going to be awesome!"

"Yeah, great." Richard's attempt to feign excitement was not successful.

But Jayden was so caught up in his own excitement, it didn't seem to faze him at all.

"So how long do you think it will take to organize this?"

"Are you kidding? Everyone's already all pumped up from this win. We're gonna do this party tonight!"

Richard was nearly taken aback, impressed that it could be done so quickly. Then he remembered who he was talking to, a man who could have very well made a living off throwing parties. "Excellent."

"So what time will you be coming by? We'll throw it here at the stadium! I'll go have a chat with the groundskeeper; he'll hook us up."

Perfect, Richard thought. *The diversion will be far enough away from the lab to increase response time, and easily a large enough event to require more officers to be called to help.* "I'll try to be there as soon as I can make it. I just need to make a stop at the lab first."

Demetri glared at Richard, who could visibly be seen cringing at himself for giving away more than he intended. Richard was never good at lying, and two lies in the same sentence seemed unattainable for him.

"You would. Still a bookworm." Jayden's voice was less enthusiastic and Richard read Jayden's posture. Jayden was now playing his part in this charade.

"Oh!" Richard had just remembered something Jayden had mentioned earlier in the conversation that was very important to him. "Bring the letter from Madeline."

"Oh, sure thing." Jayden recovered his enthusiasm. "I'll see you here! Don't be too late. I'm excited to finally party with you, buddy!" Jayden put a hand up in the air in front of Richard, the famous high five he would always give to his friends when excited about something.

Richard indulged him, slapping his hand in the air.

"Woooo!" Jayden's apparent excitement was shining through as he left the room, pausing only for a moment to wink at Elise.

Demetri closed the door and looked at Richard. "I guess I don't need to worry if he's going to do it."

Richard swallowed some emotion as guilt began to overrun his mind. He had no intention of attending this party, and he had just lied to one of his only friends to better his own situation. This was a quality he hated in other people, and he just exhibited it, to a friend no less. He felt sick to his stomach. Richard did not want to use Jayden like that. But it was the best option to complete the mission with the resources and time frame they had. Yet somehow Richard hoped he was right about Jayden's acceptance of the role he must play.

A light hand on his shoulder startled him as he looked to Jocelyn, who tried to calm him with comforting eyes. "Are you okay?"

"No," Richard said quietly. "This is not me. I don't lie."

Jocelyn nodded understandingly as she lightly rubbed his back in an attempt to soothe him.

"All right. The distraction is set," Demetri said, getting things back to the business at hand. "If we're compromised before we can finish, our part of the mission is to be aborted. That is not negotiable. Is that understood?"

"Yes, sir," Elise agreed.

"Yeah ..." Richard agreed reluctantly. He did not want to abandon this part of the mission. To him, this was the mission. He could do so much once he had those serums in his hands. He could even potentially create an antibody for each part of the serum before they deteriorated, or at least get the foundation to create one later. And saving Demetri's life was the most important thing.

Gilman ... what was his involvement in all of this? Had he always been involved? Did he know exactly what Richard was getting into? Richard had some burning questions for him but knew helping Demetri was more important. He had lied to one friend and now needed to focus on helping another.

"One more thing," Demetri said as he was about to exit. "These officers are licensed to carry firearms and are armed. Should we become compromised, don't take any chances." With that, Demetri opened the door and left the room, Nate following closely behind. Elise moved to leave as well but was stopped by Richard's beckon.

"Spire, what did he mean by that?" Richard was worried about what he believed the answer to be.

Elise lowered her head and turned it slightly to avoid eye contact with Richard as she responded. "It means if they try to stop us, kill them." She stood for a moment, knowing Richard wouldn't like that response, and then she took off.

Richard was left in silence with Jocelyn as he contemplated the consequences of his actions. If his plan with Jayden were to fail, the lives of those officers would be on his hands. No … he would not take the blame for that. Was this the kind of leadership he was to expect from Demetri? Didn't their conversation have any effect on him? Perhaps he was just making a point to his subordinates, knowing full well it wouldn't actually come to that.

"It's not your fault, you know." Jocelyn's voice drowned out the thoughts shooting through Richard's head. "They're soldiers. They're doing what they believe to be the greater good. It's their decision, not yours. They will only do what is necessary."

"I know." Richard's face turned to one of determination as he began to leave. "It's what they consider necessary that scares me."

CHAPTER 20

BLOOD WORK

"THE PARTY HAS BEEN GOING on for a little more than an hour now. It shouldn't be long before the officers are forced to respond," Demetri pointed out after looking at his watch. The four sat in the black Dodge Journey that had served them well since their escape. They parked their SUV near the parking lot where the university security van was stationed. The van was the most likely method of transportation for the officers to address the illegal activity going on at the nearby stadium. Nate had already left to accomplish his piece of the mission, handing something off to Demetri before leaving.

Demetri watched the doors to the security office like a hawk, waiting for the opportunity to access the lab. The lab was only down the hall from the security office; after all, as it was the highest security risk building at the university. This was the intended design for the location of security office. It made the task of ensuring all the security personnel would actually leave the office very challenging. Although since its inception, there had never actually been an attempt to break into the lab. The expensive equipment would be impossible to move without high-grade construction tools and at least a dozen strong men. Chemicals and smaller equipment were locked and tagged. Even if they were to be removed from the lab, alarms would go off in every police department within a five-mile radius as well as alerting their own security staff. As well, the built-in GPS in the core of the devices ensured that as long as they were functional, they were traceable. Luckily for this team, they didn't need to take the equipment, just use it. As for the locks, Demetri assured Richard they wouldn't be a problem. And Nate was going to deal with the alarm systems at the entrances before beginning his mission.

"There they go," Demetri stated. As the other three joined Demetri's watchful look outside, they could see four university officers clad in Kevlar vests and armed with sidearm pistols and Tasers. The university officers were trained similarly to police officers, as the incidents they encountered within their jurisdiction would often be just as dangerous as what local police handled. As well, the university had heightened their security since the addition of the science and technology buildings. They were equipped for the worst, but Richard had never heard of an incident where they actually had to pull their weapons, and prayed this would not be the first.

"All right, our timer starts now—let's go," Elise said in a low voice as the security van sped away just out of sight with all four officers inside. She and Demetri quickly exited, obviously under the impression they would have little time to complete what they needed to do. But if Richard knew Jayden, he would have those officers partying with the rest of them before they would arrest him for committing a crime.

"Richard," Jocelyn said in a soft voice as he was about to leave the vehicle with the others. Richard turned to her. "Be careful." A look of genuine concern on Jocelyn's face made Richard more uneasy about the entire situation.

She must have a bad feeling too, he thought as he left the vehicle, closing the door. Walking away from the car, the knot in his stomach grew tighter. He did not feel comfortable leaving Jocelyn alone in the car, especially not with the uneasy feeling he was getting. He was sure his objections would go unheard by Demetri, as her role was crucial in the case of compromise.

Richard quickened his pace to join Demetri and Elise when they were about to enter the science wing of the university, a location Richard felt most at home. He had spent most of his hours over the past few years in this very spot. Luckily, due to the football game and after-hours celebrations, including Jayden's party, there was no student activity in the science and technology wing, and the lab was locked. It was not unusual for students to be working late in the lab, but they would have to report to security to sign in and out. Tonight there appeared to be no one, as reported by Nate from his earlier surveillance. Richard was grateful for that.

When Demetri pulled out a small keychain and unlocked the door, it posed more questions. Where did he get a key?

"Let's go, Richard." Demetri waved Richard in, as Elise entered the building swiftly in a crouched and prowling position. Richard entered, trying to imitate her movement, though he could not do it nearly as elegantly. Demetri quietly closed the door and relocked it, and then turned and pulled Richard by the shirt to stand him up straight. "That's not necessary. There are no active alarms or anyone to monitor cameras. Just move quickly to the lab. Lead the way."

Learning not to question Demetri, Richard picked up the pace and with a mild jog began navigating the hallways until reaching the double steel doors to the lab, to which Demetri once again had keys. Richard gave him a puzzled look as Demetri entered the lab, holding an arm in front of Richard to prevent him from entering as Elise swept the room to ensure they were alone.

"Clear!" Elise called as she stood up from the other end after checking it thoroughly.

Demetri dropped his arm from Richard's path and entered the lab, waiting for Richard and then closing the doors. Richard could not help but notice the many cameras that were surveying the room. They had not been shut off or blacked out in any way.

"The cameras are still on," he pointed out nervously.

"Yes. But there's nobody monitoring them," Demetri retorted. "Elise has a device that can temporarily freeze the screens. The cameras currently display the empty lab as it was just before we entered. If there is nothing out of place, they will have no reason to review the tapes. Even if they do, it'll be of little consequence as we won't be visible on their tape. We'll have already accomplished what we came here to do, and we'll be long gone. As long as we're one step ahead of our enemy, they'll never catch up to us. Just a precaution that's not really needed. Wouldn't matter if they saw us. Last thing we want is for that super soldier to catch up." Demetri seemed distracted and agitated when he made this last statement.

"I see." Richard did not understand Demetri's own contradiction of hiding their presence from the border guards. How was this different? And this time it was only cameras, not living people. Richard had no qualms about dismantling a few inanimate objects to save face … literally. However, the technical explanation and intervention was satisfactory to Richard, but Demetri's actions and thoughts were becoming more and more erratic. He had a lot of work to do, and fast, if he was to protect Demetri's mind from what seemed to be further deterioration.

"What do you need?" Demetri asked Richard as he surveyed the large lab with its many cupboards, shelves, drawers and large scientific equipment.

Richard felt more at home in this room than anywhere else in the world. If he were a master chef, this would be his kitchen. He began pointing out certain cupboards and drawers that needed to be opened, and the machines that needed to be activated. The most obvious of the machinery was a large circular device with a bed placed in the center of it. The whole machine was on a moveable platform to accommodate movement of the bed and other apparatus. Its design was similar to the machines in hospitals to take MRIs. "Take off your shirt and shoes, and then lie on the bed here."

"You are going to conduct an MRI?" Demetri asked as he removed his shirt, hanging it on a nearby chair before lying down.

Richard pulled out a briefcase-size metal case, opening it on a nearby counter to show the many syringes housed safely within. This was an obvious means of transporting sensitive liquid samples safely, not warranting any sort of GPS tracking within it. He counted out the five syringes within the case and began pulling them out as he answered Demetri's question.

"No, but a similar process. This technology is far more advanced. I'm going to inject a dye into your bloodstream. You have different blood cell structure and blood types now that you have been injected with the prototype and Valour. The dye will attach itself to the different blood cells in your body, turning a different color for each different type of blood cell in your stream. It will allow me to isolate the different serums as well as your natural bloodstream. From there I can scan each color individually to take a more accurate and specific reading on the effect it is having in your body. It's going to give me a precise readout on everything with these serums, so I can study more long-term effects and solutions based on calculations conducted by the machine."

Richard poured a clear liquid into a sixth syringe he had prepared as he was spouting off his speech to a slightly perplexed Demetri. As Richard turned around with the prepared syringe, he saw the look of confusion on Demetri's face and grinned. "It's going to show me exactly what the serum is doing to you."

"I assumed as much. I don't need to know the how, I just need to know the what." Demetri smirked.

Richard put down the prepared syringe and pulled out a larger empty one. "I'll first take a blood sample for reference. I'll be able to use that for testing later on." Richard placed one hand on Demetri's inner elbow joint to feel for a vein. But oddly, could not feel a pulse. In fact, he couldn't feel his skin! On closer inspection, his hand was hovering millimetres above Demetri's skin. Richard furrowed his brow, as he was putting pressure on this invisible force, but Demetri's arm was not moving, nor was Richard's hand coming any closer to touching his skin.

"Fascinating," he exclaimed, remembering the same thing that had happened the last time he had tried to touch Demetri's skin.

"What?" Demetri asked as he raised his head to see what the problem was.

Richard removed his hand before Demetri could see what he was doing. A curious look crossed his face. "Force of will," he said quietly to himself. "Demetri, I need to take blood from your arm here," Richard stated as he motioned to where he intended to extract the blood.

Demetri raised an eyebrow in confusion. "Yeah that's fine, go ahead." He lay back down, expecting to feel a slight prick on the inside of his left inner elbow.

Richard slowly moved the needle closer to Demetri's arm again, only this time was met with no resistance and was able to pierce the skin and take the blood sample. Richard grinned with a satisfied and curious expression as he drew a large dosage of Demetri's blood. After removing it from his skin and quickly placing pressure on a cotton ball to prevent the wound from bleeding, he motioned for Demetri to keep the pressure on his arm. Richard then carefully placed the full vial into the metal carrying case he had prepared before the procedure for safe transport.

"I'm going to inject the dye now," Richard warned, not so much for his benefit but more to ensure that the needle would actually be able to pierce the skin. He removed the cotton ball and allowed Demetri to relax his arms, though he noticed that there was no longer a visible mark from the previous needle. "You're going to feel a great deal of dizziness as the dye melds with your blood cells. I suggest you close your eyes, and feel free to sleep if you feel the exhaustion."

"All right."

Richard once again slowly moved the needle into Demetri's arm, pleased that he managed to inject the dye into the bloodstream. He didn't bother with the cotton ball this time. He then moved toward the controls of the machine and activated it. It began the slow movement of the bed on which Demetri lay through the large circular scanner of the machine.

Elise seemed to take an interest now, and moved to a position behind Richard to see the control screen he was monitoring.

Richard continued to autonomously type into the control panel, watching the view screen intently as the different colors were displayed. Demetri's brain waves as well as the nervous system's functions were recorded and analyzed. Numbers and readouts were scrolling upward at an alarming pace on one of the lower screens. So fast that Elise could not follow any of it, though Richard seemed to absorb all of the information, even just out of the corner of his eye. He began to recite his findings out loud for both Elise and Demetri to hear as he pressed the print button. He wanted these results to study further at a more appropriate time.

"This is incredible," he began as he examined the scroll of printed data. "The serum has created a form of neurogenesis."

"Neurogenesis?" Elise and Demetri had asked almost in sync.

"Decan, don't speak, you could ruin the scan," Richard scolded before answering the question. "It means the serum has begun repairing damaged brain cells. In the absence of damaged brain cells, it's creating more. The cells are functioning in a similar way they would in the prenatal developmental stages." Richard continued to manipulate the controls like a maestro, but his face was confused as he proceeded. "But that makes no sense. His cognitive functions have not changed drastically. He still acts and thinks similarly to the way he did before Valour. His actions and behaviour contradict the fact that he has a much higher cognitive ability ... unless ..." Richard turned his head to more carefully read the recent text scrolling rapidly on the lower screen.

"Unless what?" Elise asked.

"Unless his ability and potential is building up in his subconscious mind. I will need to conduct more studies to know for sure. Perhaps there will be a hint in the blood analysis."

Richard turned back to the main screen for the current results. The printer continued to spit out the data. Elise gathered the printed information and rolled it tightly into a scroll, still watching Richard.

"Is he okay?" she whispered.

"I'm not sure. The serum isn't deteriorating like I had originally designed. And there is a fourth type of blood beyond his own, the prototype serum and Valour circulating through his bloodstream that was not part of the initial design. It has attached itself to every type of blood cell, preventing me from isolating it and finding out exactly what it is. It would seem as though that strand is keeping the serum from deteriorating."

"So ... he's going to stay a super soldier?" Elise exclaimed, bordering on excitement and a hint of relief.

"As long as he's alive, yes," Richard stated grimly.

Elise's face turned a pale white. "As long as he's alive?"

"The serums are performing as they should for the most part. In fact, better than intended. It would seem that Gait increases precognitive functions and reaction times as well as the increased physical agility as originally intended. Vigour has not only increased the muscle capacity without increasing their size much, it has also immensely increased metabolism and the stamina of the heart and lungs dramatically. His vital signs in every respect are performing at nearly 10 times normal capacity."

Which once again did not make sense to Richard at first, as Demetri was getting tired so easily before, suggesting his stamina had been weakened. He now knew the answer but was delaying telling Elise. He knew the feelings she had for Demetri were quite strong. "And Keen has not only increased his subconscious cognitive functions but has had an unusual effect of strengthening the man's natural aura. So strong to the point of making it a form of biological armour surrounding his entire body. It prevented me originally from touching him or piercing his skin with the needle to take blood. But when he knew I was taking it and was okay with it, I was able to take the sample. This leads me to believe he has control over this strengthened aura. And I believe with proper training, it can even be manipulated … perhaps even offensively. The only anomaly is the lack of visible signs of improvement for the cognitive functions with Keen."

"What did you mean by as long as he's alive?" Elise asked again, with more force.

"In addition to that …" Richard was obviously avoiding the question but was still genuinely interested in describing the effects of the serum to both Demetri and Elise. Although at this point Richard wasn't sure if Demetri was awake as he was making no comment.

"The aura and Demetri's blood have traces of what can only be described as liquid sunlight. It would seem the combination of Keen and Vigour have allowed Decan to absorb and even metabolize sunlight itself. This would make him immune the sun's UV rays, although it means he would be unable to tan." Richard attempted a joke, but with no reaction he continued. "The presence of the sun in his aura also suggests that if he metabolizes it, he could potentially utilize its energy."

Richard was becoming excited as he explained the effects. This was an unexpected side effect of a superhuman metabolism and could mean great strides in human evolution, though Elise was not looking impressed.

"But what about—"

"Furthermore!" Richard openly interrupted her this time, clearly aggravating her as he continued his analysis while avoiding eye contact. "The prototype serum in him is synergizing with the Valour formula, causing both formulas cells to evolve. Meaning this is not the end of his potential! The increase of his subconscious cognitive functions and synergy with the prototype formula means that with the proper training of his mind and body, his potential could be, well … limitless."

Elise had enough of Richard's dodging at this point and took position between him and the control panel, forcing his hands from it. She bent her neck down slightly to look him dead in the eyes. "Richard, what did you mean by 'as long as he's alive'?" Her tone was serious. She was not playing around, and Richard could see that now.

"The rapid evolution of the serum cells has caused a severe case of anaemia. His blood cannot maintain its own haemoglobin." Richard spoke with a sullen undertone.

"I don't understand."

"Because of the synergy between the prototype blood and the full strength of the Valour formula, there is a rapid enhancement of every muscle and organ in his entire body. When I said the serum isn't deteriorating as I had originally intended, I mean the enhanced blood is absorbing his biological cells before they deteriorate. The remaining biological red blood cells are having a harder and harder time providing the enormous amount of oxygen required to operate his now superhuman-like vital organs that only keep enhancing. The synthetic blood types don't seem to be wired to carry out that function to the capacity the body requires."

Elise's expression was growing more and more wary. "Meaning what, exactly?"

Richard took a deep breath and closed his eyes as if to prepare himself for the emotion he was about to experience coming from Elise. Reopening them, he looked her straight in the eyes, and spoke loud enough for Demetri to hear, even over the humming of the machine. "It means if we don't find a way to consistently increase his red blood cell count, and to a point that they regenerate faster than being absorbed, his organs will cease to function—and he will die."

Without missing a beat, Elise took off her jacket and rolled up her sleeve, gesturing her veins with her fingers as she offered her arm to Richard.

"You need blood? Take mine." There was a desperation in her eyes that upset Richard a great deal. He knew what she wanted to do, and he also knew it wouldn't work.

"I'm afraid it's not that simple. His immune system is too powerful now, and simply injecting blood into his stream would only cause pain as his body would reject it. His body has adapted to a new blood type now with the Valour formula, and as such would create antibodies to any other type of blood entering his system."

"Are you saying we need a super soldier's blood to save him?" Elise exclaimed in angst.

"I'm afraid so," Richard replied, the sullen expression returning to his face. "It is possible that he could metabolize the blood in order for him to acquire the necessary assets to replenish his own. But regular blood would not be sufficient in that case, as it would not have the necessary strength to sustain his organs and muscles. It would still have to be super-soldier blood."

Elise cringed. "How would he metabolize the blood?"

"By ingesting it," Richard responded factually.

"Isn't there anything you can do to prevent his cells from deteriorating?" Elise had turned around to look at the screens in a desperate attempt to see something that would solve the complications that had been revealed to her.

"I could potentially create a synthesized formula using his own blood as a baseline. But the body would construe it as viral and would eventually reject it the same as blood of a different type. The moment it is exposed to oxygen it would change composition. The body would reject it, and you wouldn't even notice it until the same symptoms of anaemia would return. And the longer it takes to form an immunity, the more his muscles and organs will enhance and require more and more haemoglobin. In other words, the longer the formula works, the shorter time it will take for his organs to stop functioning once the synthesized formula is rejected. There would be a time, likely less than a minute that his body would run on nothing but his own human blood produced itself, before shutting down completely."

"If you could do this, how long would it help him?" Elise asked, her voice breaking slightly as she looked at Demetri, who had long since fallen asleep from the exhaustion caused by the dye.

"Hard to say. With his immune system, it could be a year. Maybe two, if I can create the proper balance. Unfortunately the Valour serum as a whole is far too strong, as it is using the prototype serum to enhance his attributes at an alarming rate. But if I were to extract the Valour serum from him, he would lose the ability to metabolize the blood needed to recover his own missing blood and feed his already-enhanced organs. Ironically, the very thing that is killing him can keep him alive."

Richard didn't like the situation any more than Elise did, but he was looking at it from a scientific standpoint. And while he knew there was a way to help him, he also knew it would be difficult to create—and it would be temporary.

Elise turned around to face Richard again, her eyes slightly watering. She spoke with conviction. "Do it." She put her jacket back on and began a close watch on the door again as she stood ready to pounce on anything that tried to stop Richard from saving her commander.

Chapter 21

KARMA

RICHARD RESUMED HIS CONDUCTION OF the control panel on the laboratory equipment. He prepared the other four syringes, placing them in four separate slots on the scanner of the large machine. He programmed a small control panel below each slot. Each slot was programmed to activate the syringe to only extract blood of its assigned color from the dye and to extract only periodically as the appropriate cells were available until the vial was full. This advanced piece of equipment with the proper tuning could in fact become "the" cure for cancer, far surpassing current methods of treatment. This was ironic in Richard's mind, as he was now using it to cure what he believed to be an even deadlier disease, although it was not helpful to mankind in the way he intended.

Richard noticed that in his sleep, Demetri was breathing heavily and wheezing slightly. This hastened Richard's activity but also piqued his interest. The last time he was sleeping, Richard could not touch his skin. Perhaps if the aura truly is from the force of his will, and Demetri was indeed exhausted, it may cause the aura barrier around him to wane as well.

Slowly touching his skin, Richard nodded with both relief, and concern. Relief that he wouldn't have to wake Demetri for the procedure but concern that his friend was in this weakened state of body and mind.

Confident that he could now conduct the procedure, Richard went back to the control panel and began his technological symphony again as the machine began circulating the installed syringes in response to his commands.

"How long will this process take?" Elise asked anxiously, without taking her eyes off the entrance.

"Taking the blood should only take minutes. It will analyze the blood and synthesize a temporary cure for him that will take time." Richard responded, but with a hint of annoyance. He did not like to be bothered when he was working with such equipment, especially when the life of his friend was hanging in the balance.

The large machine began its process as each syringe was automatically designed to search for an optimum vein in order to extract its assigned blood. Before long, each of the syringes were injected and began slowly siphoning its designation. Richard did not take his eyes off the screens as he monitored the blood entering each syringe to ensure they were performing optimally. He was so engaged with the machine that he did not even notice Elise had begun slinking toward the entrance, eventually taking a defensive position just beside the doors.

Richard suddenly turned his head as the doors burst open and a human figure walked through the doors, then was tackled to the ground by Elise before Richard could even see his face. Confident the machine was performing to its intended design at the moment, Richard ran through the labyrinth of countertops to see what prey Elise had subdued. His curiosity was quickly quelled when he heard a familiar voice speak, albeit muffled.

"Whoa! That was hot!" Jayden's muffled voice echoed throughout the lab. Richard recognized his voice.

"What are you doing here?" Richard exclaimed, his pace slowing as he reached Jayden being held on the floor.

Jayden struggled to turn his face to see Richard and smiled, his voice still slightly muffled from his cheek being pressed against the cold floor. "I wanted to see if there was anything else I could do to help. Oh! And I have that letter you asked for!"

Richard could tell Jayden was making excuses; it was obvious he had a thing for Elise. He might have been interested in her, but she was too smart for him. But Richard was very interested in the letter he had mentioned and grateful Jayden remembered. This was a communication he had forgotten about until Jayden mentioned it earlier that day. That letter could very well carry the information Richard had been searching for his entire life—his origins.

Jayden looked at Elise. "If you think this isn't turning me on, you're going to be in a world of shock when I stand up."

Elise rolled her eyes with obvious disgust and released her grip, standing up but not taking her eyes off Jayden.

Returning to his feet, Jayden dusted himself off and gave Elise a wink, causing her to roll her eyes again and break eye contact.

Richard held out his hand. "The letter, please, Jayden."

"Oh, right." Jayden reached into his back pocket and pulled out the folded but still-sealed envelope he had kept safe for Richard. Richard examined the envelope and could not hide a small smile as he noticed the seal remained untouched. It would appear even though it was clearly from a woman, Jayden managed to show some class and respect.

"Thank you," Richard said sincerely as he put it in his back pocket.

"Aren't you going to read it?" Jayden asked, likely not for Richard's benefit but for his own curiosity.

Richard did want to read it. A great deal in fact. He did, however, fear it would distract him from the task at hand, and he must not get distracted. And the information held within definitely had the potential to disrupt his train of thought. There would be plenty of time to read it, after he saved his friend.

"Not right now. I have things to do." Richard turned from Jayden and returned to the control panel to check on the progress of the blood extraction, which was nearing completion.

"What are you doing?" Jayden followed Richard, much to his chagrin.

"Taking blood samples. Don't touch anything," Richard pre-emptively scolded before Jayden had the chance to give him reason to.

"Is he an alien?" Jayden asked. Richard looked at him with a demeaning glare. Then he realized Jayden was looking at the different syringes attached to Demetri and the machine that were all different colors because of the dye he had injected. Not a usual sight, but still a stupid question in Richard's mind, but he decided to accept his confusion under the circumstances.

"It's a dye to help distinguish one blood type from another."

"He has more than one blood type?" Jayden continued to ask questions. As much as it was irritating Richard, he could not help but feel the need to indulge his curiosity since as he had never seen Jayden actually show an interest toward much else but the various intricacies of the female anatomy.

"Yes. He's … special." Richard tried to explain without giving too much away. He had already made that mistake earlier. This was the very reason he was in this situation explaining his actions to Jayden as a parent would a child.

"I think he needs to get some sun," Jayden pointed out.

Richard opened his mouth to retort but stopped himself. That information Jayden did not need to have.

"I think you have a party to get back to," Richard stated coldly.

"Yeah. But I think *you* should come."

"I'm busy, Jay—" Richard looked up in his response to Jayden but realized he wasn't looking at Richard. He was referring to Elise with a sly smile.

"I beg your pardon?" Elise snorted.

"That's cool. I love it when women beg." Jayden showed some of his neatly whitened teeth with his grin.

Richard swore he saw a sparkle out of the side of Jayden's mouth.

"I'm not interested."

"Not into parties? No worries; I'm down for some private time too." Jayden began slyly moving toward Elise.

As Elise rolled her eyes in preparation for her response, her hand quickly covered her ear that housed the communications device. Richard too could hear a broken communication from Nate over the com.

"Spi ..."—static—"incom host"—static.

"What? Ghost. Repeat, I didn't copy." Elise leaned her head on the side of the earpiece as if to increase the quality. Then she looked back up to Richard. "Did you get that?"

"No. He sounded frantic though." Richard glanced back at the syringes and breathed a sigh of relief as he saw they had completed the extraction.

"We should not be getting any interference here, not to this level. Unless ..." A slow look of realization and fear quickly came over Elise's face.

"Unless what?" Richard asked innocently.

"Get down!" Elise shouted as she tackled Jayden over the nearby counter at the same moment the doors burst open with explosive force, and smoke and gunfire began filling the lab. The sound of bullets hitting metal and shattering glass resonated throughout the entire lab as Richard quickly took the advice and ducked behind the counter near the machine where Demetri was currently prone.

Richard couldn't see anything clearly as the bullets whizzed past, sparks flew and smoke slowly filled the room from some sort of grenade. He recalled the rush of adrenaline once before, when escaping the secret lab ... this feeling was similar if not identical, and so were the sounds. *Who are they? How did they find us? What are we going to do?* He cowered behind the counter as the bullets continued to strike the instruments above him, shattering the glass beakers and tubes. Terrified, Richard covered his ears and closed his eyes.

Suddenly, the force of shots had hit the back of the carrying case Richard left on the counter containing Demetri's blood sample. The case, still open with a few dents on the top from the bullets, tumbled to the floor in front of Richard. The case had been spun around so it was now open in front of him, showing the original blood sample snugly stored, undamaged from the shots or the fall.

Richard looked deeply into the syringe, and for a moment the overwhelming sounds of battle were distant to him. As he looked into the syringe, his eyes invariably turned to Demetri on the exam table and the four additional syringes now filled with his different variants of blood. Were they here for this? Is this what they were attacking for?

Demetri had begun to stir, still obviously woozy from the process, so he couldn't sit up. It was obvious he was partially aware of what was going on around him, but he would not have the strength to move himself.

Elise, behind a counter with Jayden some distance from Richard, did her best to reciprocate the gunfire to keep the enemy at bay. No voices or commands were heard, only gunfire that came in flurries. She handed Jayden her other firearm. He accepted it with terror in his eyes but began shooting in the direction of the lab door, ineffectually, but at least in the right direction.

As sparks continued to fly as stray bullets hit pieces of the machine just above where Demetri lay, Richard quickly realized if Demetri sat up in his condition a stray bullet could end his life. He also realized he had to destroy the recent data in the computer. If they got out alive he didn't want *them*, whoever they were, to have this important information.

He removed his hands from his ears and tried to clear his mind of fear. He rushed forward toward the computer where the data was stored, case in hand, and then ducked and hit the floor under the counter. He reached up for the keyboard with his arm, staying low out of the line of fire, and brought it to the floor. He frantically typed the code he hoped would delete the data and then grabbed the remaining scroll printout that lay on the floor beside him. He stuffed the scroll into his belt behind him and darted in a half-crouch for the large machine with his head down, dragging the case across the floor.

He scrambled up to the machine and grabbed Demetri by the arm, and pulling with all his might began dragging him off the machine to the floor. As the constant flurry of gunfire pelted the lab around him, he reached for the machine, careful to keep his head down, while quickly taking the syringes out and placing them into empty slots within the case.

"Rich ..." Demetri's voice was drained and desperate, accentuated by the fact he did not use Richard's code name. He grabbed Richard's arm and tried to lean up, but was forced back down by Richard.

"No! You're in no condition to fight right now! We have to get you out of here!" Richard, after securing the remaining syringes into the case and closing it, grabbed it with one hand and cupped his com ear with the other. "Ghost! Ghost where are you? We are under heavy fire in the lab! Decan is down and we have a civilian in the crossfire—*Ghost!*" Richard's pleas were answered only by static as he frantically searched for a way out.

The main entrance was where their attackers had taken up position, which only left the emergency exit at the back of the lab. It was closer to Richard but would leave Jayden and Elise far away from an escape.

He had to do something! Demetri wanted to get up but was too weak to stand. Richard placed a hand on Demetri's chest in an attempt to comfort him while simultaneously demonstrating he could be no help at this moment. Demetri then took Richard's hand to get his attention, and pointed at Demetri's nearby shirt and belt he had taken off earlier at Richard's request. Richard quickly realized he was being directed to Demetri's gun.

"Akira! Are you all right!?" Elise's voice was barely audible over the gunfire and was laced with fear, even though her words were of her concern for Richard's safety. It was then Richard realized it was not only Demetri he needed to protect. They all needed him.

"Hang on!" Richard shouted as he reached forward and drew Demetri's gun from its holster, looking at him as if to ask permission.

Demetri nodded faintly as he lay prone, "Safety ... off ..." He managed to gasp out instructions to Richard. His breathing increased in frequency as he pointed to a small switch on the gun. Richard looked to the gun and flicked the indicated switch, and with a deep breath stood up and rested his arms on the countertop. Using the counter as cover, he began firing into the smoke, which was now adversely affecting Richard and his team. His arms buckled with each shot, not prepared for the force behind the firearm. But he was determined and even tried to take aim at his enemies. It was difficult to see as his eyes burned and watered from the smoke. He could only see flashes of the enemy guns which seemed to be far more numerous than Richard had bullets. There was no visual from a few counters up where he believed Elise and Jayden had taken refuge. But when he heard her words prior, it gave him hope that he would give them an opportunity to fall back to his position.

"Back here! There's an emergency exit!" he shouted as he fired several more shots into the smoke, and then quickly ducked back down behind the counter when he heard an enormous crash. Through burning, watery eyes, Richard recognized the security van they had been surveying earlier that evening. It came crashing through the emergency exit double doors as the alarm from the door began to sound and the sprinkler system proceeded to soak the entire lab. Concrete and metal shot forward from the wall, the doors flung open then hung on bent or broken hinges, as the security van smashed through far enough that its own front doors were now accessible from the inside of the room. The lights in the lab flickered on and off from the disruption of electricity, which only adding to the chaos filling the room.

The door to the security van opened and Nate stepped out, wielding a large assault rifle. He promptly took aim, firing into the smoke. He took a few steps forward and then eased up on the trigger to speak. "Let's move! Evac! Now!" With those orders, he took cover behind the driver's side door, placing the gun through the open window and renewing his assault into the smoke. His shots had far more purpose and aim than Richard had contributed.

Richard quickly wrapped one of Demetri's arms around his neck and grabbed the case in the other. Helping Demetri to his feet, the two of them carefully made their way to the van. Knowing Demetri would be vulnerable, Richard squeezed through the small space between the van and the wall caused by the crash to make his way to the rear of the van. He used the hand carrying the case to open the two back doors and slid the case to the back of the front seats, freeing up both hands to assist Demetri, and then got himself into the back of the van.

The gunfire continued to rain on the inside of the lab as the sprinklers were dousing what few flames were creeping up from relative sparks. After ensuring Demetri was inside the van, Richard peeked around the side to see if he could catch a glimpse of Elise and Jayden. Failing that on the one side, he peeked around the other side to see the back of Nate firing purposefully into the smoke behind the driver's side door. But still no Elise or Jayden.

"Where are they?" Richard shouted to Nate, but he either did not hear or simply ignored his question. "Ghost!" Richard continued to address Nate in the midst of the combat, though his stomach suddenly dropped as he saw Nate entering the van on the driver's side and closing the door. He had not yet seen Elise and Jayden.

As he was about to shut the doors and go back into the lab to find his friends, Elise darted from the other side of the van with Jayden's arm slung over her, his head drooped.

"Help me get him in!" Elise partially handed Jayden to Richard as they put him facedown into the van and jumped in after him. Elise quickly shut the doors and banged twice on the roof. "Go, go, go!"

The van, still under fire, screeched its wheels as it pulled out of the lab. It spun around on the grass in a way Richard did not think possible, until it faced forward toward the road. Ramping off the curb in a jarring shake of the van, they began to speed away to the streets of downtown Toronto. The distant sound of other vehicles similarly screeching their wheels left the impression that this pursuit was not over.

Richard's eyes frantically scanned the van, fear in his eyes as he noticed they were missing a member of their team. "Where is Sage?"

Nate's voice could be heard from the front seat as he manoeuvred the van through the streets, "She'll be fine! They aren't here for her, nor do they know of her presence! She will meet us at the safe house! We have bigger things to worry about right now!"

Elise tugged at Richard's arm to get his attention, though Richard was on edge and not in the mood to be pawed at. *"What?"* He turned in aggravation.

Elise had a look of concern on her face, and she turned away from Richard and down to Jayden still facedown in the van. She carefully placed her arms under him and turned him onto his back, allowing Richard to see the pool of blood he had created on the floor of the van. It was from the bullet wound in Jayden's chest.

Chapter 22

DESPERATION

"JAYDEN ... JAYDEN!" RICHARD GRASPED HIS friend's limp shoulders and pressed his ear against Jayden's chest, praying this was not happening. These past several months were just a nightmare. The stress of getting the internship had obviously gotten to him ... he was simply having a nightmare in his bed. None of this was happening; it was his mind living out his most extreme fears. It was his worst nightmare coming true ... there was no possible way this could be happening. But upon opening his eyes, hearing the waning sound of Jayden's heartbeat slowing down, a tear fell from his eye as he came to the harsh realization that this was all too real.

The glass on one of the van's rear doors suddenly shattered as a bullet flew through it and of the front windshield, causing Nate to swerve the van.

Richard held fast onto Jayden's shoulders, bringing himself tight against his fallen friend's chest as the sound of gunfire could still be heard in pursuit of their stolen security van. Bullets ricocheted off the metal plates and the pavement close to the van as it screamed down the street.

Richard thought Nate's chaotic yet skilled driving seemed to be preventing them from landing any solid shots on the van or its tires, which were the likely target of their pursuers. The heavy Toronto traffic worked in Nate's favour as he could weave between lanes and manoeuvre in front of larger vehicles for momentary protection. Richard was almost unaware of the immediate danger surrounding him as he focused on the weakening rhythm of the heartbeat against his ear, which reminded him of what he was losing. One of his only friends, and in Richard's mind, it was his fault Jayden was dying.

"Dammit! Where did they all come from? Spire! Light them up!" Nate shouted from the front seat as he reached beside him to grab his assault rifle, throwing it behind him for Elise to catch. Dexterously catching it, she took one quick look of concern at both Richard and Jayden, then to Demetri, and she dropped the safety switch of the gun and pointed it out the already broken glass of one of the rear door windows. She waited a few seconds as Nate positioned the van strategically. Taking careful aim, Richard saw her pull the trigger once quickly before changing trajectories one after the other, shooting at multiple targets with what seemed to be extreme precision, even with a fully automatic weapon. After every shot, Richard could distinctly hear the sound of skidding tires followed by a loud crash, one with a booming explosion. Civilian cars were swerving, screeching and halting in an attempt to avoid this deadly encounter. Horns were honking, and people on the sidewalks were screaming as the panic-driven crowds scattered and ran for cover. Whatever Elise was aiming at, she was hitting every single time. But she did not stop firing.

The enemies in pursuit of them, whatever their numbers, were of little concern to Richard. His thoughts were of his two friends. They both lay prone in the van as if symbolizing the mortuary floor he had populated with his actions and research. Both friends were dying—and both were dying because of Richard. The sound of gunfire, honking horns from innocent drivers trying to avoid the chaos and crashing metal exploding around the van continued to fill the air, but Richard was immersed in his own helplessness and self-blame. When his darkest thought, that maybe this world was better without him, entered his mind, he was immediately shaken out of his emotional pain.

Elise glanced back to see Richard paralyzed in fear. "Dammit, Richard!" Elise shouted as she continued combat without even a second glance back. "This is not the time to feel sorry for yourself! We all need you! When your blood boils, you use it!"

"You use it … " Richard repeated as an epiphany struck him like a freight train. He scrambled on his knees to grab the carrying case for the blood samples he had stashed in the van. The van continued to swerve, causing Richard to fall against the wall of the vehicle several times, but he regained his composure with renewed vigour as he snatched the handle of the case and brought it back to his fallen friend.

"What are you doing?" An understandably distracted Elise questioned, still focused on the assailants on their tail.

"Saving his life!" Richard pulled out the raw sample taken from Demetri on the first extraction and stabbed it straight into Jayden's heart, emptying the syringe. This was his only chance, Richard reassured himself, knowing this serum could very well be the same death sentence that had befallen Demetri. But if the serum reacted quickly enough within his body, it would strengthen the heart and lungs enough to keep them functioning … even with a bullet wound. However, it would also mean that if the serum ever ran out in his bloodstream, he would die instantly, just like those soldiers the Americans pre-emptively injected with Valour.

To complicate matters further, Demetri was suffering negative symptoms. There was no telling what kind of side effects his blood would induce in someone like Jayden, especially as he suffered from a bullet wound to the chest. Even though Jayden met the physical requirements to survive such a procedure, without a profile of his DNA and blood analysis to personalize the serum, Richard knew he didn't have much of a chance. But Richard also knew that if Jayden was going to live, this was the only way it could happen.

Richard watched in angst as the serum from Demetri's blood began flowing through Jayden's limp body. Within seconds, Richard noticed slight twitches in Jayden, which quickly escalated into writhing and violent gyrating. Unconscious or not, the pain Jayden had to have been feeling would have been excruciating. It was one thing for a seasoned veteran soldier with the training and resolve to experience this, but Jayden had not asked for it. Richard whispered a silent prayer for his friend as he continued his vigil.

A large explosion outside suddenly lifted the right side of the van, tossing it on its side. The van scraped across the pavement for several yards before screeching to a halt, tossing the entire team onto the now bottom side wall of the van. Richard was in a daze, his head spinning, every muscle throbbing. It took him nearly a minute to compose himself and look around at both Elise and Nate, who had already positioned themselves at their relative exits.

The van was situated on its side across the width of the road with the roof now facing their enemies. Dozens of vehicles were stalled, abandoned or incapacitated in the fierce attack. It only took minutes for pedestrians and people who had vacated their vehicles to find shelter inside a building or behind any solid object that could offer refuge.

Without a second thought, Elise kicked out the back door already damaged in the crash, sending it flying several feet away, and proceeded to quickly vacate, armed with the assault rifle, renewing her assault at the assailants. Richard saw her take a position behind the now top of the van for cover as she continued to fire back. Nate followed suit, kicking out the windshield and leaping out the side, similarly taking cover behind the top of the van.

"Akira! Come on! You can't stay in there!" Elise shouted between bursts of fire from her rifle.

"I can't leave them!" Richard shouted, stubborn in his protection of his friends. He even began lightly shaking Demetri in hopes he would soon recover from the dye and be able to assist in the battle.

"You can't protect them from a prone state like that! Come on!" Elise's retort, while masked with malice, made sense. Richard let go of his friends and crawled to the back of the van where Elise had adequately removed the door. The van was still being pelted with bullets in short flurries, and then the gunfire would briefly cease. They were attacking from the same position, facing the roof side of the van, seemingly a fair distance away. Richard had not yet seen a visual of the attackers but could now see the front of the Rogers Center Stadium in the center of downtown Toronto.

The familiar sight filled Richard with an even deeper amount of concern. Not only were they in the middle of downtown Toronto, where traffic had already suffered many accidents due to their chase and random gunfire, it would be nearly impossible to manoeuvre around the now stationary vehicles if they were to try to get away. Then again, you need a vehicle to make an escape! Also, this sports stadium held hundreds upon thousands of spectators for any given event who could potentially be pouring out into the streets at any time. If there happened to be any kind of event this evening, thousands more people could be in danger. *So many lives at risk—and so much for a secret mission,* he thought.

"Come on!" Elise yelled again, this time reaching around the side of the van, grabbing Richard by the arm and pulling him behind it with herself and Nate, who had both taken a position with their backs to the roof. Elise poked her gun around the van again, pulling the trigger as two more bullets flew out, followed immediately by a clicking sound.

"Shit!" she cried as she dropped the gun on the ground and pressed her back on the van again, looking at Nate.

"How many?" he asked her.

"Three transports. Four agents per. All armed with two fully automatic sidearms. They are in the same attire as those who attacked the lab."

"Hardly an assault squad. If they wanted to kill us, they would have sent them with better equipment." Nate spoke with a slightly confused look.

Richard was trying to understand who was attacking them from Nate and Elise's conversation. But it just didn't make any sense. Were they Americans? Coalition agents? Bounty hunters? He swore he heard at least four or five cars crash on the way here as a result of Elise's shooting. If there were still three cars left, that would make at least seven or eight following them, not including the men that attacked them at the lab … *not an assault squad?* How could that be? What was going on?

Richard looked to the Rogers Center and then back over to the CBC news building on the other side of the street. Both sides had crowds hiding behind relative cover—cars, mailboxes, the buildings themselves. With the number of people witnessing this chaos, one thing was certain. Everyone was going to know what was going on here soon, even if Richard didn't.

"What are they after?" Elise continued the conversation with Nate, ignoring the public and the gunshots showering the underside of the van.

"That's not my concern right now," Nate stated coldly.

"They're trying to draw us out."

"Indeed. Let's give them what they want." Nate grinned as he unzipped his leather jacket. Richard saw an array of small throwing daggers scattered like armour across the entire interior of his jacket and the vest he was wearing underneath.

Elise pulled out both her sidearms, changing the magazines in each and raising them in front of her face, closing her eyes.

"You take the right flank, I'll go left," Nate said as he opened and clenched his fists several times. "Richard ... stay here. Close your eyes and put your hands over your ears!"

"Ready?" Elise asked as she kept her eyes closed.

Nate, with his back to the van, reached into his jacket and pulled out a tube-like grenade, popped the pin and tossed it into the air behind him and over the van, closing his eyes as well. After two seconds a bright flash emanated from the other side of the van, followed by a crashing noise that caused Richard's ears to ring. He had covered them but still fell to his knees in pain and confusion. He opened his eyes and saw the entire crowd doing the same thing! But not Elise or Nate.

Through his covered ears, Richard could still hear a faint and muffled, "Now!" being shouted from Nate as he leapt clear over the van with a single bound, and Elise quickly followed. These two may not have been super soldiers ... but it was clear they were still enhanced from the prototype serum.

The muffled sound of gunfire stopped momentarily but began again, only this time much more sporadic. Several shots fired in succession, and then suddenly, silence. Richard's curiosity got the better of him; he had to see. As his hearing and vision were slowly returning, he crawled over to the side of the van to look at what his comrades were doing.

He saw Elise between two black four-door cars with the doors open, her guns no longer drawn. She was engaged with four men dressed identically as the soldiers who had attacked the facility in Las Vegas. They wore form-fitting black leather-like armour, balaclava masks covering their faces, their eyes cold steel.

However, it seemed as though their eyes were quickly turning to a white glaze as they engaged Elise. All of the soldiers had already been disarmed and were now engaged with her in hand-to-hand combat. Her guns were holstered—Richard believed she must have wanted to conserve ammo, not knowing how many more of these attackers would follow. Richard could see now Elise too had similar capabilities to Nate, another alpha subject, as Jocelyn had explained.

The soldiers surrounded her, covering all four sides, one in front and back and one on each side, striking at her in succession, a punch from one, a spin kick from another, an attempted sweeping kick from the third and a two-handed haymaker from the fourth. Each was countered with little visible effort from Elise. The punch was turned aside with one of her hands as the other hand struck him across the face. Without facing the incoming kick she bent over beneath it, placing one hand on the pavement to balance herself and she raised her back leg to strike past the spin kick and hit the assailant on the chin, knocking him over. Using the momentum from the back kick, Elise lifted both hands and her remaining leg off the pavement to flip in midair over top of the sweeping kick, extending her legs in mid spin to kick both remaining assailants in the head, knocking them both to the ground, unconscious.

Richard shook his head to regain what he thought was lost composure. The actions he just witnessed happened in seconds, but to him it happened in slow motion. He could clearly see every move Elise made in her otherwise instantaneous reactions. Richard's academic mind immediately analyzed this experience, which he attributed to the fact that he was in shock.

As she landed on her feet again, she looked over to the side, likely to see where Nate was located. Richard peeked farther around the van to see the other side of the battle. As he was glancing, he saw many sidearms scattered across the ground, each one with one of the throwing daggers with Nate's name on it lodged in the barrel. Six bodies of the enemy agents were positioned awkwardly on the ground, with the same throwing daggers protruding from various vital points on their bodies.

Nate was visible shortly after, dispatching the remaining two agents. He launched a swift spin kick across the cheek of the first agent, followed by a thrown dagger to the side of the head. He then grabbed the other by the head and with a quick twist of his body, snapped the neck of the last standing agent. Richard cringed at each motion Nate made toward another agent. He knew that in this case it would be them dying if not the enemy agent, but it did not make these actions any easier for him to accept.

Although the sounds of combat were now absent from the street, the crowds on the sidelines either hiding or running were still prominent. Both Nate and Elise were combat ready where they stood, as though they expected something else to happen. Richard went to check inside on his friends, both of whom were still, but breathing. He returned to the others to converse with them as they dropped their guard and began walking back toward the van.

"We need another vehicle," Nate said as he made his way back to the van.

"Get the others; I'll procure us a suitable transport," Elise replied.

Richard stood in shock as to what he just witnessed. He was aware that these two were enhanced soldiers, but what he had just witnessed was close to the potential of the Valour serum. He could only imagine what a soldier with both serums injected inside would be capable of doing. His eyes drifted toward Demetri.

Suddenly both Elise and Nate stopped and turned toward the enemy vehicles. Confused, Richard followed their gaze to see a nearly empty road behind the enemy vehicles, just past the sea of abandoned civilian cars. There was a motorcycle in the distance barrelling down the center of the street. Richard could barely see the rider, but what he did see looked almost identical to the enemy agents they had just encountered. Only this one had the hilt of two swords visible behind his back, and the eye slit in his balaclava was covered by thick and tight-fitting black goggles. There was a slight green tint to the goggles as well, and only one visible sidearm anywhere on him. This was an odd change from the equipment of the other agents.

"Wait a minute …" Richard paused and straightened his neck from the intuitive tilt it had taken while looking at the enemy agent. He just realized the detail he could see from such a long distance. How could he see something that far away as clear as day once he focused on it? How was that possible? The object was at least 300 yards away, but when he focused, he could see it as though he were right next to it.

"Stand back, Akira." Elise spoke without looking back, focused on this new threat that was approaching them.

"Take him down," Nate commanded Elise, as she pulled out and replaced the clip in one of her holstered sidearms. She took aim and fired several shots at the fast-approaching agent.

Richard saw the agent draw one of the swords and deflect each of the bullets as though they were nothing. His eyes widened, concern growing deeper and deeper, not just for the potential danger that was about to overwhelmed them … but the sudden realization that this was not a normal soldier.

Confused but not yet concerned, Elise drew her second sidearm and began firing both guns in opposing rhythm with each other at the appropriate agent. In response, he drew his second sword and with no hands driving the vehicle began deflecting every bullet shot toward him while still driving straight toward them.

The concern on Elise's face was growing, as was Nate's. "Akira …" Elise started as her guns began clicking repeatedly, out of bullets. "*Run!*"

Suddenly the motorcycle the agent was riding launched into the air off one of the cars that had remained on the side of the road. The agent leapt off the vehicle and in mid-air drew his pistol to shoot at the motorcycle moments before it hit the ground in front of the three of them. This caused the motorcycle to explode with the force of a grenade, throwing Richard into the van behind him.

Richard's muscles ached, and his mind was hazy. He was not able to see straight for the first few minutes, recovering from the force of the explosion. He was still sitting on the ground with his back against the underside of the van. As his vision began to clear he could see Elise and Nate engaged with this enemy agent. The agent had sheathed his swords and was fighting them unarmed. Richard could tell they were fighting at a speed beyond what normal humans could accomplish, but as he watched, the rest of the world seemed to slow down, and he could see their movements as clear as day. And he could see that even two against one, Nate and Elise were outmatched.

Every strike they made was countered with minimal effort. It almost seemed as though he was toying with them. But every time either Nate or Elise was knocked down by their enemy, they would instantly kip up and reengage. Their determination was far beyond anything Richard had seen in a human being before. Overpowered and outmatched, they fought with every fiber of their being to stay the onslaught of this enemy who threatened them and their friends.

It was not long before the agent took one of Nate's throwing daggers in the midst of a strike counter and turned to stab it into Elise's left leg. She let out a cry of pain but quickly bit her lip and endured. However, the following kick from the agent was with such force that it sent her flying several feet, crashing into one of the cars on the street, leaving a large dent in the metal as she fell limp to the ground in front of it.

"Akira! Get out of here!" Nate screamed as he grabbed a throwing dagger for each hand from his arsenal and renewed his assault on the enemy, putting the agent on the defensive. Nate held the daggers on such an angle so that each time the enemy agent blocked his hand strikes, they would pierce his skin. Richard saw Nate begin to draw blood as the agent showed signs of pain. Each block the agent made prevented him from countering the strikes.

The agent, who was now growing increasingly aggravated, managed to grab one of Nate's arms, putting him in an arm lock with one arm as he began striking his face with the free hand. A swift lift of his arm caused a loud snap as Richard could audibly hear Nate's arm break. Nate, obviously in pain only gritted his teeth, while blood dripped across his teeth from the repeated strikes to his face. After a few more strikes, the agent released his arm and leapt off the ground a few feet in the air to strike Nate with a spinning kick, driving him into the wall of the nearby CBC building. His impact left a hole in the concrete where he hit, and a few loose bits of the wall landed on Nate's body. Nearby civilians ran into the building screaming after seeing the force of this attack.

An ominous silence followed for a few moments as the distant sound of police sirens could now be heard. The terrified screams of civilians were becoming more distant as the curious and brave alike were now the only ones remaining in the vicinity.

The agent looked toward Richard as though about to approach him but stopped suddenly and entered a combat stance.

Richard was confused at first, but then out of the corner of his eye he saw movement. As he turned to look, he saw Demetri leaning one arm against the back of the van. He was standing, breathing heavily and using the van as support to stand from his recovering exhaustion. But Richard could see that his ragged breaths were not from exhaustion but from anger! He looked to the two injured bodies of his comrades and then glared at the enemy agent, his heavy breathing stopping the moment he met the agent's gaze.

Richard may not have known Demetri for a long time, but he knew not to cross him. And from what he could see, exhausted or not, this agent was about to be the target of Demetri's long pent-up rage!

Chapter 23

CLASH

DEMETRI'S COLD HARD STARE CONTINUED as he stood away from the van and began walking toward the agent, completely ignoring Richard's presence. He was focused, and Richard understood that. And although Richard was told many times by Elise and Nate to run, he was compelled to stay. He needed to be with his team, not just to protect his friends but for the experience—he had to see this! Richard needed to observe as a scientist and mentally record his data and conclusions, but more importantly use this data to help Jayden, Demetri and the cause for which he stood!

The two soldiers stood across from each other in a stare-down for what seemed like an eternity. The crowd was still in a panic, and distant police sirens could be heard, slowly growing louder as they approached the scene. The two soldiers began circling each other, sizing each other up without a word. They moved with the stealth of two black panthers ready to pounce on a most formidable enemy. The enemy agent slowly drew his swords as he continued his deliberate footsteps around Demetri. Even he could tell Demetri was not going to be an easy prey.

Suddenly, without even a visible spring from their legs, the two soldiers leapt in a single stride toward each other, immediately engaging in hand-to-hand combat, each striking at the other with the masterful prowess of a martial arts champion. Neither seemed to be able to land a hit on the other; it was almost as though each of them could anticipate every move of the other and block or dodge every attempt. Even while their eyes deadlocked onto each other's gaze, they moved with a grace and finesse Richard did not think possible. Any other onlookers (with the exception of Nate and Elise) would not see the details of this phenomenal encounter as the soldiers' movements were much too fast for the ordinary eye to process.

The combat between the two progressed faster and faster. Their movements began to widen from the original small circle where they first engaged, becoming more aggressive and forceful with each strike. As their movements quickened, their strikes had more time between them as they stepped back to put more force behind a strike, or leaped back to spring forward for a kick. The force of their strikes was so great that it tossed debris for a wide circumference and even shook the vehicles in their immediate vicinity, resulting in sudden gusts of wind.

The enemy agent's blades danced around him like a performance piece, making it difficult to discern where the next strike would come from. As each strike came, Richard could see Demetri anticipate it and avoid it, if only by the skin of his teeth. It was becoming increasingly apparent that Demetri was indeed fast, but the enemy agent was faster. His reaction time seemed greatly enhanced as well, though his strikes did not carry the same force as Demetri's, nor did his awareness of his surroundings seem as keen as Demetri's. Demetri would avoid the huge cracks in the pavement as they engaged, but the enemy agent was tripped up by them more than once. He was obviously enhanced, as was Demetri, with at the very minimum Gait serum characteristics.

"That's impossible," Richard said in quiet realization to himself. This man was not only in possession, but a product of a piece of the very serum Richard had been working on for months. How could he have access to it already? Did the Pacific Coalition have a similar project in the works? The similarities between this man's enhancements and the Gait serum were far too numerous for it to be a coincidence. The fact that it was sold on the black market recently didn't logistically allow enough time for it to be in use!

If it were true, that would mean Demetri should be just as fast as this man, unless this soldier had more time to train with it and develop his abilities. But that still meant Demetri would have superior strength and cognitive functioning. It was possible they didn't have access to every piece of the serum—if he was missing Keen and/or Vigour, that could give Demetri the edge he needed. Not to mention that the enemy agent would not have the protective aura around him that Demetri did, though it seemed Demetri was too physically drained for his to be currently active. Did Demetri know this? It would be a tactical advantage, wouldn't it?

The two soldiers disengaged each other for a moment as the city's police force began arriving in full force around the scene. The police blocked all roadways and created a perimeter around the site. The officers began pouring out of their vehicles as some took cover behind their cruisers, taking aim at the two combatants while the others assisted civilians to get clear of danger. The Tactical Unit of the Toronto Police placed themselves strategically behind protective barriers in optimal position to stop the threat of harm. It was obvious the authority's main concern was the protection of the people. The officers attempted to help the obviously injured and dazed Elise and Nate, but both refused the help, pushing the officers away stating they did not require assistance. The officers reluctantly complied, but still took defensive positions around them as other civilians were beings escorted to safety.

Both Demetri and the enemy agent continued their renewed standoff, completely ignoring the directions from the police given to them from the established sidelines. "Police! Don't move!"

"Decan!" Richard shouted over the police sirens and panicking people. He needed to take this break in their fight to ensure Demetri was aware of his pending advantage over his adversary. "He is only infused with Gait!" It was not a lot of information, but Richard did not want to give too much away to the masses, and he knew Demetri would know what it meant. After all, Demetri had been there from the beginning of the development and knew each serum and its attributes. He knew it would mean he could take advantage of his greater strength and awareness over the enemy agent.

Demetri turned his head slightly back toward Richard after he said that. He saw Richard leaning against the underside of the van. His eyes narrowed, and he nodded both in understanding and thanks before turning his full attention back to his opponent.

"Put your hands behind your head and get down on your knees!" the police commanded, assuming their lack of movement was in response to their previous request.

As if in open defiance of the police request, Demetri suddenly lunged forward at his opponent before he could react, shoulder checking him into the CBC building behind him and causing him to drop his swords. The force created a large hole in the side of the building as hunks of concrete fell from all sides of the impact area. The enemy agent immediately began kneeing Demetri in the chest in an attempt to get him off.

Demetri stood up and blocked the following punch from the agent, countering with his own. But the agent quickly ducked and rolled as Demetri's fist went right through the concrete behind the agent. The enemy agent stood from his roll and faced back to Demetri to take advantage of his fist in the concrete. He was met with a large cinder block that struck him in the face, shattering it, as Demetri had physically ripped it out of the wall and aimed it directly at his head.

The agent was thrown off balance from the sheer force of the block, cinder dust floating around his eyes. Then Demetri charged at him, punching him in the stomach, followed by a cross to his head. The agent was obviously still dazed from the strikes but managed to begin dodging Demetri's blows. He ducked under one of Demetri's cross punches and then spun and kicked Demetri in the gut with enough force to knock him back into one of the enemy agent cars near Elise.

The police renewed their efforts to continue clearing people away from the increasingly growing battlefield as the enemy agent car was moved back several feet from Demetri's impact. Two officers continued to offer assistance to Elise but she repeatedly denied their assistance without a glance as she focused on the fight at hand. The officers were forced to resume their protective and on-guard stance.

As Demetri stood up, he could see the enemy agent was about to spring into a charge toward him. He looked behind him, and then turned quickly to dig his hands into the metal of the car's front end. With a single motion he tossed the car toward the enemy agent a few feet off the ground. He then leapt high into the air. At the same moment, Richard noticed the enemy agent charge toward Demetri and slide under the car as it passed over him, and hit the police barricade on the other side of the street behind Richard.

Just as the car passed over the enemy agent, Richard could hear a loud thud and crumble of concrete as the very ground beneath him shook for a moment. Demetri had landed knee first on the agent's chest just as he passed under the car, and proceeded to punch him repeatedly in the head.

The police scrambled to protect the people still in the vicinity as the flying vehicle struck the barricade; however, officers who had their Tasers trained on the fight had now opened fire on Demetri. As trained in protocol and procedures, the police were obligated to intervene in a physical fight when one party appeared to have the advantage. This action was intended to prevent serious injury to the disadvantaged party.

As several Tasers struck Demetri's back, his assault on the enemy was immediately halted. The Tasers appeared to have some effect as he was holding his chest, but his body was not convulsing. Sparks of electricity emanated from various parts of his body as the Tasers continued their assault; the electricity more and more rapidly becoming visible across his body before slowly dying down, almost melding into his skin. He turned and stood quickly with one quick swipe to knock the Taser's wires hard enough to move them away from his body, but quickly fell to his knees with quick rapid breaths as he clenched his chest. Several further shocks of electricity visibly sparked from his body as he fell.

The enemy agent, though bloody and disoriented, was not the object of the police assault, and he capitalized on the situation with a strong mule kick from his previously prone position. He landed on his feet after striking Demetri across the head, sending him to the ground. He began a series of flips and somersaults, making his way to where he had dropped his swords. The police attempted to similarly target him with Tasers as several officers began advancing on the fallen Demetri to take him into custody.

Grabbing his swords, the enemy agent leapt into the air toward Demetri, avoiding the police Tasers with ease. He landed on Demetri's chest, plunging a sword into his chest. Demetri cried out in pain.

Seeing this show of lethal force, the police responded in kind and began firing on the enemy agent, who had begun his advance on them, engaging the police in a one-sided fight as he dodged and deflected the bullets with his remaining sword.

As he weaved through the police barrage, the police had trouble keeping up with his movements, firing where he was a second ago, never where he actually was. Richard clearly saw his movements, but it became apparent the police could not.

Richard looked in shock at his fallen friend with a sword through his chest. His friend whom he tried to help, tried to save. Demetri's cries of pain were loud and piercing to Richard's ears, each time causing more pain to him than the sword embedded into his own heart ever could have.

When the cries of pain suddenly stopped, it was if the world itself had stopped spinning for Richard. Everything he had set out to prevent, everything he had set out to do ... was gone. Gone in the single dying breath of one of his best and only friends! He shut his eyes tightly as a tear trickled from his eye, the one tear he thought he would never shed. The one tear for the friend he tried to save.

But when he opened his eyes, he saw Demetri sitting up from his prone position with the sword still lodged in his chest. Without a word or even a wince, Demetri grabbed the blade of the sword with his hands as if mocking the agent's attempt to kill him. A large electric pulse shot through Demetri's arms and through the blade of the sword as he ripped it out of his chest, throwing it on the ground beside him.

Richard's eyes grew with relief but quickly waned as the reality of the situation began to sink in. The pain ... the pain he was feeling had triggered something. Something he wanted to prevent! This was no longer Demetri. This ... was Decan!

Getting on his feet, Demetri glared at the enemy agent who was slaughtering the officers trying desperately to protect the people around them. Without so much as a word, the enemy agent stopped in the middle of his attack and turned back to Demetri. Sword still in hand, he lunged from what seemed to be a hundred yards away, still closing the distance in a second. Demetri grabbed the blade of the sword, stopping the enemy agent dead in his tracks right in front of him. Blood trickled out from Demetri's hand as he raised the sword with the agent still holding it, and with a quick twist of his wrist snapped the blade at the hilt!

Shocked but not submissive, the agent began striking at Demetri with every limb, moving around him at lightning speed, seeking a vulnerable spot. But Demetri could now stop every one of his strikes with what seemed to be no effort.

Richard was sure of it now. This is what he had hypothesized! The horrors Demetri had experienced all those years ago in Siberia had created a completely separate personality from his own, one who slept in his subconscious until it was triggered by the same thing that had created it—agonizing pain. When he experienced this pain, his other persona—a ruthless, remorseless super soldier—would take over. The abilities of a super soldier would be limited by the brain's ability to adapt to the body's inherent capabilities enhanced by the serum. Normally years of constant training, self-awareness and battle experience would be required to unlock the full potential of a man injected with these kinds of serums. But for Demetri … a dual personality evolved, one of which resided deep in his subconscious. The true extent of his full capabilities were perfectly synchronized, body and mind in this deep subconscious state, leaving some characteristics of the serums still evident in his daily persona.

A loud scream resounded across the streets as Demetri grabbed the agent's arm and snapped it, followed by ramming the end of the sword he was holding into the agent's leg, clearly an eye-for-an-eye retribution for his team mates Nate and Elise. Demetri then grabbed him by his neck and lifted him off the ground. He turned the agent's head slightly to the side, brought his neck close to his mouth and bit into it like a wolf.

Richard looked on, horrified at the sight of his friend with another man's blood dripping from his mouth. But his hypothesis was further justified. The personality wanted to survive, and it knew it needed to ingest super soldier blood to do so. As horrific as this was, it was necessary for Demetri to survive. Richard had no love for the man who had attacked him and his friends and killed numerous police officers, but he wouldn't wish this kind of fate on anyone.

As Demetri finished his feast, while still holding onto the agent, he looked up into the sky with an open mouth. Blood still dripping from his mouth, a smile formed as he closed his eyes and basked in his newly acquired health.

A familiar car suddenly skidded to a halt after it had manoeuvred down the sidewalks of the CBC building and around the police barricade. Richard could see Jocelyn behind the wheel of their Dodge Journey, which was now idling beside the destroyed van. Surprised, Richard ran toward the vehicle's driver side door and was greeted by Jocelyn, getting out of the vehicle, beckoning the team to join her. "Come on! Let's go!"

"What are you doing here?" Richard protested her presence, though he was relieved to have her back with the team.

"I heard what was going on over the police bands, and I wasn't about to leave you guys stranded. Now come on!"

Both Elise and Nate were already on their feet, taking advantage of the chaos amongst the police who were recovering from the devastating attack by the enemy agent.

"Get Jayden!" Richard barked at Elise as she made her way to the van.

"Move!" With his good arm, Nate shoved Jocelyn aside, away from the driver's seat as he got in. "Sage, Akira, get in the back!" Jocelyn followed his direction and hopped into the back seat. However, Richard ignored him and ran over to the van to help Elise bring Jayden's body into the backseat of the SUV, but not before Richard reached in and grabbed the case with the blood samples from Demetri.

When they reached their rescue vehicle, Elise urged, "Just get in and we'll lay him on top of you! Hurry!" Elise took the full weight of carrying Jayden as Richard hopped into the backseat beside Jocelyn, who was sitting on the far side. Richard placed the case at his feet before helping Elise place Jayden over their laps as she joined them in the cramped backseat.

The police were beginning to reform on the barricades as the doors to the Dodge Journey closed, and Nate drove up beside Demetri, who was still basking in his accomplishment. "Come on!"

The police were positioned behind Demetri and were now beginning to recover from the enemy agent's onslaught. They opened fire on Demetri. The bullets did not even touch his clothing; they simply stopped within a centimetre of him and fell to the ground. Demetri did not even notice the bullets harmlessly falling at his feet. But after seeing the means of transportation waiting beside him, he slowly turned around and tossed the body of the enemy agent toward the police.

The bullets were still deflecting harmlessly to the ground, when Demetri raised an open hand toward the agent's body on the ground in front of what remained of the police barricade. Demetri's body began to pulse with the same electricity that had encompassed him when the Tasers struck, and it then began to flow into the palm of his hand. A small but bright-yellow light began to form in his palm and grew larger as the glow from the rest of his body fed into it. A quiet humming could be heard, even over the gunfire and radio communication of the police bands. The humming grew progressively louder, resembling that of a power generator as the light grew brighter.

Richard was in utter disbelief. Decan must have already metabolized the electric currents from the Tasers into his body.

This second personality knew how to utilize it to its full extent, the power could be so ... destructive. Was it possible that he could already materialize what he has metabolized?

"Everyone out of the vehicle! Hands behind your heads! Down on the ground—now!" The police commands were becoming increasingly hostile as they now feared for the lives of everyone there.

A grin creased Demetri's face. "Close your eyes, Ghost." Nate quickly complied as a beam of yellow light burst from Demetri's palm toward the fallen agent and police barricade. The moment the beam of light connected with the ground, an enormous explosion erupted as a blinding light rivalling the sun itself filled the sky. The car shook violently. Richard rubbed his eyes, trying to recover his vision. Seeing nothing but a bright yellow light, he heard the passenger side door open and close, followed by Demetri's voice. "Drive."

The car then suddenly sped up, weaving recklessly back and forth. Richard heard the scraping of metal on metal from both sides of the car as it weaved through what must have been stationary traffic.

The sounds of the police sirens grew faint as the car sped off in a direction Richard couldn't determine. Through his own orientation, he believed the barricade would have prevented them from going in the direction in which he thought they were going. Did that blast move the cars? Did Demetri just kill police officers himself to secure their escape? With everything that had just happened, Richard had far more questions than he would ever expect answers to. Answers he feared.

It took several minutes for his vision to return. When it did, they had already merged onto the Gardiner Expressway and were merged with traffic speeding on their way. Wouldn't the police have pursued them? After everything they caused, they would be more wanted now than before. Yet they seemed unimpeded as Nate weaved in and out of lanes like a commuter who had just worked a double shift, rushing home, driving like nobody else was on the road. Was it possible that because Jocelyn came in so suddenly, Demetri's "blinding" technique prevented the police from establishing a vehicle make and model in time? With the amount of time it took Richard to recover his sight, he would imagine the police would be in the same boat.

In either case, Nate and Demetri seemed to have the situation well in hand. And now Richard had yet another concern to contend with, the friend who was lying on his lap, numbing his legs. Richard saw Jayden's chest heave up and down, and he breathed a sigh of relief. Even after everything that had just happened, he may have succeeded in saving two lives—two lives who were in danger because of him! It was a small victory, but at this point Richard was willing to take what little victories he could get. He thought of all the losses that had been sustained and all the lives that were just lost. It was hard for Richard to keep the bigger picture in mind when he could not get the image of dead bodies out of his head.

Nevertheless, the team had just had its first encounter with what could be a long-term adversary and won. But there was a nagging feeling in the back of Richard's mind. The enemy agent they fought was equipped with a piece of the serum he had worked on for America, he was sure of it. If they had one agent who was experienced with the serum, how many more did they have? Could they make more? Nate and Elise may have been enhanced, but even they didn't stand a chance against a fully crafted super soldier.

Richard looked down at Jayden, breathing slowly, even with a bullet wound in his chest that had since healed. The bullet remained in his body, but the wound had already healed over it in such a short time. He looked at Nate driving with his broken arm, then beside him to Elise bandaging up her leg using the first aid kit under the seat. Then his eyes drifted down to the case at his feet, holding the other four vials of blood samples from Demetri. The four samples of super soldier serum ...

Richard lay back against the seat and closed his eyes, trying to remove the recent images from his mind. In a few hours, they would be at another safe house. In a few hours, they could plan their next move. In a few hours ... they would have a lot to discuss.

Chapter 24

DESPONDENCE

S EVERAL HOURS LATER RICHARD WOKE in a daze from a deep slumber, a rest that was long overdue from his tiring ordeal. His rousing was warranted only by the sound of the car doors opening and shutting around him as the other members of the team exited the vehicle. He looked around to orient himself and quickly realized his situation. He recalled that once they were well on their way out of Toronto traffic, he, Jocelyn and Elise carefully put Jayden in the cargo space behind the backseat, his body limp and unresponsive but breathing. The bleeding had stopped. Demetri took position in the back of the vehicle where the door was opened and carefully took Jayden from his resting spot. Elise was already out of the backseat ready to assist Demetri. Richard and Jocelyn still remained in the vehicle momentarily. Richard rubbed his eyes as he further regained his awareness, and then slid his way out of the vehicle, followed closely by Jocelyn.

He gazed the large cottage before him, situated in the middle of a very dense wooded area. Richard came to the obvious conclusion they had reached their destination, a safe house somewhere in Northern Ontario. They were in the Canadian Shield, a geographic area with dense forest and large mountainous rock formations and outcroppings. The cottage was surrounded by a blend of deciduous and coniferous trees, the former with most of their leaves fallen to the ground but some in full array of beautiful fall colors still clinging to their branches. There was nothing to see except more of the same, endless forest. About two hundred yards behind the cottage was a huge rock formation that connected to other similar hills that looked much like a small mountain range. These outcroppings of rock, however, had large patches of vegetation from mosses, to grasses, to small shrubs, to large trees covering its surfaces. The cottage seemed protected by its immense surroundings.

The stained-brown wood of the exterior revealed its age. Although weathered and worn, the cottage seemed solidly built to endure the harsh conditions of Canadian winters. The front porch was bare of any furnishings; only dried leaves and forest debris decorated its wooden floor. There were no telephone wires or visible means of electricity to provide for this reclusive cottage. The sheer majesty of endless trees on all sides of the cottage and a barely visible path of folded grass where the car had entered the clearing gave a solid meaning to the word "isolated."

The others made their way inside following Elise's lead. She had opened the door easily as it wasn't locked. Richard paused and reached back into the SUV to grab the case he had been carrying with him since the university. Before picking it up, he looked intently at it for a moment where it lay on the floor of the back seat. He secretly contemplated the thoughts circling through his mind and remembered the events that had occurred around the acquisition of the case's contents. Shortly after, he joined the group who had already entered the cabin, leaving the door open for him to follow.

Inside, Richard was greeted again by an immaculate and similar physical layout to the safe house in Las Vegas where they had stayed not so long ago. Demetri took Jayden down the hall, to what Richard assumed to be a bedroom, to lay him down. Nate sat on the couch with Jocelyn, who tried futilely to attend to his broken arm. Nate refused any assistance, insisting it would heal itself within a few hours. However, he finally relented when Jocelyn pleaded with him for her to check that his bones were in the right position to fuse and heal properly.

Elise's wound seemed to have healed very well as she and Jocelyn had attended to it during their drive to the safe house. She was now ravenously hungry and immediately opened the fridge in the kitchen to a wonderful array of fresh vegetables, cooked meat, fruit, beverages and condiments decorating the shelves inside, not even questioning how these cupboards were also fully stocked with fresh food.

Richard noticed a small generator servicing the small fridge and providing electrical power for the lighting in the cottage. Elise already stoked the fire with the available kindling and wood piled beside the old-fashioned woodstove. Water was available at the kitchen sink from an unusual-looking tap that first needed an electrical switch to be turned on to generate a water pump. There was extra clothing for everyone, including warm jackets, hats, gloves and boots. The thought of this being an emergency safe house was fast leaving Richard's mind. This was prepped recently, which meant they knew they were going to be using it, and they knew when! The question now was, did they know exactly what was going to happen right from the beginning?

Demetri closed the door to the room where he had placed Jayden and began to make his way back to the living room when he was suddenly confronted by Richard, physically standing in his way. Demetri stopped curiously at the courage Richard was demonstrating in the face of a man who was quite literally bullet-proof. Although Demetri's demeanour was now subdued, his appearance was still very menacing and intimidating, especially with the bloodstains still visible on the front of his shirt and jacket.

"Did you know what was going to happen?" Richard accused. Demetri stared back into Richard's eyes and knew that only the truth would appease his accusation.

"Yes," he replied bluntly, walking by Richard to sit on one of the couches surrounding the circular table in the center of the living room. Jocelyn and Elise were in the kitchen area preparing a tray of food for the group within earshot of their voices, and Nate was already seated on a couch across from Demetri.

"Then why the façade? If you knew this was going to happen, then why did you help create it?" Richard had followed Demetri to the couch, leaning down to him as he raised his voice. Jocelyn looked in Richard's direction with empathy and concern.

"You're an intelligent man, Akira." Demetri stood up to look down at Richard as he addressed him almost condescendingly. "If you're going to work with us, you should be able to think like us. Knowledge is power, and I wish to know my enemy."

Richard turned his head and closed his eyes for a moment. *I wish to know my enemy*, he thought. Did he mean the super soldiers? Being at ground zero of Project Valour would certainly give Demetri intricate knowledge of what he would be up against. Perhaps he knew from the beginning he would be the first test subject? Literally becoming what he would be fighting, would give him the ability to effectively combat his enemy. Or perhaps he was referring to another enemy? One who had not revealed itself yet in Richard's eyes! Perhaps the one who had orchestrated the attack on the facility, and the one who framed Richard with the false identity!

"We will speak no more of it now. We have already been through a lot, and we will need to plan our next move," Demetri stated as he sat back down.

Jocelyn and Elise brought in a tray of fresh food and set it in the center of the table, and then Elise sat with the group.

Jocelyn went to Jayden's room with a medical bag in her hand.

The intensity of the moment lessened as everyone reached for some food. Richard absentmindedly took a few bites of a sandwich, totally engrossed in this thoughts.

"We *are* going to stop the mass production of these soldiers, are we not?" Richard demanded, as though the answer was obvious.

Nate leaned forward toward Richard. "I don't know if you were paying attention, kid, but from the looks of it, they already have that capability in other installations. God knows how many more have been created already. How can we stop something all but one of us can't compete with?"

"By becoming something greater," Richard stated proudly.

Nate sat up straight with an inquisitive look. "What do you mean?"

Richard marched over to the front door and retrieved his treasure. Swinging the case, he placed it on the table in the center of the room beside the food tray and opened it, displaying the four remaining samples of the different serums taken from Demetri's blood earlier that day. "Perhaps we should level the playing field."

A grin creased Nate's face, which he quickly hid from view. "You think those will do that for us?"

"In all honesty, I'm uncertain. All I know is that if you encounter another soldier who rivals Decan's power, you won't survive. What I'm offering is an alternative that will likely kill you as well … but not before you complete your mission."

"Are you saying your dying university friend in the other room is going to become like Decan?" Nate asked.

"If he survives, yes, that is very probable." Richard appeared grim in his response, with the obvious notion his friend may not survive the night.

Jocelyn returned to the living room. She was able to set up an IV for Jayden with the emergency medical supplies in the cottage. His vital signs remained the same.

"So you and Jocelyn would take two, as would Elise and I?"

"No," Richard retorted bluntly. "Neither Jocelyn nor I have the physical requirements to survive such a process. And again, without proper DNA analysis, the dosage given to you could very well be fatal and should therefore be limited to one vial. There are no guarantees you would even survive the process. However, with the prototype serum already in your system, I believe it will react similarly in your blood as it did with Demetri's by enhancing all of your attributes to a level beyond what any serum by itself could do. In addition, I believe each of you will achieve a unique, extremely enhanced specific skill as determined by the vial you receive. Therefore, the other two vials should be saved for Paul and Anthony."

"What about Decan?" Elise asked from the kitchen as she gathered some fruit for the food trays. "Do you not need to create something to assist his ... problem?" She was clearly trying to approach the subject delicately.

"With what he ... ingested earlier," Richard's face cringed as he explained, "his blood should be self-sustaining for a little while. With the amount he ingested, I would estimate it could be anywhere between a week and a month. I cannot be certain. It should be plenty of time for me to concoct a solution of sorts, if only temporary, and *if* I can access a lab and obtain the right materials. I'll keep a small sample from each vial, plus I have pertinent information from the computer printouts I managed to grab before our escape. I've also committed much of the information of the formulas to memory, so we'll have a good starting point."

"Won't we need it as well?" Nate inquired.

"I am unsure of your potential needs, Nate. It may differ for each of you. I will have to take blood samples and test the results once you have been injected. Demetri is a unique case. The remaining four vials are samples of the various serum injections from Demetri's blood. It seemed to be the interaction of something in Demetri's blood that reacted poorly with the serums which then created his problem. I do not believe any of you will have the same reaction," Richard said confidently, but hid the fact that the vial injected into Jayden carried Demetri's blood, not just a serum, knowing that even if the others didn't need it, it would still be a priority to ensure Jayden's longevity as well as Demetri's.

"Then don't worry about a solution," Demetri said coldly.

"You'll need it in order to survive, Decan," Richard explained.

"You said yourself I have become self-sustaining with what I did. I don't require a cure."

Richard's face grew more worried. "Temporarily. This is not a permanent solution."

Demetri glared at Richard and spoke in a deeper tone of voice. "It means I would have to regularly ingest enemy super soldier blood, the very people we are going to be hunting, a motivating factor in finding our prey. The only time it will no longer be a solution will be when there are no more enemy super soldiers left, at which time I will wither and die, correct? Sounds to me like the ideal solution."

Richard did not like his reasoning, but he could not argue his point. He was right. The only time there would be no chance to ingest super soldier blood, aside from enemies trying to hide from him, would be the lack of their existence—at which point, Demetri's "services" would no longer be required! From a scientific and professional standpoint, it was perfect. From a personal standpoint, however, it was unacceptable. Richard found himself questioning his better judgment, knowing Demetri was providing a perfect end-game solution, but not willing to accept it as the solution. He could keep his reluctance to himself for now. There would be plenty of time to discover an alternative before the time came.

"Would we have the same abilities as Decan?" Nate asked, sounding almost excited now.

"I honestly can't tell you," Richard said. "With the dosage and DNA differential, your reactions will likely be unique and unpredictable. It will take a good deal of self-awareness and training to discover and learn what you will be able to do … if you survive the process." Richard did not enjoy pointing out the potential for failure, but he felt it necessary to keep emphasizing it so they would be aware of the dangers of the process, although Nate did not seem fazed by it in the slightest.

Elise walked into the room with a bowl of fruit, tossing an apple at Nate, who caught it with his good hand. Taking a bite while Elise sat beside him, they both looked at Demetri. It was clear Elise had many of the same concerns Nate had but was letting him speak as the agent while she gathered the essential nutrients for everyone.

"What say you?" Nate asked as he slowly chewed.

Demetri looked at Richard and then at Elise and Nate sitting across from him. "A pack of wolves is far more likely to catch its prey than the lone hunter."

Nate grinned at Demetri and then nodded at Richard as Elise followed suit.

"All right." Richard began, "Then I suggest both of you continue with your hearty meal as you will need all the strength you can muster for this process." He closed the case as he swallowed his emotion. He couldn't believe what he had just suggested. He was going to create more of the very monsters he had helped design, filling the world with more of these "attack dogs." And this was a group that he had not known for longer than several months. Was he making a mistake? No, he told himself. The real mistake would be to do nothing. This group was his last and best chance to put a stop to a potential plague of super soldiers that could dominate the earth. If the bastards who created these soldiers in the first place wanted a war ... Richard was intent on giving them one.

"Then it's settled." Demetri stood up. "Akira, you should have a rest before we begin the process. I want to make sure you're fully alert before I put my comrades' lives in your hands."

Richard believed that Demetri was trying to make a joke, though Richard did not find it funny.

"I'll show you to your room."

Demetri headed down the hallway, expecting Richard to follow.

Richard turned to look at Jocelyn, who had now locked eyes with him, sharing a moment of mutual concern for the coming tide of events they would soon have to face. It looked as though Jocelyn wanted to say something, but a quick glance at Elise and Nate beside her stopped the words from escaping her mouth. She sat back and looked away from Richard as though disappointed she could not share her thought in the present company.

"Sage, perhaps when you have a moment you could join me in my room to discuss a few details regarding the coming process?" Richard did not need to speak to her about it, but for once he recognized the social need of another and offered a solution to her desired interaction.

Jocelyn looked back to Richard and smiled. "Yes, I'll join you shortly—after I check on Jayden," she said softly.

Richard nodded and walked down the hall to meet Demetri standing in front of a now open door in the hallway, leading to a well-furnished bedroom. "Thanks," Richard offered as he walked into the room, stopping halfway through the doorway and turning back to Demetri, his head tilted to avoid eye contact. "My parents ... they'll be targets."

"I know," Demetri responded. "But they'll be taken care of."

"I need to see them." Richard nearly cut off Demetri's statement. There were few things in this world Richard truly did care about intimately. His adoptive parents were amongst those few, and he needed to see for himself that they would be safe. "They need to know the truth about me not committing the crime of treason against the US government, plus the ridiculous accusations of me being Akira, a Japanese spy!"

"They will, Richard." Demetri used Richard's real name to emphasize his understanding of Richard's point. "Trust me."

Richard got right to the point. "There's a second team, isn't there?" There was no other explanation for this safe house being stocked with fresh food this conveniently. He had to know how many people were supposedly working with them.

Demetri paused for a moment as if searching his thoughts for an appropriate response. "We're not alone in this endeavour, Akira. We have prepared for this eventuality."

Richard furrowed his brow and looked past Demetri. Without raising his head, he glared upward. "You lied to me. You told me you wanted to give me the chance to stop it. But you knew it couldn't be stopped."

"No, Akira. I'm the only one who has been honest with you," Demetri said with a deeper meaning. It was a meaning Richard could not yet decipher and dreaded to think of what he was referencing. "I asked you to hold the leash." Reaching to the dog tags wrapped around his neck, he ripped the chain off. He took Richard's hand in one of his, placed the tags into his open palm and walked away.

Richard looked down at the tags again as Demetri walked away, reminded of the first time he saw the same tag lying across the table in the hotel conference room. He read the tag quietly to himself again. *Decan.* He looked down the hall at Demetri as he walked away, then back at the tags, gripping them tightly in his hand for a moment while sitting on the bed.

There was more to this than Demetri was letting on. What possible use could Richard have for his dog tags? Was Demetri just losing his identity? Or perhaps gaining it back? The steel was cold in his hand, a temperature that no amount of body heat could change.

A knock at his open door quickly shook him out of his thoughts. Jocelyn stood shyly at the door.

"Come in," Richard said, cupping his hands to hide what he had been given. Jocelyn walked in and closed the door, sitting beside him.

"I think Jayden's going to live. Though the state of his body is another matter. You may want to make your own assessment soon." A look of concern overcame her as she looked him in the eyes. "Are you sure this is what you want?" she asked, clearly referring to the decision to spread the very virus he wanted to control.

"On the contrary," he began. "I'm certain I don't." He looked back down at his hands. "But I can't do nothing! The very fact that our enemies have created this intricate ruse of my fake identity and what I have done to their country ..." Richard turned his head back to meet Jocelyn's gaze. "It means they consider me a threat. It means they believe I can do something about it. So by god, I'm going to!" Richard spoke with self-assurance and conviction. He displayed a confidence he didn't know he was capable of.

She smiled at his words and nodded in understanding. She placed her hand on his as she leaned forward and kissed him softly on the lips, sending a warm feeling through both of their bodies. It was Richard's first kiss. He felt a strong connection with Jocelyn as their lips met, and it was not on the intellectual level he was used to. There was an awkward moment of silence between them as they gazed softly into each other's eyes.

She stood from the bed and walked toward the door. She opened the door, looking back with a smile. "I'm here for you, Richard," she said, and then closed the door.

Richard reached up and touched his lips, as if to confirm what had just happened was reality. Then he noticed the dog tags still in his other hand. Shaking his head for a moment he placed them into his back pocket. "What the?" Richard felt a piece of paper in his back pocket as he placed the tags inside. The letter! That's right, Madeline's letter to Richard! Jayden had given it to him at the university, and then all hell broke loose! Richard had completely forgotten about it.

He pulled the letter out, reading the return address as Madeline's, in her handwriting. Was this the information she had offered to get for him in his apparently, inappropriate questioning of his parents? It was the plan he and Madeline, but mainly Madeline, devised to avoid the emotional pain of discussing Richard's heritage with his parents. Perhaps Madeline was able to shed some light on his origins. Richard suddenly felt a pang of overwhelming emotion as he held the letter in his hands. His professional inner turmoil was now further complicated by his personal inner turmoil. He struggled with his fond feelings for Madeline and his sensual feelings for Jocelyn.

He opened the envelope and pulled out a folded letter, and two attached documents. He realized she must have had some success in her search but decided to read her letter first.

> *Dear Richard,*
>
> *I hope this letter finds you in good health. I have attempted to contact you through other means, but have been met with silence. I am assuming you decided to work the government contract you had been offered, in which case, congratulations! I'm very proud of you for making this decision, and I know that it will be the best thing for you in the end. I know it must be difficult, but as you had always said to me; if it were easy, it wouldn't be worth doing.*
>
> *I have worked very hard to acquire the information you desired, and called in a lot of favours*

with various friends I've met over my years here at Princeton. I was not able to get all of the information yet, as I hit quite a few roadblocks. But I did manage to find a few pieces of information that prove to be very interesting. I have included a copy of the original adoption profile provided to your parents at the time of your adoption issued by the J. C. Hope Adoption Agency. It appears the contents were modified or just incomplete, not meeting the standards and regulations of our Canadian laws. It appears your birthmother was the source of the information on this document. It also seems as though there were a few things that your birthmother did not feel necessary to share, or perhaps it was excluded by the adoption agency. But remember, Richard, your parents love you. Anything you read in this document or ever find out about your birth parents should never change your feelings toward Adam and Isabella. You are their son, and they will always love you. Please remember that.

Anyway, I will continue to dig in my spare time and see if I can fill in the remaining, puzzling blanks! Please call me when you get back from your job. I want to hear all about it! Talk to you soon!

Madeline

Richard flipped Madeline's letter under the two other pieces of paper in his hand. He scanned his adoption profile, first noting the letterhead with the name and address of the J. C. Hope Adoption Agency. This was the document Madeline had recovered. The introduction included general legal information required in the process of adoption. It was the profile that had been highlighted by Madeline and immediately drew his attention.

Child DOB: June 13, 2001
Place of Birth: Toronto, Ontario
Mother: Adelaine Montrose
Mother DOB August 21, 1972
(Deceased June 1, 2002) died of heart attack
Father: Hiraku Yuu
Siblings—none
Relatives -----
Child's development: met all physical milestones of physical
development in his first year; happy and healthy boy.
Genome scan attached
*MOTHER'S WILL STIPULATES THAT SHE WISHES
HER SON TO BE ADOPTED BY PARENTS WHO
WOULD AGREE THAT HE BE THEIR ONLY CHILD.

Richard paused and reflected. No siblings or known relatives would only support a theory like being a test tube baby. And why did his mother insist on Richard being adopted by a couple who would only ever have one child? This confused him. Was it so that he would get all the love and attention he possibly could from two loving parents? Was that his mother's way of making sure he would have his gifts properly recognized and not be lost in a litter of children?

Richard quickly flipped the paper to the second document, his genome scan. He was satisfied that the scan revealed healthy genes with no anomalies or potential future disease. His mind was trying to process this new information as he flipped back to the adoption profile.

So far the paper had raised more questions than answers. His eyes trailed back up to the top of the page, noting again the address of the adoption agency in Ottawa. This he already knew.

Suddenly Richard's eyes widened, and his heart quickened, his breaths almost turning to hyperventilation as sheer shock paralyzed him.

The paper drifted to the floor after Richard read the first line over and over in his head ...

Child's Name: Akira Yamarito.